RUTHLESS SCANDAL

A REGENCY ROMANCE

GUARDIANS OF THE BONES

K.J. JACKSON

AWD PUBLISHING

First Edition: April 2024
ISBN: 978-1-940149-93-6

DEDICATION

– As always, for my favorite Ks

CHAPTER 1

HADDINGTONSHIRE, SCOTLAND, JULY 1828

Faster.

She had to be faster if she was to beat Lord Hedstrom back to the manor house.

Her legs pumping, her dress and boots gripped in her right hand, Nemity dodged trees on the trail through the woods.

The last time she'd been late to one of their meetings, he'd threatened to make her move to his castle on the coast. On the *coast.*

Far from Springfell Manor. That would be disastrous.

Stuck with the sea wind biting her skin every time she set foot outside of the dreadful place. She'd be a prisoner inside the cavernous, cold stones. Not that Thomas hadn't modernized it, warmed it where he could. But still, the castle was a monolith to a time long ago. Most people loved Ravenstone Castle.

She had a differing opinion.

The last thing she could let happen was to be late. To have Thomas watching for her at the top of the south lawn with his foot tapping. Always tapping his foot, he was.

If he was already at Springfell, she was sure his ire had reached overwhelming proportions.

Especially after what had just happened a week ago.

If she could just be a little quicker, she could maybe—*maybe*—beat him into the manor. And if she was even luckier, her shift would dry as she ran so her dress wouldn't stick oddly to her body when she threw it on.

She jumped to her right at the tree with the lump on its left side and a sharp twig jabbed into her heel. Squeaking in shock, she hopped, the pain sizzling up her leg.

Damn her boots that took far too long to lace up. She thought she'd be faster in bare feet—and she usually was—but now this.

She stopped for a moment and flipped the sole of her right foot upward.

Blood was already flowing from the sharp end of the stick currently embedded in her heel. No time to take it out properly. Leaning her shoulder into the nearest tree, she grabbed the stick and yanked it out of her heel, hoping the cracking sound she heard didn't mean part of the stick decided to find a new home in her foot.

Shaking her head, she hobbled forward a few steps, then started into a full run again, ignoring the pain grinding into her heel with every other step.

Not too much farther.

Up and over the lane near the entrance to Springfell and she could make the last stretch along the forest to the bottom of the south lawn in record time.

She darted out of the line of woods onto the roadway and instantly tumbled over, landing on her back as a giant black horse sent its front hooves flailing in the air above her head.

"Pharaoh!" A deep voice grunted out. A man atop the horse fought the beast backward and the front hooves landed only a breath away from her arm—a breath away from crushing her.

The horse lifted into another rear.

"Dammit, Pharaoh." The man on the saddle swore as he yanked back on the horse, keeping the flailing hooves from stomping down on her. Pulling the reins hard, he made the horse hop a step away from her. Angry, the beast pawed back and forth in place, still aggravated.

"Bloody hell, woman." The man was a giant. A giant on a giant horse glaring down at her.

Nemity scrambled backward on the road, her fingers clawing at the dirt and rock as she tried to distance herself from the flurry of hooves that could squash her. She glanced up at the man. A man that looked like he was about to descend death upon her.

"I am a good screamer." Scrambling for her feet, her words spat out, panicked. "My screams will carry far. People are waiting for me."

A stupid thing to say. But what did one say to looming death?

And it was true—her screams would easily carry all the way to the manor. She *was* a good screamer. Been blessed with wide, healthy lungs.

"Pardon." The one word barked out as the dark-haired giant eyed her curiously, his colorless eyes running up and down her body. Her wet, soaked shift clung awkwardly to her skin. Probably transparent in all the wrong spots.

Unseemly of him, as a gentleman would look away.

This man was no gentleman, his stare eating into every speck of her body and refusing to look away.

His hand flung out, motioning forward. "The lane is yours."

She started, her look whipping over her shoulder at the

lane through the forest. She looked back to him. "No need. I'm just passing through."

The lane was slow. She needed the shortcut through the woods at the moment.

His eyebrows cocked, making him appear extra angry as he looked into the line of trees where she had emerged, then to the forest on the opposite side of the road. "Just passing through?"

"Yes." She nodded.

Best to just end this whole interaction before it turned into more than a passing moment. Time had been against her since she'd left the waterfall pool, and it had conspired with fate to make her even later.

Her dress still tangled around her arm, she grabbed her scattered boots from the roadway and darted off the opposite side of the lane. Hobbling and only able to put weight onto the ball of her right foot for the splinters that were surely embedded into her heel, her run was reduced to an awkward trot as she weaved through the rest of the trail back to the manor house.

Lord Hedstrom was going to murder her.

CHAPTER 2

The second his horse reared, Callum knew it was his fault.

Near asleep, he'd only seen the slightest flash of white before his stallion jerked, flinging its front hooves upward and doing its damnedest to throw him off the saddle.

He needed to be done with this damn mission.

All he'd been doing for the last half hour was staring at the rocks in the roadway, thinking about sleep.

Sleep.

A full night's worth. That would be nice.

He was accustomed to squeezing in sleep at any time—day or night—whenever there was a chance to sleep, he had to take it in his line of work. Guardians didn't need sleep—or at least that was what he always told new recruits.

Told himself.

Been told.

But the last eight months had started to take their toll on him three months ago, and he would near slit a man's throat for his bed and twelve hours of uninterrupted sleep right now.

This damn job had stretched on far too long. He hated missions that went on for months with no end. Hector knew that, yet he'd still stuck him on this assignment, tromping after a wastrel of the *ton* without a speck of sense.

He needed something new—anything new that would stop rotting away at his brain.

It'd been months of the same thing. Gambling and drinking every night in London. Gambling and drinking every night from there to Scotland and back again. Back and forth. More and more gambling. More and more drinking.

An unending cycle he could see no way out of.

Hector, head of the Guardians of the Bones, had said Callum would be able to sort out everything quickly—whether or not this younger brother was after the older brother's earldom.

Whether or not those three random accidents that had nearly killed the earl were truly accidents or if something else was afoot. In the first accident, a stairway along the edge of the cliffs by his castle had given way during his morning walk down to the ocean. With the second accident, a carriage wheel had randomly come off the earl's curricle while he was in it. The third accident was the most suspicious, when a billet of his saddle had been cut half through and snapped while he rode—his *new* saddle.

The earl, Lord Hedstrom, was convinced three accidents where his neck was on the line couldn't possibly be happenstance, and he approached the Guardians of the Bones for help.

Callum tended to agree with Hector's initial assessment about the younger brother, Charley, being the likely suspect. So Callum had wormed his way into Charley's life, becoming his new favorite friend. Always up for carousing. For late nights in seedy clubs. For dragging Charley's dead drunk ass home morning after morning.

Charley thought he'd found a new best friend. While Callum couldn't wait to call this job posing as Charley's new confidante done.

Eight months he'd been waiting to call this mission done. Investigating every thin thread that could possibly implicate Charley, and never uncovering any solid evidence. Nor had Charley said a word about his brother that indicated he was trying to off the earl.

Charley was mischievous to a fault. A boy who'd never grown into a man. But a killer? Callum had his doubts.

Still, Hector and Lord Hedstrom weren't convinced. And since Lord Hedstrom was paying the Guardians of the Bones a hefty sum to sort the threat out, Callum was stuck in place, sticking close to Charley to protect Lord Hedstrom from his own brother.

He was sick of it.

And now this bizarre turn of events.

Lord Hedstrom had requested that Callum focus on an entirely different matter—guarding his distant cousin, a spinster of all things, who had recently been abducted from the road by her home, but had escaped unharmed.

Probably a play for attention, if he had to guess. Spinsters were rarely abducted.

Whatever it was, it was a completely unwelcome distraction. Especially because it was rather hard to protect the older brother from the younger brother when one was twenty miles away.

He was awake now, at least.

Trying to keep his horse from killing a slip of a woman, yes, but awake.

The woman scrambling on the road out of the way of Pharaoh's hooves was rambling, saying something to him that he couldn't hear over Pharaoh's snorting and thundering as Callum tried to control him.

It took a moment for Pharaoh to calm and Callum stared down at the woman splayed out on the road, glaring up at him. A wood nymph if he'd ever seen one. No regard to propriety of dress or hair in place or common courtesy. A flitty, little dragonfly quick to scare the beast under him. For all of Pharaoh's might, dragonflies had always made his horse skittish.

Below her wild, dark red hair she wore only a shift. A wet white one that clung to her breasts in an indecent way that he had a hard time averting his eyes from.

Hell.

It'd also been eight months of celibacy, because with Charley, there was never a night off.

And the image of this nearly naked wood nymph he wanted to lock into his memory for later.

Except that there was the look on her face.

The look that always undid him. Made him feel every inch the monster that he was.

Fear in her blue eyes.

His look jerked away and his hand whipped out. "The lane is yours."

She scrambled to pick up the boots she'd dropped. "No need. I'm just passing through."

Then the flash of white darted off the roadway and into the forest.

She looked to be limping.

Funny, he didn't think wood nymphs limped.

CHAPTER 3

Her heart thudded hard in her chest after that interaction with that giant man on that giant, snorting black stallion.

Not exactly a giant, but he was big.

And not local.

The whole of him—the extra height of him on that massive horse—reminded her of nightmares she'd had as a child of death coming for her.

If death was a hulking man on a black horse.

Fear flickering relentlessly in her chest, Nemity attempted to stomp it out. She was only five more minutes from the manor. There was no way his horse could navigate the thick grove of trees as fast as she could on foot.

She looked back only twice after darting into the forest, but the man seemed to have no interest in pursuing her.

Not a threat.

Plus, he definitely wasn't one of the two men that had abducted her. He was too big. They had been too scrawny.

The forest was nestled closer to the manor on the east side of the house, so she stayed in the treeline, instead of running up the south lawn that lined the main garden, as she aimed for the side door that would allow her to slip up the servants' stairs and to her room unseen.

Racing through the trees, she quickly glanced toward the front of Springfell.

Blast.

Lord Hedstrom's carriage. How long had it been sitting there?

Her distant cousin liked to be early. Controlling. Not like his father.

She darted from the edge of the forest to the side door, then opened it as quietly as possible, which wasn't easy given the thick iron hinges holding the heavy oak door squeaked like a mouse in the jaws of a cat every time it shifted.

Stepping into the cool confines of the hallway that ran the length of the east side of the house, she drew a deep breath into her hungry lungs as she set her boots onto the floor. Turning left, she just had to make it fifty short steps and she'd be hidden away in the dark stairwell and could escape up into her chambers.

Mrs. Jorge was surely covering for her right now in the drawing room with Lord Hedstrom.

Change. Hobble downstairs. All would be well.

She started down the hall and a leaf fluttered down past her nose from where it had been caught in the front of her hair.

Her fingers lifted, pushing back the hair around her face and she plucked out two more small leaves that had lodged into her locks.

She didn't even want to think about what her hair looked like.

Didn't have time to think on it, much less fix it.

All would be well if she didn't look in the mirror and just made it downstairs to the meeting.

Step forty-two. Almost there.

"Nemity." Lord Hedstrom's stark and extremely annoyed voice echoed down the hallway toward her.

She stopped, spinning around slowly, drawing her dress up in front of her to hide the fact that she was wandering about in her shift. Her wet shift. Never mind that he surely saw exactly how she was dressed from the backside when she was sneaking down the corridor.

Lord Hedstrom's arms clasped over his chest, his face pinched in disgust.

Why did her cousin always make her feel like she was five years old? A very naughty five years old. He was only ten years her senior, she'd known him her whole life, and still, she felt like nothing but a bug to be squashed when he was staring at her like that.

"Thomas." Her chin tilted up regally as she inclined her head to him. For all he made her feel worthless with one look, she wouldn't let him see it on her face.

"You're a disgrace, though what should I have expected." The elongated sigh that eased from his lips turned the air sour around her, even at this distance.

His words stung, more than they should, for she really didn't care for Thomas. Not like she did for the rest of his family. His brother, Charley, and their father, Heddie, the ninth Earl of Hedstrom, who had been her guardian for much of the last four years. Heddie, as she'd called the earl since before she could walk, had been a lovable bear her whole life. The only father she'd ever truly known. Heddie had been one of her father's dearest friends and a distant cousin on her mother's side, and he had become trustee of her fortune when her mother had died.

But then Heddie had died a year ago. Which had left her under the guardianship of Heddie's eldest son, Thomas.

A bloody raw deal, if she were to voice it out loud.

Which she would never do. Thomas had all the power over her, had control of her fortune, and they both damn well knew it.

Her chin lifted higher. "My apologies. My walk in the woods lasted longer than I intended."

"Walk in the woods?" He looked her up and down, at the dress hanging in front of her damp shift, and his glare landed on her bare feet. "It appears a might bit more than that."

"It was nothing. Fresh air."

He hated her.

Hated everything about her and how she went about in the world. Said she was a wild, unpredictable heathen every chance he got. But she'd never minded his pious, supercilious judgement because it had never affected her. Not until a year ago.

"Your current state did not result from fresh air." His lips pursed. "We talked about this, Nemity. You can't go wandering out by yourself onto the estate after what happened. If you cannot listen to simple directions—*for your own safety*—perhaps Ravenstone is the place for you after all."

There it was. Right to the threat. He'd been threatening it for months. Dragging her to Ravenstone and making her live there under his thumb until he could suitably marry her off to one of his equally stuffy friends. Never mind that she was quickly slipping into spinsterhood. Already there by some accounts.

How Thomas ever ended up being the exact opposite of Heddie, she would never know.

Her hands clasped the length of her dress in front of her to her body. "Please, Thomas, just give me five minutes to right myself and I will join you in the study."

He stared at her for a long moment. "No. No, I don't think so. I think you'll join me in the study right now, as you obviously intended to be seen as you are. For if you were intending to make yourself presentable for company, you would already be so."

Her brow furrowed. "How long have you been waiting?"

"Forty-five minutes."

Hell.

Her lips drew inward. Thomas hated, *hated,* tardiness from anyone. Least of all his hoyden ward.

She pointed over her shoulder to the stairs. "Truly, Thomas—"

He cleared his throat.

"Lord Hedstrom. Please. It will only take me a moment to change."

"Get the dress on, Nemity." His arms still clasped against his chest, he turned around to give her privacy, but didn't leave the corridor. Not taking the chance she would escape him again.

Her hands fumbling through the fabric of her peach day dress, Nemity quickly pulled it over her head, wiggling into the fabric that was determined to not properly slide down her wet shift. Her arms into the sleeves, the dress was still half askew when she heard footsteps approaching the hallway.

"There is the little hellion." A voice she loved echoed down the corridor and she leaned to her left to look beyond Thomas.

"Charley," she squealed, forgetting about her crooked dress. "You're here. I didn't know you were coming." A smile beaming wide on her face, she skirted around Thomas and darted toward Thomas's younger brother.

"Miss an opportunity to say hi to my favorite cousin? Never." He threw his arms wide and bundled her up into a giant hug, swinging her feet in a wide circle. "You're soaked, Pip."

She laughed, squeezing him hard. "I am."

He laughed in her ear. "If I know you as I think I do, I would say you're merely hugging me to get me wet."

She leaned back, laughing, batting her eyelashes innocently at him. "You think I would do that?"

"I know you would do that." He set her onto the floor, the grin on his face telling her he didn't mind one bit her slightly evil streak.

Taking a step away, but still squeezing his left arm, she looked up at him. "I didn't even know you were coming up to Ravenstone, and then to here. I thought you were in London."

"I just arrived last night."

Boot heels clicked on the floorboards past them. "To the study."

Nemity looked at Thomas walking past them. "Surely there is time for me to change."

Thomas didn't slow his stride. "No. You'll come with me now. Wet and cold. And you will suffer the consequences of making me wait. We have matters that need to be discussed."

Her mouth clamped closed.

There was no arguing with Thomas. It wasn't a fun way to spend time and she'd never, in all these years, nudged him away from whatever he already believed in his mind. Stubborn. Always right.

Not like Charley, whom she loved to argue with.

Thomas continued down the hallway, not even glancing over his shoulder to see if she and Charley were following. He already knew they would.

And thus, she was stuck in this limbo. In this awful existence of her parents' making, where she was a mistress unto herself, had Springfell Manor at her disposal, a fortune at her fingertips, yet all of it accessible only through this odious guardian.

Not willing to raise the stakes on the confrontation and

annoy Thomas any further, she bit her lip, following him. Charley fell in step beside her, grabbing her hand and threading it into the crook of his elbow. He at least cared, which was more than she could say for Thomas.

Into the study at Springfell. Her mother's study.

She imagined it had at one time been her father's study, but she only had memories of her mother in here, handling all the affairs of Springfell Manor.

It still smelled like her mother, years later, especially when a waft of rosemary would drift into Nemity's nose when she moved a pillow or opened a drawer that her mother had kept packets of rosemary in.

Thomas always looked out of place in the study because her mother had chosen furniture that fit her petite frame. Thin lines on the chairs. Two delicate peach damasked sofas that faced each other in front of the fireplace. A beautiful rosewood desk with cherubs and scrolling vines carved into the wood.

It was a woman's room and she had to stifle the urge to shove Thomas out of it every time he stepped foot in it.

Charley, on the other hand, she never had the urge to push out of the study. Charley was at ease in any room he ever entered. Always fit. Always was welcome.

"I truly do not have the time for your antics today, Nemity." In front of her, Thomas strode into the middle of the study, swallowing the space as he railed at her. "I have a hundred other things I could be doing at the moment."

Looking down, Nemity tugged on the side of her dress, still trying to right it. "You are the one that demanded this meeting."

"Demanded?" He turned around to her, stepping to his left. "I wouldn't have had to insist on anything if you would just keep yourself out of trouble."

His last words dissipated into sounds that meant nothing,

for she had glanced up and her look had transfixed on the sofa that faced her.

What in the hell was that—no—*who* in the hell was that?

The man with the dark hair in the woods. The giant on the giant horse, now a giant in her mother's favorite room.

CHAPTER 4

Thomas followed her stare to the stranger. "Good you have arrived."

The man's eyes narrowing, the stranger hadn't looked anywhere but at Nemity since she'd spotted him. His stare locked on her, his gaze didn't even flicker to Thomas as he spoke to him.

He fully recognized her as the one that had almost gotten him thrown from his horse.

Or the one that had almost trampled her, depending on one's vantage point.

The stranger stood, polite at her entrance, though his eyes still bored into her.

She'd seen eyes like his before.

Eyes determined to crawl inside her, trying to discover all her secrets in one glance, like she was a simple puzzle to solve. Solve and then own.

Nemity tore her gaze away from the giant.

One, because she couldn't quite handle his stare. Two because she'd just realized how thoroughly Thomas had meant to humiliate her.

Punishment for her tardiness, he would tromp her out in front of a complete stranger in the wet and disheveled state she was in.

Her gaze sliced into Thomas. "You could have let me go to my room to change. Especially knowing you'd invited a visitor into my home."

Thomas puffed out a breath that sounded exasperated to the hilt. "I thought it better that Callum know exactly what he is getting here."

Her head snapped back, her eyes blinking furiously. "Getting here? What do you mean?"

She looked over her shoulder to Charley, who had stopped by the doorway. He stood, observing but not intervening, as was his way. No one was more fun than Charley when one wanted to have fun. But Charley was not one to insert himself into anything uncomfortable. And the very air around Thomas was uncomfortable.

Her look darted back to Thomas. Staring at the cold set of his jawline.

He couldn't actually think...to marry her off...sell her like cattle...

She advanced on him. "What are you talking about, Thomas?"

"I am talking about what happened a week ago. And I can see from your actions today that you've taken no heed to the danger you are in." His head shook, his lip curling into a snarl. "Leaving the manor house. Utter stupidity."

Nemity winced.

She'd rather hoped Thomas had calmed from his initial reaction about the incident a week ago.

He didn't need to worry about her. And he certainly didn't need to bring a giant into her home because of it.

Thomas grabbed her upper arm and turned her toward the man. "Callum is a friend of Charley's that has graciously agreed to stay by your side until we know where the threat came from."

She didn't look to the man, her focus still set on Thomas. "You are making too big of a deal of the whole incident. I was fine. I am fine."

"You were only fine because Mr. Youngstrom happened to be out putting one of the horses through its paces. Those two men already had you a mile away from here. If Youngstrom hadn't seen your hair hanging out of the back of that wagon, they would have gotten you. And who knows what they would have done to you."

Dropping her arm, Thomas looked to Callum. "Mr. Youngstrom is the stablemaster here at Springfell Manor. He broke his arm getting Nemity out of that wagon and the men that took her got away. We were lucky they weren't willing to fight him."

Callum nodded. "Charley told me." His look dropped to Nemity. "You were fortunate they didn't escape with you."

She shrugged. "Luck is usually on my side."

Next to her, Thomas grunted. "Luck isn't going to keep you safe—not until we know who exactly those men were and what they wanted with you."

Her head shaking, she looked to the coffered ceiling. "How are you possibly going to find that out? I'm sure those men have long since left the area."

"I have several people investigating that very thing, trying to find them," Thomas said.

Of course he did. Thomas was nothing if not controlling to a fault. A big fault.

Thomas's mouth pinched. "Though your description of those men gave us very little to go on."

Her hands flew up at her sides. "I was in the gardens and they threw a bag over my head. I don't have eyes in the back of my head. I didn't know I was about to be snatched and tossed like a bag of turnips into a wagon."

"And that is exactly why Callum is here. He will be the new eyes in the back of your head."

Her teeth gritting, she seethed out a long breath through her nostrils. "Except I don't need eyes in the back of my head. I am fine. Mr. Youngstrom is here on the estate, and he has been very studious in knowing my whereabouts."

"Mr. Youngstrom also has a broken arm." Thomas pointed at Callum. "Callum does not. He's the one that's going to be here to protect you."

She glared up at Thomas. "You think a man with brawn and no brain can protect me?"

"I have both, actually." Callum's deep voice suddenly sliced into the room, his look cutting into her. "I am also one of the men helping with the investigation and the more I know of you, the more I know where the threat is likely coming from."

Her arms folded in front of her damp dress as she met his stare. "That means you intend to know me. A bit presumptuous, don't you think?"

"Nemity." A warning shot from Thomas.

Her looked whipped back to her cousin. "What? I think I have the right to ask who and what this man is that thinks to insert himself into my life. Plus, the incident happened a week ago, and now you think to sic your lapdog onto me?"

"I've had men patrolling the outer grounds for the last week."

Her eyes snapped open wide at him. "You have? You could have told me."

"It was better that they told me they lost track of you constantly, when you were supposed to be staying in the manor." Thomas seethed out a sigh, pinching the bridge of his nose. He did that a lot, pinched the bridge of his nose when he was around her.

His hand dropped away from his face. "Would you rather I bring you back to Ravenstone? That is the other option on the table."

Her jaw clamped shut.

"Exactly. You don't want to be at the castle. And I don't want you there."

Her head tilted to the side and she gave him a sickeningly sweet smile. "Coming from anyone else, that might sting."

"Good that it is coming from me, then," Thomas grunted out.

She paused, holding the snide smile as her mind whirled, searching for a new argument.

Her hand flung out, pointing at Callum. "Except this won't do at all—what of the propriety of it? I am an unmarried woman, here by myself, and you think to have an eligible bachelor living here with me?"

Thomas scoffed. "You and propriety parted ways long ago. Don't cry foul on it now."

"And what makes you think I am a bachelor?" Callum asked.

Her look swung to him, her words stuttering. "Well...I just imagined...are you not?"

The smallest smile quirked the edges of his lips. "I am."

"Then why even bring it up?" Her hand flew up at her side. "It isn't right, a rogue gentleman here at Springfell Manor."

"I can stay at Springfell," Charley offered.

All eyes swiveled to Charley leaning casually on the wall by the door.

She'd almost forgotten he was still in the room.

"Yes." She glanced at Thomas and then looked back to Charley. "Yes, that is the perfect solution. Charley can stay and keep me safe. He is a cousin, and is far more appropriate than some random man."

Thomas shook his head. "If your safety is my top concern, which it is, I would not entrust it to Charley. No offense, brother."

Charley lifted his hand. "None taken. I merely meant I could stay at Springfell with Callum to help entertain Nemity while she is under lock and key. He protects her, I entertain her." He looked to her. "What say you, Pip? The longest party we ever had?"

"Yes. Yes, please," Nemity blurted out. Charley was the only one that was going to make this bearable.

Thomas looked to his brother, his head tilting down, his stare pinning him. *Don't get involved*—a very clear message etched into his face. "Except I need you at Ravenstone, Charley."

Charley pushed off from the wall, stepping farther into the room. "For what? You never need me for anything."

"I do." Thomas pointed to the door, his voice not to be argued with. "Let us discuss this outside."

Charley shook his head. "Thomas—"

"Now, Charles." Thomas started toward the door, and he glanced at Nemity. "Nemity, take a seat. This may take a while."

Thomas left the room, assuming, as he always did, that the person he was ordering about was following him.

Charley rolled his eyes as he gave her a look. He knew just as well as she did how his older brother could be. He tromped out of the study after him, closing the door on his way.

Which left her…alone with the giant.

Still standing in the middle of the room, she glanced about, wondering how much time she could waste looking everywhere but at the man.

If she didn't look at him, she didn't have to acknowledge he was about to become her jailer.

"You could sit, Miss Wheldon." His low voice had gone softer, almost like butter, when he wasn't barking words out. "Thomas is no longer in the room to battle against."

She didn't look at him. "I am fine standing and waiting."

"It might be better for your carpet if you sat."

"What?" She looked down at the blue and tan Axminster carpet that stretched across the wooden floorboards. Splotches of deep red were scattered into the fibers.

"Dammit." She swore in a low whisper as she picked up her right foot and twisted her heel upward.

The shard from the twig she'd stepped on in her mad dash back to the manor had embedded itself so deeply, blood had pooled around it and smeared across her heel.

She glanced across the carpet. Blood was hell to get out of a carpet like this. She knew that well enough.

Hobbling over to the two sofas on the ball of her right foot with every other step, she attempted to not let any more blood drip onto the carpet as she moved. She lunged the last long step to the sofa on the left, landing hard on the cushions.

As she righted herself, Callum took it upon himself to sit next to her and grab her ankle before she could bring her foot up onto her own thigh so she could pick at the splinters.

He pulled her foot onto his lap, setting her calf on his thigh.

Pushing her damp skirts down around her exposed leg, she tugged at his hold, trying to free her ankle. His meaty paw didn't give her the slightest bit of freedom.

She forced a half smile. "Truly, you don't have to help."

"I also don't have to sit by and watch you bleed all over the sofa as well." He reached his free hand into an inner pocket of his dark coat and pulled out a handkerchief.

She nodded, staring at the neatly folded white linen cloth, an insignia she couldn't identify sewn into the corner—not letters, but an emblem of some sort.

"The handkerchief is clean," he muttered.

Her look lifted to his face. "I didn't assume it was dirty."

He grunted. "You have done nothing but assume you know everything about me in the fifteen minutes we've been in this room together." He set the cloth to the bottom of her foot, wiping away at the blood.

"I did n—" She stopped herself.

She *had* assumed quite a bit about the man. When she actually knew nothing.

His hand moved to curl over the top of her foot and he lifted it higher for a better angle to see what he was doing.

She eyed him for a long moment.

Curious.

What sort of man would grab the bare foot of a woman he'd just met and start cleaning it?

Maybe he wasn't death on a giant horse. Maybe he wasn't an idiot oaf.

He still was big, though. His hand easily covered most of her foot.

She cleared her throat. "My apologies. I did assume some things about you and I shouldn't have. This was a surprise—the most unwelcome sort of one, with Thomas coming in and setting you upon me like I was a five-year-old child that needed a nursemaid. You suffered the brunt of my reaction to him and his supercilious, overbearing ways."

Callum nodded without looking up at her, as his gaze was still set directly on the bottom of her foot. "I deduced as much fairly quickly, Miss Wheldon."

She nodded, more to herself than to him, since he hadn't glanced at her face since sitting down next to her.

Her forefinger resting on her thigh flicked out to him

"Since you already have my bare foot in your hands, I imagine we need to catch up on pleasantries that should have previously been taken care of by my odious cousin, such as what is your family name?"

"Lonstrick. But everyone calls me Callum or Cal. I am not one for formality, Miss Wheldon."

Yet he called her Miss Wheldon.

She frowned, staring at him dabbing away at the blood on her heel.

On that score, she could see why Charley liked him. Charley hated the formality of their world—he always had. And he loved moving through London with a friend the size of Callum at his side. It kept escaping the mayhem his debauchery caused —whether with wine, or women, or at the hazard tables—all the easier.

"And you are Charley's friend?"

"I am."

"For how long?"

His shoulders lifted slightly. "Seven, eight months or so. We have gotten on well."

"I imagine. Charley likes to have muscle at his side."

"He does enjoy himself." Not taking her baited words, his voice was bland, like he was describing a tablecloth.

"That is putting it mildly." She chuckled. "Charley likes to skirt to the edge of everything. It is why he is so well-loved. He's never known any bounds and people love that about him."

"You love him?" His voice didn't change from the bored indifference it had been set to.

"I do."

For how much she loved Charley, she saw him deeper than anyone else.

She was wild, while he was a step beyond—out of control, most of the time.

Probably because, as the second son, Charley knew this world of society would not be his to pass down to his heirs. He knew that within generations, his descendants would be the poor, distant relations that would need to be begrudgingly taken care of. He'd accepted his lot early on in life and most days, when he wasn't drunk and reflective about it, he moved through life as if it were one grand ball—never enough wine, enough women, enough fun. He was going to squeeze every last drop out of this life while he could.

She couldn't blame him.

Callum's eyes flickered to her face, then back down to her foot as he lifted it higher to catch the light from the window across the room onto her heel.

"I noticed Lord Hedstrom is a bit stern with you."

"He is." Her arms wrapped around her middle as she glanced over her shoulder at the door, wondering when her cousins would reappear. "The sad part is that I used to like Thomas."

That statement pulled his full attention away from her foot and onto her face. "You did? When?"

"Before he disappeared years ago. Did Charley tell you that of him? That he disappeared?"

Callum shook his head. "No. He didn't mention it. Always just said his brother was an arse."

She shook her head, blowing out a long sigh. "Thomas hasn't always been like this. He used to have streaks of kindness in him. He's ten years older than me, so he never paid me much mind growing up. But between him and Charley, he was always the levelheaded one. The calm one. Charley and I are peas in a pod—we both love to laugh and get ourselves into predicaments that we shouldn't. Thomas was always there to make sure we didn't fall on our heads and crack our necks when we were doing something stupid."

Callum looked to the door, a vertical line between his brows deepening. "What happened to him?"

"He disappeared seven years ago. No one knew what happened to him, where he went. He just disappeared. Then a few months before his father died last year, he reappeared." She shook her head. "But he came back to us mean. I don't know what happened to him, but now he's just...mean. At least to me." Her shoulders lifted.

Callum looked to her. "He's that way with Charley as well. I've seen it."

"I suspected as much. Charley is as loyal as the day is long, so would never say anything. But I suspect Thomas has been treating him in much the same way. To my great disappointment, Charley now tries not to spend too much time in the North. So I only get to see him when I'm in London."

He angled her heel to pick up more light and he set his face close to it, studying it. "I can see the slivers—no, it's more of a chunk of a branch."

He set the bloody handkerchief on his leg and moved to pluck it out.

She jerked forward, grabbing his arm. "Wait, I should probably do it."

He cocked an eyebrow at her. "Don't think I can pull a sliver?"

Her lips pursed as she shrugged. "You don't have the smallest hands."

He ignored her and pinched his fingers together at her heel. A jab of pain and then relief—the chunk of the branch was dislodged. She hadn't realized how painful it had become until he'd pointed out the dripping blood.

"There. The blood will flow for a bit, but I imagine it will scab soon." He picked up the handkerchief and held it to her heel where blood had started to flow fast again.

He set her calf down onto his thigh, holding the cloth tight to her heel to stem the flow.

Nemity looked at him, her lips pulling to the side.

She was usually a good judge of character, except when it came to men. Handsome men. Even if the man sitting next to her was a giant, she had to admit he was handsome in a brutal, feral way. Dark hair with a shadow of dark stubble across a hard jawline. A strong nose with a bump in the middle that looked like it had been broken at one time. Eyes that were canny and colorless—except not truly colorless, more grey.

Her immediate judgement on him may have been all wrong. Upon further reflection, he wasn't an oaf. Wasn't an idiot. He had gentle hands, no matter their size. And didn't appear to be Charley's lapdog.

"Are you actually soft?" she asked.

His gaze locked onto her, the hard planes of his face tightening into indestructible iron lines. "The look in your eyes—don't make that mistake. I'm as hard as they come."

True, his ministrations on her heel had been so nonchalant, it was clear he'd dealt with blood a lot in his life. Had she mistaken that for softness?

She studied him for a long moment.

He knew blood, but he wasn't death. Not like she'd first thought when she'd darted in front of him. Far from it.

He might even be kind.

Or he might be using his connection through Charley to get close to her.

He wouldn't be the first.

She settled her back against the side arm of the sofa, her fingers picking at her damp skirt. "How is it that you met Charley? I've never heard him mention you."

"We met in London in late January."

She nodded. It made sense since she hadn't seen Charley

very often since early January, except at the opera or the park a few times. She'd been far too distracted this last year with things beyond the realm of parties and balls.

"We both served under Edward Paget in the army at different times. A happenstance meeting at Boodle's."

"And you enjoy his company?"

He half shook his head. "I do. Charley is…Charley."

She chuckled. "A never-ending source of mayhem and fun."

"He is that. And he likes my company well enough. And you are right about the muscle. I am good at getting him out of the scrapes he gets himself into."

She smirked. "At the tables?"

He shrugged. "Among other places."

"Your shrug was just dismissive enough for me to wonder what those other places are."

"Other places not to be spoken out loud."

Nemity laughed, leaning forward, grabbing his forearm with her eyes aglow. "You've gotten him out of a married woman's bed, haven't you? When the husband has shown up?"

His eyes went wide, his stare settling on her. "How in the hell do you know that?"

She laughed, leaning back against the side of the sofa. "Charley has told me of the many times he's found himself in that predicament."

Disbelief, and maybe a tiny bit of shock, wrinkled his brow. "Why in the world would he tell you about that?"

She grinned, folding her arms across her ribcage. "We don't have a lot of secrets, Charley and I. If you've spent any time at all around him, you know he doesn't have a filter on his thoughts."

He lifted his forefinger to point at her, a quick grin playing at his lips. "That, I do know."

"Plus, he doesn't treat me like I'm breakable or a thorn in his side, which is how we're both treated by Thomas. So I guess we combined forces long ago to survive my cousin."

She flipped one hand outward, waving it between them. "But all that doesn't answer the question."

"What question?"

"Why in the world would you agree to do this? Play protector for someone you don't know?"

His left brow rose as his eyes met hers. Grey eyes. Devoid of color, but in that simplicity, the color looked so alive. Almost a glinting silver that picked up the colors around it. Her blue dress. The shard of orangish light coming in through the window. The red of the blood on the handkerchief.

Not just grey eyes—silver eyes that reflected the world around him.

"Honestly?" he asked, his face serious.

"Please."

"There are some gambling debts I have in London that Thomas will erase if I do this. He knows of my background in the army, knows I can get Charley out of scrapes, and this seems a pretty simple trade. I know well enough how to protect a lass such as yourself. All it will cost me is some of my time."

"Except that—I repeat from earlier—I don't need anyone to guard me."

He nodded, his fingers wrapped around her ankle twitching. "You may think that. Thomas does not. And he's the one that will clear my debts."

"I could clear your debts."

"Could you?" His head tilted to the side as he considered her. "Doesn't Thomas have to approve such a measure? He does control the purse strings, does he not?"

"Don't remind me." She tried to jerk her foot out of his grasp. He just held it in place, staring at her.

She sighed, lifting her right arm to balance her elbow along the back of the sofa. Her fingers dug into her still damp hair. "Would it matter in the slightest if I said that I don't want a guard?"

His lips pursed as he looked away from her for a long moment. His gaze returned to her face. "It would matter if I was the one making the decision in this case. I'm not. So I'm not the one to talk to."

Her jaw jutting outward, she blew a big breath upward and the hair alongside her face moved, tickling her cheek. Thomas wasn't to be swayed—she'd never accomplished it before. "I will just have to act as though you don't exist, then."

"I think we both already established I'm a hard one to miss."

"I do think I can manage it." She smiled sweetly at him and then yanked her foot back toward her.

This time, he let her escape his grasp.

She swung her leg to the floor, about to get up, but then paused, looking to him. "You may have just plucked the thorn from the lioness's paw. But that doesn't tame me. Far from it. I'm still going to fight this."

"I never imagined it would." He smiled. Smug bugger.

Yet in that moment, he looked classically handsome. A smile that managed to erase the brutality from the hard lines of his face.

Not that she noticed.

Not that she wanted to notice.

CHAPTER 5

Luck wasn't on her side.

Callum had watched, tired, yet oddly entertained as Nemity had spent an hour switching back and forth from railing at Thomas, to pleading with Charley for his assistance. Charley abandoned her after the first twenty of those minutes, mumbling something about getting back to Ravenstone.

Whatever Charley and Thomas had talked about out of earshot had crushed Charley's mood to the point of sulking.

A sulking Charley was no fun for anyone.

Even, apparently, Nemity, who seemed to adore him.

Which made him wonder just what Thomas had said to Charley to make him heel.

Thomas had let Nemity's spoiled rantings go on for an hour before leaving. Which was an hour longer than Callum thought he was going to allow Nemity to plead her case.

That had been two hours ago, and since then, Callum had been given a quick tour of Springfell Manor, a short walk around the grounds, and then was shown to a bedroom on the opposite end of the sprawling house from Nemity's chambers.

The woman may be spoiled, but was polite, if nothing else. Though aside from noting the basic placements of things on the tour—"here are the gardens... here is the drawing room... here is your chamber... here are the kitchens... here are the stables..."—she'd said little else to him.

Across the table from him in the conservatory where she took her meals, Nemity pushed the asparagus tips around her plate, forming them into a ring around her cut of beef. Apparently, she had little appetite when she was sharing dinner with her new jailer.

She was now stuck alone with him. Him with no Charley to soften the blow.

His feelings might be bruised if he had feelings to hurt. Which he didn't. He'd been in this position before, protecting people that didn't want to be protected. Nemity was just the latest in a long line of jobs.

She was probably the most headstrong of all the women he'd ever had under his care—he already recognized that about her. Also one of the most beautiful, though he'd recognized that when Pharaoh had almost trampled her on the lane.

Chewing on a bite of beef, Callum sighed internally. Best to start chipping away at the frost in the room, or time was going to drag on and on in this place.

He looked up from his nearly empty plate to her. "We can eat in silence for as long as it takes, but I think you're going to eventually break if you are as akin to Charley as I believe you to be. That man always needs to be talking."

Her blue eyes that drifted into purple along the outer edges of her irises lifted to him. "What you know of Charley and what you know of me are nowhere near the same thing."

His head angled to the side as he studied her. He wasn't going to argue the point, even though he was pretty well assured Nemity and Charley came from the same cut of flamboyant cloth. Flippant and carefree and not accustomed to any of life's harsh realities.

He set the tines of his fork onto his plate, giving her his full attention. "How are you two different?"

"Charley doesn't like to think, Charley likes to do." She pushed a piece of asparagus to the middle of her plate to snuggle with her beef. "I have a slightly more well-honed sense of danger afoot, which is another reason you don't need to be here."

"I thought that particular conversation was over with upon Thomas's exit."

She glanced up at him. "Just because he was done arguing doesn't mean I was done arguing."

Callum grabbed his glass of wine, stifling a chuckle at that comment. This woman was salty to no end.

But one could be lulled into thinking everything from her mouth was sweet. She had a light Scottish accent, like she'd been schooled by an English governess and spent much of her time in London, but there was just enough lilt that he could make out she was a native of the north. The lilt of it was entirely too pleasant, the type where she could swear up and down like a sailor and he wouldn't even notice what she was saying.

She jabbed an asparagus tip with her fork with as much malice as she could muster. She took the bite, chewing as she stared at him. She swallowed. "Tell me, whose husband have you saved Charley from recently?"

Forehead scrunching, his head shook. "I'm afraid that is information that must stay wrapped under the silence of the code."

"The code?"

"The code that says I never tell who I see coming or going from any bed. It's not my business."

She nodded. "It's a code I would adhere to as well. Charley doesn't have a code like that. He loves to tell me of his exploits."

He tilted his glass of wine toward her. "Just like you and Charley are very different people, Charley and I are very different people."

"Why do you spend time with him?"

"He's easy to get lost with." Callum lifted his shoulders. "Lost from life."

Her jaw shifted to the side as she nodded slowly at him, her look running over his face, studying him. "That, I understand." Her voice came soft, almost a whisper.

But in the next instant, she shook her head. "It's easy to get lost with him, but repercussions can be the cruelest rubbish. For as much as you think Charley and I are alike—living lives of madcap revelry—I've learned about repercussions in life. Charley never has."

"What repercussions have you learned of?"

"Well..." She grabbed her glass of wine and leaned back in her chair, holding the fine crystal between her fingertips, but not drinking it. "For a start, I've learned that if I ever get control over my own fortune, I will be very specific about not putting any restraints on it for my heirs. And I will certainly not force my grown daughter to have a trustee such as Thomas controlling her money."

"Yet you have no heirs. Thomas said you were a spinster?" This, he had been surprised at once he saw Nemity up close. If ever there was a woman that shouldn't go down the path of spinsterhood by looks alone, Nemity would be it. Her dark red hair, wild like it was earlier in the day, would be enough to send any man to his knees, begging to get lost in it. High cheekbones and a delicate face framed her blue eyes that never lost that indescribable spark of life—not when she was arguing with Thomas, and not even when she was sulking and giving him a tour of Springfell.

Though it was seared into his mind, he hadn't allowed himself to conjure back up the image of Nemity in that transparent white shift, taut rosy nipples straining against the cloth, the swell of her hips—it was a body meant to be explored and worshipped.

In short, most men wouldn't think twice about bedding her.

A damn brutal shame she was off-limits to him.

"Spinster." She echoed the word, a laugh on her lips. "I do like that word even if it's awful. But freedom comes along with it, so I'll happily take the title."

"You never met a man you would like to marry?"

She took a sip of her wine. "I spent plenty of time in the marriage mart. But I never met a man that I could convince myself I would like for the rest of my life."

"Not love?" He was genuinely surprised by that statement. He figured during her early London seasons she would have been a fanciful young chit with dreams of a grand love in her eyes. Much like how Charley moved through life, emotion dictating every decision in front of him.

She snorted a guffaw. "Love doesn't exist for a single young woman with a fortune. The only thing that exists for someone like me is the pressure to be ever vigilant so as to not be trapped into a marriage with a fortune hunter by a brutal scandal. Love has always been far beyond my grasp—I knew that. I was settling for like, and even at that, the pickings were slim."

"Better to just live alone for the rest of your life?"

"I have plenty of friends in London and I entertain most of them here at Springfell Manor throughout the year. I'm not alone." She took a sip of her wine. "Besides, I'm mostly just biding my time."

"For what?"

"For some of the wives of all the men that had to marry for money to die."

He choked on the wine going down his throat and had to cough it out of his lungs. "You're waiting for people to die?"

She flipped her hand in the air. "Well, not all the wives, of course. That would be sad and some of them are my friends. But inevitably, some wives will die in childbirth or an illness will befall a household. My theory is that many of the widowers will no longer be beholden to marry for the coin, for they have already done so once. That leaves opportunity for their true characters to thrive. I imagine some of the men on my dance cards were truly honorable people, and I imagine some of them were vile creatures with masks of gentility. But it was impossible for me to know what was in front of me at nineteen, or at twenty, or at twenty-one. Even when I was twenty-two and in the last season where I was seriously entertaining the idea of a match, I couldn't tell the vipers from the virtuous."

He stared at her. Bloody fascinating, this creature was.

He set his wine glass down on the table. "So you wait on death?"

"I wait. As morbid as it sounds." She nodded, a determined half-smile slipped onto her lips. "I do hope to have children, so I hope I will not be waiting forever. But I also refuse to settle and marry and lose all control over my life and money, especially if it is a viper I have fallen for."

"It is morbid." He nodded. "But also, I understand the reasoning. People aren't what they appear."

He ate the last bite of his beef, setting his gaze on the fireplace behind her, watching the flames as he tried to not stare at her. Tried to not peel back her layers and figure her out.

Nemity was already proving to be nothing like Charley, even if she herself had said they were alike.

Maybe this latest assignment from Lord Hedstrom wasn't going to be nearly as taxing as tromping after Charley's flamboyant ass.

A nice break. Real sleep. All he really wanted at the moment.

Finished chewing, he looked to her. "Tell me what happened when those men tried to kidnap you."

She leaned forward, setting her glass down and picking up her fork. "It was nothing, truly. Like I said earlier, Thomas is making far too big of a to-do about it."

His eyebrows lifted. "Having a sack thrown over your head and being tossed into the back of a wagon was not a big to-do?"

"It is only of consequence if I let it be. Mr. Youngstrom stopped them. If he hadn't, I imagine I would have found a way to untie my hands and jump from the wagon. I'm quite nimble."

"If you had escaped, you don't think they would have come after you? Then what was your plan?"

She shook her head, dismissing the question as she popped a bite of beef past her lips and chewed slowly.

Not afraid to shove food into her mouth as an avoidance tactic.

Try as she might to play it off like it was nothing, her very avoidance of the topic told him she'd been shaken by the situation.

The other guardians, Rory and Seth, that he had brought up from London to help investigate had better come up with some leads on the men that had abducted her, and quick.

Quick, because he didn't want to be here at Springfell Manor longer than necessary. For he was beginning to rather like Nemity, and any emotion, good or bad, was never welcome on jobs like these.

It rarely turned out well.

CHAPTER 6

Her stomach growling, Nemity flipped back the sheets on her bed, crawling out and reaching for her wrap.

She should have eaten during dinner—eaten her full meal—for now she was awake and unable to sleep for the angry pangs in her stomach.

She knotted her wrap loosely around her waist, yawning as she lit the candle next to her bed.

Picking up the candlestick, she looked to the center of her windows where she'd left the curtains open and had cracked the window for fresh air. The moon was shining bright tonight—she hadn't seen that in weeks for the constant cloud cover.

Not bothering with slippers, she moved to her door, opening it, and promptly tripped over a large mass directly outside her door.

A squeal erupted from her mouth as she went down, the flame of the candle going out as the candlestick flew from her hand. She landed hard on her side, the impact knocking all the air from her lungs.

"Bloody hell." A low growl. Movement in the dark hallway shadows.

The mass belonged to Callum.

She rolled herself up to sitting. "What in the hell are you doing?"

"Sleeping." He barked back. "What in the hell are you doing?"

Rubbing her upper arm that had taken the brunt of her fall, she glanced down the hallway. There was just enough light coming in from the window at the end of the corridor to see the outline of Callum as he sat up. "I was hungry so I was about to visit the kitchens."

He rubbed the back of his head, his voice sounding perplexed. "In the middle of the night?"

"I couldn't sleep."

"I could."

She puffed out a sigh, moving to her knees to reach for the candlestick she'd lost grip on. "You do this often?"

"What? My job?" The growl hadn't lessened in his voice.

"Sleep on the floor outside a room."

"I do what is necessary."

"You do what a creeper would." There. Her fingertips touched the metal of the candlestick. She grabbed it and looked at him.

In the scant light, she saw the smallest smile lift his cheek.

"Truly, Callum. Why aren't you in your room? Was it not to your liking? You thought to lie out here so you could tell me first thing in the morning?"

"I told you, I'm doing my job." He got to his feet and held a hand down to her.

She took it and he pulled her to her feet. "Your job entails sleeping on a hard floor when there is a perfectly suitable, *comfortable* bed waiting for you? Thomas is really demanding a lot from you."

"He didn't demand anything. I demand it of myself." He didn't let her hand go and he started tugging her along the hallway. Without thought, she followed him, still trying to see the full of his face in the low light. "My job is to protect you, and it is damn hard to do so from the other side of this house. I'm at least five minutes away, even running through the corridors."

"You timed it?"

He shrugged. "I counted the steps."

"You what?"

"Counted the steps along each hallway from there to here. I know how fast I can run, and the corners would slow me down."

They started walking down the left steps of the split identical curved staircases that ran from the second level down into the grand foyer.

Her jaw dropped slightly at his statement. "Well, there is no need for that. No need to count steps or sleep in front of my door. No one would dare sneak into Springfell in the middle of the night."

"You are sure on that?"

"Well, yes." Her lips pursed, then she nodded. "Fairly sure. And even if someone did come in, they wouldn't know where to go to reach me."

"I imagine one could lurk about in the shadows in this place for quite some time." They turned down the corridor that led to the kitchens. "Not a single person on the staff saw me set up camp at your door, much less asked me about it. Lurk about, look in rooms—it would be easy enough to do at night. How many exterior doors are there here at Springfell?"

She counted in her head. "Six—no, seven."

"Not to mention the windows one could sneak through. I noticed open windows in the library, study, dining hall, billiards room, and the third drawing room you showed me, what was it called?"

"The Neptune Drawing Room."

"Yes. That one. Who closes all those windows at night?"

She stared up at his profile dipping in and out of the shadows as they walked. She didn't have a good answer for him. She imagined no one closed them at night.

Was she really living in that much delusion? Danger around every corner? Her life forfeit at any moment?

At her silence, he glanced down at her. "Why don't you want me here? Why such staunch resistance?"

They took a few steps before she answered him. "Many reasons."

"Tell me one."

She sighed. If she started telling him things, she didn't know if she could stop. And that couldn't happen.

Still, she could offer him something. "Here is the only place I am free. Not under Thomas's nose. Not under the wagging fingers of the *ton*. One would think after my many seasons, I would be a curiosity they had brushed aside, but I am not. Here I get to be me."

"It is an interesting concept, being oneself. I tend to think one is oneself no matter the circumstance or what airs are put on."

"Then you have never stood before the old biddies of the *ton*. Their pinched faces alone set a rod of straight iron into one's spine."

He chuckled. "You like to slouch?"

"I like to be *able* to slouch when the mood strikes."

They walked down the stairway to the kitchens and he led her to a roughhewn table in the middle of the wide space, pulling out a stool for her to sit on.

He unclasped his hand from the hold it had on hers, and

it wasn't until that moment that she realized he'd held her hand the whole walk down to the kitchens.

Unthinkable.

She snatched her hand to her belly, her fingers curling inward.

How did she possibly let that happen?

She set the candlestick down and he took it, moving about in the near dark. A spark in the void and he lit a spill, then set spill to wick.

Light flickering in the space, he used the candle she'd brought to light five more candles set on the table.

Without a word, he went to the side larder and pulled free a loaf of bread, finding a knife on the counter next to it.

He set the bread on the table in front of her, cut two slices from it, then moved to the larger larder at the rear of the kitchen and pulled a block of cheese out, setting it on a plate. He grabbed a bottle of wine and a tin cup as he moved across the room back to her.

She watched him curiously as he set it all down on the table and grabbed the knife to cut the cheese.

He knew his way around a kitchen.

"Thank you. Though I could have made it down here and pulled all this out. You didn't need to come all the way here, as I'm sure you want to get back to sleep."

"It is not a problem." His head stayed down as he sliced thin strips of the cheese. "I'm awake now."

She opened the wine bottle and poured the cup full, pushed it toward him, then hopped from her stool to grab another cup and fill it. "But there isn't any danger down here in the kitchens."

"Call me thorough." He grabbed another stool and sat around the corner of the table from her, pointing at the food as she sat. "Eat. Unless you want me to dig around and see what else your cook has left about?"

"No, this is good. Thank you." She took a sip of wine and then picked up a cheese slice, layering it on the bread. Exactly what she would have pulled out for herself, though he didn't need to know that fact about her.

She took a bite, swallowing it as she watched him take a sip of the wine from the simple tin cup. "What is your job, exactly? I mean, I know what Thomas sent you here to do, but aside from this, are you usually a man without a care? A man of leisure like Charley, who just got into a spot of trouble at the gaming tables?"

"I wouldn't exactly say that I am a man of leisure like Charley, though I do spend a lot of time with him in London. Honestly, my only concern is what is in front of me—my task to protect you." He lifted his tin cup to her. "So, I will do that to the best of my ability until it is no longer necessary."

She nodded, taking another large bite of the bread and cheese.

"Hell, is that wax?" She reached out across the table to his cheek and flicked her thumb across his skin, dislodging hardened wax from where it had splattered onto his face. "From my candle—I am sorry. It must have happened when I tripped."

He stilled as her fingers touched him, looking at her oddly, then shook his head. "It is nothing."

She pulled away, flicking out the wax that had caught under her nail. "Yet it was hot wax. It must have stung."

He shrugged. "Pain and I have a unique relationship."

"Which is?"

"I ignore it."

A faint smile touched her lips, her eyebrows drawing together. She waited, but he didn't say anything else.

What an odd man. And abrupt when he didn't want to answer questions.

And sinfully attractive, though not in a classically handsome way. Something emanating from him that she couldn't quite pin down, but felt in the air.

Her friends would not be quick to call him handsome. He was far too gruff. Too big. Too…manly. But she. She would. Maybe it was something one had to feel when one was sitting on the floor next to him to understand, but there it was.

Attraction.

Attraction that made her mouth water and swallow hard.

Attraction that palpitated down to the crux of her, blood rushing to her folds.

That it was the middle of the night and she couldn't sleep didn't help.

What was she thinking?

Moreover, why was she thinking with parts of her body that shouldn't have any say, in any matter, ever?

She needed to get rid of him. Stop encouraging him to even talk to her.

Her fingers fumbling, she gathered her plate and set the cup of wine on it. "Maybe I'll just take this up to my room."

His shoulders were still stiff from her earlier touch and he nodded. "That would probably be wise." He stood, swallowing the full of his cup, then returned the bread and cheese to the spots he found them.

She blew out the extra candles and picked up her candlestick.

Silently, they walked back up to her room.

He pushed open her door, stepping inside before her, and looked around, presumably to check for the imaginary brute he was sure had slipped into the house.

He stepped back, motioning her inward.

Turning sideways to step past him in the doorway, she stopped as he grabbed the door handle.

She glanced down at the floor just outside her door

where a rumpled blanket had been shoved to the side. "Are you still going to sleep out here, even though it's not necessary and I wish you wouldn't?"

He nodded, his voice gruff. "You guess correct."

She nodded. "Good sleep to you then."

He closed the door and she had to take a deep breath.

She knew what the man was doing, worming his way into her thoughts so that he could discover her secrets. Secrets she wasn't about to share with him.

Setting the food down on the small round table by the open window, she turned around, staring at the door for a long moment.

She didn't imagine sleep would be coming quickly for her.

But that didn't mean it wouldn't for him, even on that hard floor.

She looked to her bed and sighed. Defeated in this one small way, she went to her bed and pulled one of the extra pillows free.

Going to the door, she paused for a long breath, then cracked the door and thrust the pillow out into the hallway.

She held it in the air for an awkward moment before he grabbed it.

Another grunt from him.

Probably a thank you.

Blast. Sleep would escape her for some time, she imagined.

But that would give her time to imagine up ways to avoid him tomorrow, and every day after that.

Avoidance was key in this situation.

CHAPTER 7

There he was.

His feet stomping. His arms swinging long, the set of his wide shoulders heaving.

Heaving in anger, if she were to take an educated guess.

It only took Callum a good five hours to find her.

He looked like the harbinger of death again. Death sweeping across the land, dusk settling behind him as darkness took over the earth.

A sight she wasn't sure she liked or not, for if that raging ball of fury was the fury currently protecting her, she felt safer than she ever had in her life. She just didn't care for how it was currently directed her way.

Bracing herself, she poked at the logs in the wide firepit in front of her at the head of the large brick-lined pond in the middle of the expansive gardens. The wooden poking stick in her hands nearly the height of her, she stuck the blackened point of it into the fire, shifting a log along the edge so it would catch better flame.

"Where the hell have you been?" Callum's growl reached her well before he was near her.

She looked from the fire to him, watching in silence as he stomped the rest of the way toward her.

He pulled up, his breath heaving. "Where in the hell have you been?"

"Around."

"Around?" Snarling, his right hand ran through his dark brown hair, pulling at the strands. "That isn't an answer, Miss Wheldon."

She looked to the fire, poking the stick into the embers, sending sparks flying to drift up into the sky. "You need to call me Nemity."

"I don't *need* to do anything." His look pinned her. "Where were you?"

"I answer my friends. I don't answer strangers."

He hissed out an exaggerated sigh. "Do tell me where you have been, *Nemity.* You've been gone from the house for hours after you sneaked out behind my back."

"I did no sneaking. I quite properly walked out the eastern door of the house." Her head fell back, her gaze on the darkening blue-grey sky. "Is it so wrong to want just a moment to myself to breathe properly? I went for a walk."

"A moment isn't hours. You also could have told me exactly where you were going so I wouldn't have spent the last five hours searching every damn place for you."

She dropped her gaze to him. "Well then, success. You found me. Well done."

"You're being a spoiled brat."

A smile went wide on her face. That wasn't the worst thing she'd been called in her day. "Am I?"

"Bloody boorish insolent woman," he spit out through gnashed teeth and spun away.

He took three steps before she called out. "Cal—Callum. My apologies. Please stay. A fire by one's lonesome is…well… lonesome."

He stopped, his right hand curling into a fist and uncurling. It looked like it took monumental restraint to not take another step away, and then his feet crept around, his body following suit. He looked at her, his glare at her in no way mitigated.

"Please?" Her eyebrows lifted, pleading. "Keep me company. I shouldn't be out here in the gardens by myself. You never know who will come along."

Obnoxious abuse of the situation, but she didn't care.

His eyes went to slits on her, knowing full well what she was doing, but he let her get away with it.

He took a step back toward the opposite side of the fire from her and threaded his arms across his chest.

Animosity rolling off of him, he refused to look at her, his gaze scanning the surrounding landscape—along the tall evergreen hedges bordering the gardens, to the many formal raised squares of various flowers, to the allée of cherry trees, and then down the length of the long, rectangular man-made pool lined with heavy limestone blocks to keep the water in. The center grand pool was raised, a holding pond providing the necessary water for the many plant beds coming from this main source.

His eyes never stopped moving, looking for danger in every corner, in every shadow.

She watched him across the fire for several full minutes in silence. In the dark, she had to admit he was even more handsome. The dark shadows hid the animosity that usually lined his face when he was dealing with her.

She was beginning to understand he didn't want to be here at Springfell any more than she wanted him to be here —that much was evident on the sour look always lining his eyes.

But in the dark, those hostile lines smoothed away, and he

looked almost young, almost innocent. Odd, for how big he was, that he could still possess a shred of innocence.

She stuck the sharp point of her stick in the ground, her right palm wrapping around the top of it as she leaned her temple to rest on her hand. "You are taking this guarding job seriously, aren't you?"

His look finally peeled off their surroundings and settled on her. "As seriously as you should be taking your own safety. Seriously enough to want to wring your neck."

She guffawed. "That wouldn't exactly be protecting me, then, would it? You becoming the exact thing you're trying to protect me from."

He seethed a breath, his top lip curling as his head shook. "Woman, how many men have you sent to bedlam?"

She laughed, the sound echoing into the night. "Only one."

"You are serious?"

Her laughter died and she shrugged. "He was only in the asylum for a short while. And I really couldn't be blamed for it, though his mother tried to place the fault solely on me. He was unstable as it was, long before I met him. Charley will verify that fact. But that was my first scandal in London. Certainly not the last."

His eyebrows cocked. "You left a trail of broken hearts in London?"

"I don't know about hearts, but broken coin purses, yes. I don't ask, don't encourage gifts, yet some men will gamble their last desperate coins on silly baubles that they think will impress me. Why, I have no idea. Nor, I learned, could I control it."

"Men will gamble on things they think they can win."

"They wouldn't have to gamble if they just asked my opinion on the matter." She shook her head. "Then they would have known I wasn't about to marry them. That message should have preceded my entry into society—wealthy heiress, not looking for a husband."

"Plenty of men would still play those odds."

"Then that was their problem, not mine."

He nodded. "I imagine it was."

His countenance relaxed slightly, his legs shifting as he widened his stance. He pointed toward the fire. "At least it was easy to find you once this was lit."

She smiled, looking at the pool next to the fire to watch the reflection of the tall flames dance across the ripples of the water with the slight breeze. "I do love evenings like this, when it isn't too cold or damp and the fire keeps me the perfect temperature."

"You like to be outside, don't you?"

"I do." She flipped her fingers back toward the manor house. "Truly, Springfell is a lost cause on someone like me. Some people would go in there and never want to leave. While I cannot wait to get outside the walls every day. But that has nothing to do with how grand the house is."

He glanced up the gardens toward the house, considering it. "It echoes lonely, I would imagine."

"It does. But that's not the manor's fault. It was meant for grander things than me living here by myself."

"And a staff of eight."

A chuckle bubbled up past her lips. "Yes, they do make it less lonely."

She looked over her shoulder at the house. The high torches lining the gravel pathways were already blazing in the dark air. "The manor was built over the medieval castle of Lord Oppler. The castle was crumbling a hundred years ago, when they tore the stones down and built Springfell."

Turning back toward the fire, she pointed to the rectangular raised pond next to it. "They used the stones to build the pond. And this, the fire pit, the gardens were designed with this as the center. It's one of the same fire pits that they used hundreds of years ago when tournaments were held here and knights roamed the land."

He moved a step closer to her. "Knights had tournaments here?"

"Aye. Or so goes the history that was passed down to me." Turning toward the fire, she leaned on the long stick in her hand. "Mr. Youngstrom usually starts a fire for me, he knows how much I like them."

Callum looked about. "Where is he?"

"He went to bed when he saw you storm into the stables. His broken arm was aching. He figured I'd be in safe company soon enough."

His mouth pulled to a tight line. "Did he know your whereabouts today?"

She shrugged. "He usually doesn't keep track of my whereabouts, nor would I expect him to do so. He has been more vigilant since the incident, though. Why, did you ask him?"

"I did. And he mumbled something about you being on the estate."

"Not much help, then?"

"Far from it. And I think you know that."

She lifted her shoulders. She may have asked Mr. Youngstrom to be evasive with Callum, and Mr. Youngstrom was nothing if not loyal to her. He'd been stablemaster here at Springfell since before she was born.

She flicked a finger out at him. "You mentioned your background in the army—what did you do in it?"

"I went where I was needed. Fought, of course." His voice dropped slightly, slowed. Barely noticeable, but it was there. "I observed and reported. I investigated. That's why your cousin wanted me in particular to come here and not only protect you, but to help discover who would have attacked you."

She eyed him, attempting to decipher what he wasn't saying. "Were you a spy?"

His right cheek pulled back in a strained smile. "I did what I did."

Her left fingers went to her chin, tapping as she stared at him. He could be just as cagey as she was. "Were you always known as Callum Lonstrick, soldier, at these mysterious, various locations?"

His look swung to her, staring her down.

She smiled.

His eyes lifted upward and he shook his head. "No. Sometimes I was a coachman. A footman. A gamekeeper. A sailor. I did whatever was necessary to blend in."

She nodded, staring at him, trying to read his impossibly hard-to-crack façade. "I imagine you played all those parts well. Even with your size drawing attention. You've been here for a few days and I still don't know a thing about you. Were you good at it?"

"Yes. People see what they want to see." His gaze sank into her, pointedly.

She laughed. "Yes, your huge, thick fingers are capable of grasping tiny slivers from a foot. I think we established that."

He chuckled and the low sound rumbled effortlessly from him, making her own chest vibrate with the sound. A warmth she wasn't expecting came with his laughter, filling her lungs.

The grin didn't leave his face as his eyes locked on hers. "Just as long as you know how capable my fingers are."

Well...hell.

Was he flirting with her?

He was here to protect her.

Thomas hadn't said one word about Callum trying to

charm her into marriage. Though Thomas wouldn't confess to such a thing. Even if he wanted her married and out of his hair more than anything.

Hell, Thomas could have been the one to send those men to kidnap her, just so he could contrive this very situation.

She pinned Callum with a look. "What are you really here at Springfell for?"

His bottom lip jutted upward. "What do you mean? I'm here to protect you."

"No other reason?"

"What other reason would there be?"

"Thomas didn't send you here to seduce me? To trap me into marriage?" She lifted the stick and jabbed it into the ground by her feet. "For if he believes a little tryst with you is enough to trap me into marriage, he has another thing coming. Clandestine trysts have never forced me into anything. I'm even more careful about them than actual marriage."

Callum coughed, his eyes going wide. "You partake in clandestine trysts?"

Her hand flew up at her side. "No. Not at the moment. But I have. I am a spinster, after all. No proper mama of a lord looking for a respectable rich wife would now let me anywhere near her son. Which means I am currently in the position where getting caught with any of those men in a compromising situation would be enthusiastically overlooked."

"You choose to have trysts with men that will marry for money and are honor-bound to please their mothers?"

Her mouth pulled to the side. This sounded like a trap. "Maybe."

He moved closer, leaning past her to take the long stick out of her hands and he stuck it into the fire, rolling a log that was close to breaking and tumbling out of the fire onto her foot. "It sounds like you're partial to picking fairly boring gentlemen—ones that are still hiding in their mother's apron strings."

Her jaw dropped and she swatted his arm. "You don't know a thing about the men I've enjoyed company with."

He jabbed the stick into the ground and rested his elbow atop of it, looking at her. "Your description just told me anything I ever needed to know about any of them."

"Yes? And what is that?"

"That they probably didn't know what to do with you. You are a lot, Nemity Wheldon, and not for the faint of heart." His chest expanded in a deep breath, and he leaned closer to her, his voice dropping into a low rumble. "I imagine they didn't know how to make your heart thunder. Didn't know how to make your skin prickle under their touch. Didn't know how to kiss you properly enough that it swept you into a dumbfounded state of mind. Didn't know how to slip a hand down your body so slowly, it sparked every single one of your nerves alive."

She'd leaned towards him, her lips parted, her breath quickening on its own accord. "And what would you know of what those men did or did not do to me?"

He met her gaze, and the heat in his grey eyes nearly stole all the breath from her lungs. "You like to argue with me, so I know if any of them had had that effect on you, you would already be defending them. You aren't. You didn't even interrupt me, and you do love to do that. Am I wrong?"

She held his gaze for a long moment before she broke.

Broke, because he wasn't wrong. Most men didn't have a clue what to do with her.

But she would never admit that to him. So instead she did the only thing she could.

She inclined her head to him. "Good eve, Callum."

She spun and stepped around his body, stiffly walking up the expanse to the manor house.

Never once did she dare to turn around and look at him, for she wasn't sure what she would do in that moment.

Bait him some more? Probably, it was too much fun not to.

Touch his arm, flirt? Most likely.

Kiss him? Almost definitely.

None of that would do.

She chewed her lip as she walked, all of her nerves on fire for exactly what she knew he could deliver. It took her long seconds before she shook her head to herself.

No.

She wouldn't go there. Not with him. Not with someone Thomas stuck in front of her when he only wanted to auction her off.

Callum was far more dangerous than she first deemed him to be.

She needed to get rid of him before this whole debacle of protecting her took a turn she couldn't afford.

CHAPTER 8

Three more days she'd managed to avoid Callum.

She'd written Thomas several letters, still pleading her case—that she was in no danger and Callum wasn't necessary.

None of them had been answered.

The likelihood of getting rid of Callum anytime soon was slim, what with Thomas's notorious stubbornness. So this was the next best option.

Avoidance.

She'd managed that very thing, day after day. Telling Callum after breakfast she was drowsy and going back to bed, then veering out the eastern door. Slipping out of the library when he was talking with her butler, Mr. Flourin, about an impending storm. Outright telling Callum to meet her at the stables for a ride after she changed into her riding habit, and then scampering out to a trail in the forest instead.

His glowering face when he found her each and every time didn't even faze her anymore. It was actually somewhat endearing, the simmering rage vibrating under his skin when he would finally set eyes on her.

For as brutal as he appeared when he was vexed by her, there was not any true, vicious malice in him. She hoped.

After yesterday and slipping away from him three times, she almost figured he'd given up on traipsing after her. She wasn't worth the effort. Exactly what she'd been telling him during dinner every night.

So when she had her boots in her hand and slipped in the east door of the manor, she wasn't expecting Callum's hulking form to be waiting in the shadows of the corridor.

"It's dark out. Where have you been?"

She jumped at his voice—his voice that wasn't pitched to his usual bark.

No, this time, his voice was low, lethal. Something she'd never heard from him before.

Setting her brightest smile on her face, her voice went sweet as she attempted to move past him in the corridor. "None of your business."

He caught her arm as she darted past him, stopping her cold. His grip tight, his fingertips dug into her muscles. He leaned down over her, his words slow and low. "You cannot continue to disappear on me like this, Nemity."

"Why not? It suits me rather fine. Thomas is the one that wanted you here. I did not."

"I've asked you time and again to cease this…this…this infantile game you are playing at hiding from me at every corner." The growl in his words was unmistakable.

He'd reached his limit. Finally.

All he needed was a few more pushes to topple him over the edge and he would leave her, leave Springfell. Leave in disgust, yes, but he would leave.

Her gaze dove down to his hand gripping her arm, then lifted to him as she batted her eyelashes. "Infantile?"

His lips pulled tight. "Yes. Infantile, immature, foolish."

"Or maybe I just don't like you hovering over me."

"Or maybe you're a spoiled rotten chit that needs to be locked in her room."

"Or maybe you're an overbearing ogre with nothing better to do than make my life miserable. You don't need to be here, Callum. Go. Go to Ravenstone Castle. Go to London. I don't care. I'll tell Thomas to pay off your debts and he will. At this point I don't think he cares if he marries me off or if I die, as long as I'm no longer his responsibility."

He seethed in a breath. "If he wanted you dead, why in the world would he bother to have me here? I'm here to keep you safe, and you're making a mockery of it."

She glared up at him. "How many times do I have to tell you? What Thomas thinks is safe and what I think is safe are very different things."

"No, they're not. There is one route and one route only, and that is the cautious route after you were abducted. It isn't too much to ask, it isn't outside the realm of common sense. Thomas hired me because he's doing the bare minimum to keep you alive and well. While you're running around here without a care for your own safety when you don't have the first clue as to what can happen to someone like you."

"Someone like me? What does that mean?" She dropped her boots to the floor, ready to wedge her arm out of his grasp.

He leaned over her, the rage simmering below his skin starting to bleed out. "It means you are small and weak and easily overpowered and you never look around at your surroundings to make sure they are safe. You wander through life assuming—no, I don't even think you are assuming anything, I think you just believe it to your core—that someone is always watching out for you. That someone is going to save you from yourself. You don't know the cruelty that the world has in store for someone like you."

Her head snapped back, stung. The ass didn't know the first thing about her. "I don't?"

"No."

Her top lip curled, a sudden boiling ball of anger surging into her chest. "You don't know the first thing about what I do or don't know."

His voice rose to match her own. "You don't know anything of the horrors. If you did, you wouldn't be acting this way."

"No. You do not get to tell me who I am, what I know." She yanked her arm free from his grip, stumbling a step backward with the force, her voice pitching in a scream. "For I know exactly the cruelty this world holds. I saw my mother gutted—a knife splitting her open. I saw her die slowly. Blood pooling around her. I saw that."

Her hand thumped onto her chest with every other word. "I was the one that felt the life in her blood soaking into my fingers, knowing I couldn't do anything to save her. I'm the one that had to watch the tears in her eyes when she told me she loved me for the last time. Told me to never bow, never settle. I'm the one that lived that horror. So yes. *Yes.* I damn well know what this world can do to someone weak and ignorant and stupid like myself."

His face had shifted from rage to shock in a matter of seconds. "Nem—"

"No." Her hand flew up to stop him. "Knowing what this world can deliver—what evil can do—and living in fear of it are very different things. And I will never..." Her eyes closed, her head shaking. "I will *never,* as long as I have breath in my body, choose the fear. I do so, and I fail my mother. I fail her in everything she taught me, in everything she was. She was a beautiful diamond that embraced life—on her own terms—and she made damn sure I did as well."

She whipped around and ran down the corridor, tears blinding her as she took a right and aimed for the closest servants' stairs. Fumbling with the small doorknob, she yanked the door open and stumbled into the tight, dark space, then sank onto the second step, leaning against the wall, tears streaming down her face.

She heaved a breath. Then another one.

She'd never told anyone that.

How she'd watched her mother die.

That her mother was alive when she'd entered the room.

Mrs. Jorge had travelled back to Springfell with her that day, instead of travelling with her mother. Mrs. Jorge was the one that had found Nemity curled into her dead mother's side. Pulled her away. Held her.

But even Mrs. Jorge didn't know Nemity had watched her mother die.

Had heard the gurgled breaths, the last fight for life in her lungs. In her eyes.

She'd wanted to live so badly. She had so much still to tell her. Nemity could see it in her eyes, and then watched it all… just…slip…away.

She'd never spoken a word of it, of those moments twisting between the planes of life and death with her mother. It was her time to hold just to herself, for she could never afford to let it bleed outward.

Except she just had.

She crumpled over, pulling herself into a little ball, heaving sobs wracking her body as her mother's blood washed everything in her mind a tinge of red.

Out of nowhere a hand on her back.

A thick hand. Warm. Fingertips curling into her.

She didn't look up. Couldn't.

Couldn't bear to face the pity in Callum's eyes.

A handkerchief appeared, wedged in just under her fingertips.

And then the warm hand disappeared, footsteps receding and the door to the staircase closed.

Leaving her be.

CHAPTER 9

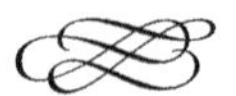

He found Nemity in the study, curled up close to the fire on one of the matching sofas.

The same one where he'd plucked that twig from her heel.

A book with a tooled leather cover was on her lap, tilted toward the fire, like she was reading, but her fingers were nowhere near the pages and her gaze was set solidly on the flames.

In her night rail and a wrapper cinched tightly at her waist, she rested her chin on her knuckles, the glow of the fire highlighting the red in her loose hair that tumbled over her shoulders. Her cheeks flush, the heat of the flames made her look like she'd just tumbled naked and well-satisfied out of a man's bed.

He heaved a breath at the thought, then pushed it out of his mind.

Off-limits. One didn't touch a client.

Still, he stood just outside the door of the study, studying her for long minutes.

Maybe he was a creeper.

Or maybe he just wanted her to take her own safety as seriously as he did.

She didn't have the slightest sense that he was lurking about, that danger could be near. She should have at least heard his footsteps in the hallway. Should have at least turned her head toward the door to see if she needed to run.

True, his feet were bare—he'd just had on trousers and a lawn shirt when he'd gone to settle in for the night outside her door, then checked in on her room only to find her bed empty. But his weight alone made the floorboards in the hallways creak with every step.

Yet there she sat, almost in a trance. Possibly even asleep with her eyes open. It was deep into the morning hours and he hadn't seen her since he'd left her alone in the stairwell.

He'd made sure she was in the house, though. Checked with Mrs. Jorge to verify she was in her rooms earlier.

She'd taken dinner in her chambers as well. Left him to an empty table.

An empty table he didn't exactly relish.

He'd eaten as quickly as possible and then went to stand outside her door, not satisfied until he heard movement within.

With her securely in the manor, he'd made his way down to the stables to meet with the other two guardians, Rory and Seth, that were working on finding the two men that had abducted Nemity.

They didn't have much to report.

Two leads that didn't lead anywhere, and they were on the trail of another lead.

Not what he wanted to hear.

He wanted the bastards caught. And soon.

He'd been on edge since Nemity had yelled at him in the corridor by the east door.

He'd had no idea her mother had died in such a horrific way.

A pertinent fact that Thomas had left out when he'd asked Callum to shift focus and guard Nemity.

Her mother had died years ago, Thomas had mentioned. But *how* she died was a fact that should have been top on the list of things he'd told him about Nemity.

Thomas also should have told him that Nemity was a flitty little dragonfly that would drive him straight into madness.

And that she was headstrong to a fault, and would try to evade him at every turn.

And that she was entrancing, and rather hard not to stare at. Probably because of all those other traits. But also because of the way sunlight seemed to ooze from her pores, even on cloudy days—a smile almost always on her face, whether she was eating or working hard at sneaking off without his knowledge.

She did it all with an odd enthusiasm for life and a laugh at her lips.

All traits he was unaccustomed to.

People weren't like that.

People were dour and sad and angry and foolish.

They weren't sunshine.

He was used to fights and blades and blood and broken bones. All the worst humanity had to offer. Not grins and laughter and teasing he had no idea how to decipher.

Nemity didn't think like other women of society—at least not the ones he'd encountered. Fiercely independent. Embraced scandal. Happy to be a spinster.

He'd worked with plenty of female guardians, and while many of them were headstrong and uncompromising, they were strong. They knew how to fight. They knew how to survive.

Nemity didn't have the slightest instinct in any of those categories. Especially how to survive.

Other than her "luck" as she'd put it, which had kept her alive thus far. As though optimism and cheer would somehow deflect a blade aimed at her chest.

Callum still wasn't quite sure what to make of her. Other than he deeply, agonizingly, wanted to strip off her clothes and set his hands all over body.

Still, no matter how imbecilic her need to court another abduction, he'd been out of line earlier when scolding her. He'd assumed things about her when he'd chided her for doing the very same thing to him—assuming she knew him.

He stepped into the study and her head finally swiveled to the doorway, her eyebrows arching.

"Oh. It is you." She looked around the room as she closed the book and slid it to the side of her leg by the arm of the sofa. "You can see I haven't tried to sneak out from under your wary eye. Just here, like a good, docile little dove."

He chuckled, moving across the study. "I don't think you know the slightest thing about being a docile dove. But I do like that you didn't sneak out into the wilderness at this hour."

She looked over her shoulder at the window across the room. "I thought about it."

"I imagine you did." He sat down onto the sofa she had curled onto, leaving plenty of room between them. "I have figured that out about you—some people were not meant to be forced into houses."

"Or cages." The smile on her face told him she wasn't so much blaming him for wanting to cage her in, as much as she was teasing him. He was starting to recognize her smiles now. When she was teasing him. When she was attempting to play him. When she was genuinely gleeful at something.

He turned toward her, bending his left leg up onto the

cushion as he set his left arm along the back of the sofa. "You couldn't sleep?"

"It was elusive."

He pointed to the book she'd wedged between her leg and the side cushion of the settee, mostly out of view except for a worn corner of the leather cover. "What were you reading?"

"Nothing of note." Her eyes looked haunted for one moment before she twisted away from him to grab a tumbler of deep amber liquid from the side table and took a sip. "Usually I sleep like a well-fed wee one when I'm not hungry. It was not the case tonight."

She offered the glass to him and he took it from her.

In his experience, a woman drinking alone in the middle of the night was never a good thing.

Better that he drink with her in this instance.

He took a sip. Cognac. Bold of her. Though everything about her shouted bold.

He let the liquid slide down into his belly, then cleared his throat. "I am sorry."

She settled back against the cushions, facing him as a frown pushed up her lower lip. "For what?"

"For assuming you were one thing instead of realizing that people have layers, you included."

Her tongue pushed out the side of her cheek. "You thought I was a silly, imbecilic girl?"

"Make no mistake, I think you aren't putting enough attention on your surroundings for someone that was recently abducted." His gaze dropped to his fingers twisted around the thick cut glass in his hand, shards of light from the fire catching the angles and sparkling. His look lifted to her. "But that doesn't mean you don't know pain. That was where I went wrong and I'm sorry."

Her blue eyes drifted to sadness as she nodded an acceptance of his apology.

"But please, hear me when I tell you this, Nemity. You need to be more wary of your surroundings, at least until we track down who abducted you."

Her look dropped to her hands, her fingernails picking at each other. "You think you will be able to find them?"

"I know it, actually. I have two of the best trackers I know on the job, combing every nook and cranny and hell hole in the area looking for the vermin."

Her gaze lifted, setting hard on him. "You sound confident."

"I am."

"Then I shouldn't really need to worry, or be more wary of my surroundings now, should I?"

His fingers flexed around the glass, ready to strangle her until he saw the slightest tilt of the right side of her mouth.

Mischievous hoyden.

He took a large swallow of the cognac because he damn well needed it when dealing with her and he handed her back the glass. The grin fully appearing on her face, she took another sip of the drink, then set the glass on the side table.

His finger flicked toward her. "Is your one aim in life to drive me stark mad?"

"My aim in life is to have fun." She shrugged, the grin not leaving her lips. "To enjoy each moment as it comes to me. Sometimes the opportunity to tease you is so big and bountiful it is hard to resist."

He shook his head. "We haven't found those men. It is not yet time to be lighthearted about the situation. You need to be more careful."

"Why?" She gave a dramatic sigh, her face tilting up to the ceiling. "Why live like that?"

His gaze sliced into her, his voice grave. It seemed impossible to instill fear into her, but he needed to do it. For her own safety. "It will keep you alive. That seems like a good reason."

Her look dropped to him. "I thought you were keeping me alive."

"I will if I know where you are. That is the key part that is currently missing. You need to let me know when you are leaving the main grounds. Just promise me you'll do so."

Her head angled to the right, the side of it pressing onto the high back of the sofa and almost touching his resting hand. In an uncontrollable instinct, his fingers flexed, brushing against a lock of her hair.

The smallest gesture and one he instantly wished he could take back. One he wished she didn't notice, but her look flickered toward him, the light blue of her eyes glowing from his rogue touch or heated from the fire, he wasn't sure.

She smiled. "I'm sure it will be much to your amazement, but I'm not fully ignorant of the situation."

"You aren't?"

"No. As much as you think I am a wild, ignorant hellion, I have taken precautions. Anytime I am in the gardens, which is where those men stole me from, one of the staff knows where I am—either Mrs. Jorge or Mr. Youngstrom."

"And when you're not in the gardens?"

Her mouth pulled to the side. "If I am unfindable by you, I doubt I am findable by a couple of imbecilic brutes trying to capture me."

"Why do you think they are imbeciles?"

She scoffed a laugh, pulling her head away from the rear of the sofa. "For the ridiculous way they tried to take me. They threw a bag over my head, tied my wrists together and threw me under a blanket in the back of a wagon, but didn't bother to truly hide me. And then Mr. Youngstrom merely had to sidle up his horse next to the wagon, lean in, and grab my arm to pull me from the wagon. Just as I tumbled out, his sleeve got caught on a board of the wagon and it unseated him from his horse. That's how he broke his arm. He didn't even have to fight them off."

His eyebrows lifted. "And you landed on the road? You must have been injured."

"Some bruises, nothing more. I don't feel that I was ever in mortal danger." Her hand flipped up from her lap. "I never would have even told Thomas it happened, but Mrs. Jorge wrote to him without my knowledge." Her head shook. "I swear, sometimes I think her loyalty is still to my mother instead of me."

He nodded, suddenly glad he hadn't found her sleeping in her bed earlier. She'd told him more tonight than she ever had. He doubted she would be this honest in the middle of the day, since that was her favorite time to sneak about evading him.

His gaze ran over her body, and she looked so damn tiny curled onto the couch in her wrapper. Lonely, even. "Is it so wrong, people worried for you?"

She shrugged. "I am not sure why they would, save for I pay their salaries."

"Why is it that you think your own worth is defined by your inheritance?"

Her eyebrows lifted. "I think that?"

"I've known you for a week, and yes, I can say with certainty that you do think that."

Her lips pulled back in a smile that wasn't a smile as she scoffed a laugh. "Maybe I do. Maybe I am. Aside from my few close friends in London, I have been defined by little else other than my inheritance since my mother died. It is why people want me."

"Is it so wrong, people wanting you?"

"When they want you for the wrong reasons, it is."

He nodded, his gaze set on her. Then words he had no control over tumbled from his mouth. "What if they want you for more basic reasons?"

She blinked.

Blinked again as his words sank in.

There was no taking the words back. Not that he wanted to, for the energy that exploded between them in that moment stilled his heart beating in his chest.

With a shuddered intake of breath, she leaned forward in the same instant he did.

Their lips meeting in some odd magnetism that both of them fought but were powerless against.

Heated and raw and primal.

His fingers went deep into her loose hair, digging into the waves, strands of silk teasing his nerves. He'd wanted to get lost in her hair for far too long. Feel her breath against his. Her body pressing into his. Kissing him with just as much carnal impulse.

He tilted her head for better angle as his tongue slid past her lips, tasting her. A slice of heaven on his tongue. A trace of the cognac mixed with something that made him hungry, deep in his gut, for more of her body, more of her lips, more of her breath.

The softest guttural mewl came from her throat as she kissed him back, her tongue tangling with his, and his cock pressed hard against his trousers. His body, his fingers wanted more.

Wanted all of her.

Stripped down and raw and exposed to him. The purple in her irises bleeding into the blue as she watched him above. As he slammed into her.

Fucking hell.

Too much.

One little taste of her and he wanted too much—all of her.

Something he knew he couldn't have.

He ripped himself away from her, his head shaking. "I—I cannot. My apologies for..." He growled, rubbing his hand across his face, looking up at the coffered ceiling. Searching for willpower he knew damn well he should possess but had suddenly deserted him.

His gaze dropped to her. "There are promises I swore to Lord Hedstrom. Lines I cannot cross. This is one of them."

Her dark red hair sat ruffled from his fingers in it, her cheeks flushed, and her lips had gone puffy, bruised. Had he done that? Made her look like he'd just made her body come alive? Made her look like she'd just been thoroughly ravished?

All with one kiss?

Great fucking Zeus. One kiss and that was the result. What would she look like if he actually bedded her?

Her hand slipped down from his shoulder to trail down his chest, pure seductress. "You take this job that seriously?"

For how much he wanted to grab the back of her neck, drag her to him, and show her exactly what his body actually wanted to do to hers, he couldn't do it. Oaths sworn. Promises made.

He could only set a stony façade to his face, refusing to move an inch toward her. "I take playing with other people's emotions that seriously. I am here, but I won't always be."

Her shoulders lifted, her tongue swiping out to lick her lips.

Good hell, he wanted more of that. More of her.

She leaned closer to him, her voice low. "Are you playing with my emotions if I willingly go into it?"

He dragged a steadying breath into his lungs. "I'm playing with emotions because I will never be in one place for very long. There is always the next task that I will be called onto."

"A man with no home?"

"Exactly."

Her fingers tapped along his bare chest above the cut of his lawn shirt. "So you won't be around in what? Four weeks, four months, four years?"

He half smiled, shaking his head. "I'm not doing my job if it takes four years for us to discover who attacked you."

She pulled her hand away from him, nodding to herself, then her gaze lifted to him. "What if you never find out who did it—does that mean I'll be in perpetual danger? What then?"

He shook his head.

This he knew—he *would* find out who tried to abduct her. It was only a matter of time. "It's not going to happen. I will find them. Find out why they wanted you. And then I'll be gone."

She leaned onto the back of the sofa, folding her right arm against the sofa and tucking her head against it as she stared at him. "It doesn't bother me. The fact that you'll be gone soon enough. I am not an innocent, Callum. I am too many years and too many clandestine trysts in dark arbors beyond that. When one is put on the shelf, the whole world opens up to her. I do what I want."

Bloody hell. His cock was about to explode. He had to get out of there.

He shoved himself off from the couch, looking down at her. At her long lashes against her smooth skin, at the wild intensity fully on fire in her eyes.

For one weak, brutal second, he nearly broke—could almost feel her body under his as he pushed her back on the sofa and sank his cock deep into her.

He snapped his stare away from her.

"The problem, Nemity, is that you are an innocent to me. And I would rather keep you that way."

His legs heavy, a thousand stones of regret vibrating down his muscles direct from his swollen shaft, he turned and exited the study.

Better to leave her untouched.

Better for both of them.

CHAPTER 10

It'd taken far too long to finally discover where Nemity kept disappearing to.

Days, and it wasn't until he pretended to not be paying attention to her and then followed her from a good distance behind that he finally found her hiding spot.

Deep in the forest that surrounded Springfell Manor.

The pathway through the woods had twisted and turned, but there hadn't been very many forks on it and he managed to stay on her trail. For as slight as she was, her boots still left footprints and broke sticks in the path just like anyone else's.

He'd found her.

But he hadn't been expecting this. Hadn't even imagined this.

The brook that ran through this side of the estate cut into a shallow ravine in front of him, and just beyond the pathway, the water disappeared over a waterfall. From his spot higher up on the trail, he could see the wide pool beneath the waterfall. The black shawl that Nemity had been wearing when she slipped out of Springfell when she thought he wasn't looking was now neatly folded and set atop of a large boulder. That boulder was one in a set of three at the side of the waterfall pool that looked like they had been rolled into place on purpose for their odd positioning next to the water.

But no one would put the effort to roll boulders of that size in the middle of a forest.

The sound of the waterfall in his ears, he moved off the main trail and onto the pathway that lined the brook and then swung out a short distance to go down the hillside beside the waterfall.

It wasn't until the pathway veered back inward toward the pool of water that he realized the trail had twisted outward to go around what was a large cave next to the pool.

The entrance to the cave faced the pool and from this angle, he could see that the water of the pool bled into the cave.

But where was Nemity?

He moved toward the three boulders near the edge of the water and picked up the corner of Nemity's shawl. A waft of citrus and honey floated up to him with the touch.

Her shawl. He'd know the scent anywhere.

Was that her dress folded under it?

Her boots at the base of the boulder.

He looked around.

No movement. Only the gentle cascade of the water splashing downward in the short waterfall.

Hell, she couldn't have drowned in there, could she?

His look frantic, he searched the water, desperate for any sign of Nemity when a shard of sunlight cut through the overcast sky, shining through the trees, and something bright reflected into his eyes.

He turned toward the cave, only to see a bright white light reflecting directly into his face.

"What in the..." he muttered to himself as he moved toward the entrance to the cave.

He stopped. Frozen in place.

All along the interior walls of the cave, shells were mortared into the rock wall. Shells of all sorts—shiny ones, white ones, iridescent ones. All of them mortared onto the walls in intricate designs that created beautiful motifs. Circles and swirls and flowers created with the varying shells.

A shell grotto.

And standing in the middle of it, Nemity.

Faced away from him, her wild hair tied back with a string of leather, she stood in the water that reached up to her mid thighs, without the slightest clue he was standing behind her. Her white shift floated about the water around her before pulling inward to cling to her legs, fully transparent in the light that came in through the other opening of the grotto to his left.

His cock jerked to life.

A damn Venus emerging from the sea. A goddess.

A goddess he wanted to drag down onto his shaft, have her riding him until screams came from her lips.

Bloody errant thoughts. Lock them down.

He swallowed hard. Now was the time to exit. Get out of here while he could.

He didn't need to replay the scene from two nights ago in the study. It had taken a monumental effort to walk away from her when she was willing and mostly clothed.

To walk away from this—he'd be stark raving mad to do so.

Except wait.

What was Nemity holding in her hands? Why were her shoulders heaving?

His gut dropped.

She was crying.

Crying, every breath sending a shudder across the

smooth plane of her bare shoulders. And what was in her hands?

He squinted. In her right hand, a bucket filled with something thick and white, and in her left...were those shells?

His look flickered back to the interior of the cave.

The grotto was full of the shell designs, but in front of her, the cave wall was still bare.

She was finishing the grotto.

Her shoulders gave a heave, and an audible sob reached him.

All thoughts of backing away before she knew he was there left him.

Until the other night in the stairwell, Callum didn't think her capable of sadness. He'd only seen her happy. Lighthearted. Teasing. Not a care in the world.

His mistake.

Everyone was hiding something.

She was just better at it than most.

His stare not moving from her, he pulled off his boots, his coat and waistcoat, and then rolled up the sleeves of his lawn shirt.

His focus refusing to shift away from her slumping shoulders, he moved to the edge of the cave, where the ground gave way to the water gently lapping against the rocks that formed natural steps down into the pool.

"Why are you crying, Nem?" His voice was low, soft, set not to scare her.

She jumped, whipping around.

So much for not startling her.

Her eyes went wide as she met his stare and she shook her head, swiping at her cheeks with the back of her wrists. White mortar speckled her hands.

Her look dropped and she spun away from him, the water sloshing along her thighs and making her shift cling tight to her upper thighs. Her movements jerky, she shuffled to the far end of the cave where a pile of shells and mortar were balancing on a stack of flat rocks near the other entrance to the cave.

Callum stepped into the pool. Warm.

The water was unnaturally warm. A hot spring.

A hot spring tempered by the water running through the cave from the brook.

No wonder she could sit out here well into the chill of the evening air.

No wonder her dresses always looked wet when he would see her coming back into the main house. Just like that first day he met her.

He moved across the water, sending it sloshing as he got to her before she could set down the shells and bucket of mortar in her hands. He grabbed her arm, stopping her as he rounded her.

"Why are you crying, Nem?"

She glanced up at him. Then looked away. "'Tis nothing. Nothing." She forced out a bright smile, but her eyes were still red-rimmed and puffy, red splotches dotting her forehead.

"It is something."

She pulled her arm free, taking three steps around him toward the mound of shells, and she dropped the three white cone shells in her fingertips onto the pile and set the bucket of mortar down.

Her head bowed, she stared at the pile of shells for a long time. "This is where I disappear to. Obvious to you now, I imagine."

He looked around at the cave and the bright white shells glinting light where there should be none. "It is beautiful. Though it doesn't explain your tears."

Her look cast downward, her arm shifted outward at her

side, her fingertips trailing along the water top, sending little swirls scattering. "My mother started this project two years before she died. We always loved to swim and play in this hot spring—no matter the time of year—it was our favorite place." She pointed to the entrance closer to the main pool of the waterfall. "We can move the rocks on this end so the cold water doesn't invade in the winter."

She heaved a sigh, her look skittering about. "This place was laughter. It was silence. It was peace."

She reached out to a wall, her fingertips running along the edge of an iridescent shell. "When she died, this was where I came. I sat in here and would sleep by the rocks with my toes in the water. Mrs. Jorge sent Mr. Youngstrom out here to bring me blankets. I stayed in here for three days."

"Were you wrinkled?"

Her gaze jerked up to him, her brow scrunched. "What?"

"At the end of three days—I imagine you were wrinkled."

She laughed, sudden and wholeheartedly, shaking her head at him. "I—I guess I was. Mrs. Jorge eventually came herself and pulled me out of here. I don't remember much during those days."

The laughter was real, and his chest warmed at the thought that he'd somehow managed to produce it, but he was almost sad to see the melancholy in her dissipate. The sadness had been real—a true glimpse into her—and he already knew she covered up far too much with smiles and laughter and nonchalance.

He nodded. "Why do you come here if it makes you this sad?"

Her bottom lip jutted upward in the middle of her melancholy smile. "It doesn't make me sad. Not usually. I was just overwhelmed by thoughts of my mother today. I found something of hers in my room that I thought had been lost. But I'd had it all along."

"What did you find?"

"A missing earring. From her favorite pair. A broken pair for the last four years, now reunited. It's a pearl drop—big, but still elegant, with diamonds surrounding it and leading upward to a simple diamond stud."

"Finding it didn't make you happy?"

"It made me happy, until it made me sad." All energy seemed to drift out of her and with a long exhale, she moved to sit on the bench submerged along the side of the grotto, her white linen shift pooling about her. The bench was low enough that the water came up just past the peak of her breasts.

Callum locked his stare onto her face, not allowing his look to drift downward.

He did that, and he'd have one hell of a painful walk back to the main house.

Her arms swished back and forth under the water and she flecked off a piece of mortar that had stuck to her hands. "As long as that earring was still missing, I had hope."

The lower half of his trousers was already under the water—he may as well fully commit. He yanked off his lawn shirt and stepped back to the opening, tossing it back to the pile of clothes at the entrance to the grotto. Moving through the water toward her, his toes searched the way along the pebble-filled bottom of the grotto to the bench that lined the back half of the cave and he submerged himself, sitting next to her. The smoothest curved shells pressed into his back—a gentle massage.

His gaze centered on her. "Hope for what?"

She looked down at his bare chest and the slightest hitch of her breath made her lips part. "I looked for it right away after her death—the missing earring—but it was gone." Her gaze lifted to meet his. "One was in her ear. One was missing. I always thought that someday I would find the missing earring and it would give me answers—or at least a clue—as to who killed her."

"Where did you find the lost earring?"

"In my room. I didn't even know she had been in my room that day—we had taken different carriages from London, and she arrived here earlier than intended—no staff was here and our driver had gone into the village and the countryside beyond to fetch cook from her cousin's home, our footman and butler, and the other maid from her daughter's home. Mrs. Jorge and I were only hours behind her, but we arrived before anyone else. Mrs. Jorge went down below to see if staff had returned while I went looking for my mother." She heaved a shaky breath. "You know what I walked in on."

He nodded gravely.

"That was the only thing out of place on her, other than the knife wound straight to her belly. The only thing that wasn't where it was supposed to be. Her earring."

Could be a clue. Could be a completely random happenstance.

But he was beginning to wonder if her mother's death had anything to do with the men that had abducted her.

His mind started to churn, listing out the things he needed to do.

He needed to get on Rory and Seth to push them on their search for Nemity's abductors. Needed to find out why Thomas—or Charley—never mentioned Nemity's mother dying in such a way. Needed to find out why no one ever caught whoever murdered her mother—if it was even investigated.

Thomas was as cold as an iceberg, so Callum could see why it wouldn't register with him how devastating losing her mother in that way had been for Nemity, or even that she would still be feeling the loss this many years later.

Nemity hid so much between quips and smiles and laughter that Thomas probably never even thought to ask her about her mother after he returned to England.

Charley might have information. That was an option he needed to explore.

His mind had rambled off into work and he didn't notice it was happening until he saw it plain on Nemity's face—she was near to crying again.

He didn't want her to have to sink into it. Not when she expended so much energy trying to hide the sadness—when she clearly didn't want to feel it.

He looked around, his elbow dipping into the water as he lifted his hand to touch the wall between them. "This truly is artwork. How long have you been working on it?"

"Years." Her look followed his and she took a deep breath, then smiled, the edges of her eyes crinkling. "It should be done by now. But I often come out here to work on it, then end up just sitting in the waters. Silent. It is peace that I don't get anywhere else."

"I can see why."

She nodded, reaching between them and running her fingertips over the smooth back of several shells in the wall, her gaze centered on the curve of the line of tiny round shells that swooped into a giant fleur-de-lis. "It is the peace that slows me—or it may very well have taken me this long because I just don't want to finish it. It is my last real connection to my mother. I can trace where her fingertips pressed shells into the mortar. Remember watching her do so as I sifted through the pile of shells finding just the right size she needed next."

"You sound like you were very close with her."

"We were." Her gaze shifted to him and her eyebrows drew together. "Is this how you find out answers from an unsuspecting maiden? Pretend to care?" She grinned, flicking water at him, and the droplets landed on his chest.

"I'm not above it." He grabbed her hand before she could splash him again, and he met her gaze, his stare piercing into her. "But in this instance, no. I find myself, against my own staunch intentions and moral code, caring. Caring about you. Caring about the smile on your face and the sadness in your eyes. And not able to stop it."

Her jaw dropped slightly in a sudden breath, her right eyebrow quirking as the tip of her tongue slid out to wet her lips. Her hand in his palm twisted around and she slid her fingers up the length of his forearm.

For the life of him, he couldn't quite stop himself for wanting—needing—to slip his tongue past those parted lips to taste her again.

A force there was no defense against, he dipped his head down toward her, his lips meeting hers in a kiss that started soft.

Just one taste.

One and he would be done.

Her lips parted to him and the kiss deepened. His tongue touched the tip of hers.

In that instant—with one taste—he was lost.

Useless against his own code of valor and right and wrong.

The softness in the kiss was discarded as quickly as it began, the kiss turning searing, rabid. She met him as an equal with every breath, every guttural moan deep in her throat echoing his.

Her reaction to him only goaded him onward, willing him to ignore every speck of decency that managed to still live within him.

There was no pulling back, and the kiss turned feral, his

need to devour her from toe to the crown of her head overwhelming.

She didn't deserve to have a monster like him in her arms, yet here he was.

His hands ran down the sides of her torso, locking onto her hips, and he lifted her through the water, sliding her onto his lap. A satisfied growl vibrated deep in her throat and he plunged his tongue deep into her, then left her mouth, his lips dragging down her neck.

Her legs straddling him, she arched back against his grip as his lips moved downward from her neck, onto her chest, and he pulled free the right strap of her shift, baring her breast to him.

He locked onto her nipple, teasing the bud, sucking it, until it was hard and taut under his tongue. Her fingers threaded behind his neck and she pulled the crux of her against his raging cock in his trousers, her bent legs clamping against the outside of his thighs.

Hell, the woman was going to be the death of him. Yet he couldn't pull his mouth away from the sweet taste of her skin.

She shifted, her fingers dragging slowly down his bare chest, setting his nerves on fire, and she slipped her hands down between them. Flicking free the buttons to his fall front, his hard cock spilled into her waiting fingers and he had to still himself for the heaven that was coursing through him.

As much as he wanted to sink into her, he wasn't convinced she was ready for that—so he'd settle for her coming under his hands instead—not that she needed any help. Her hand had slid down the length of his shaft, pressing it into her folds and she slid up and down along the length of him, holding him tight to her.

Damn glorious.

She gyrated up and down, her lips parted, ragged breaths coming from her at every peak until he slid his fore and middle finger between his cock and her folds, finding her nub. Her body jerked at the touch, her scream hitting the air as her head dropped back.

Up and down, teasing along both sides of the nub until she was writhing, every cry from her mouth a begging please.

Except she didn't need to ask, didn't need to beg.

He was taking her there—taking her breath away—if it was the last thing he did.

His tongue swirled along her left breast, and he clamped down lightly on her nipple. A scream, louder than the rest, and he bit down harder.

An instant reaction, and her body tensed, then shuddered a violent release, her savage scream echoing off the grotto walls.

The sound of it, the feel of her body under his fingers, the way her nails scratched into his back, and he was sunk. She was the sun exploding all around him, and he'd never been in light like hers before.

So caught up in watching her come, his cock had strained to painful proportions.

She rode his fingers for a second more, then looked down at him, her lips parted with shuddered, rapid breaths. "I'm not doing it alone." A raw whisper, but he heard it all the same.

Her eyes flooded in pleasure, a smile came to her lips and she descended on him, her hand sliding in along his cock and she pressed the length of him back against her folds. Riding out her own pleasure, her fingers held his shaft tight against her, rubbing up and down along the back side. Pressure one way and then the next, until he was growling, grabbing her hips to grind his shaft hard against her.

His balls started to tingle deep, rabid, and her lips met his, swallowing his roar as he exploded under her hand. Surge after surge mixing in with the warm water surrounding them.

He was in hell or heaven, it didn't matter which in that moment.

Her head dropped alongside his face, her lips burying into the crook between his shoulder and neck, her breath hot and rapid on his skin.

"That." She purred out a satisfied groan into his neck, her hips still shifting back and forth, drawing the last vestiges of pleasure from her release. "That took longer than expected."

His fingers wrapped around her lower back as he chuckled. "Longer? I thought I had you screaming in record time."

She laughed, full and hearty, her body vibrating against his, and something deep in his chest cracked at the sound.

Cracked, merely because he had put the laughter in her throat.

He hoped to hell and back the crack didn't have anything to do with the solidly crafted stone walls he had firmly in place to protect him from feeling any emotion. Those walls were thick on purpose and had never been breached.

Never would be.

Her body still shaking with laughter, her wet hair landed on his shoulder as she turned her face toward his, her lips along the line of his jaw. "You did perform better than expected. Or maybe it has been a long time since I've let a man touch me." She angled her face to look up at him. "No. I meant I thought I might corrupt you sooner than I did. You held on an admirably long time to your morals."

"You've been seducing me this entire time?"

"When I wasn't trying to get rid of you." Her finger came up to sweep along the line of his jaw. "Once I accepted that you were here whether I liked it or not, I decided I may as well make the best of it. And can you blame me? Society is not here to judge me and you are a rather handsome warrior. How could I resist?"

"Minx."

He leaned down and raked his teeth along her neck in a mock bite. Damn, she tasted good. Like the water from the spring on her skin somehow quenched a thirst he never knew he had.

She squealed, trying to squirm out of his grip, but she was only able to pull back, looking at him. Her eyes dropped to his torso as her fingers traced the tattoo on the left side of his chest. "This—what is this?"

He didn't need to look down at the ink to know exactly what line in the circular emblem she was following. "The past."

She nodded, leaning forward and kissing a circle around it. Not pressing for answers.

Her lips trailed upward, across his chest, along his neck, and she pressed the most gentle kiss he'd ever experienced onto his lips. A kiss that could have gone on a thousand years and he wouldn't have dared stopped it.

With a giggle, she pulled away and the slippery little water sprite managed to slip out of his grip and was to the opening of the grotto in a flash.

"Come. We should get back to the manor. Mrs. Jorge was expecting me a while ago and I don't want her to rouse Mr. Youngstrom to come find me. I feel bad enough that his arm is broken."

He stilled, staring at her. "They always know where you are, don't they?"

"They do." She tossed the words over her shoulder with a smile.

He should have known.

She wasn't an idiot. Wasn't completely careless—though she was still far too careless for his liking.

Her staff was loyal to her above all else. Especially above the constant questioning of a rogue gentleman always inquiring after her whereabouts.

That alone was telling. People didn't inspire loyalty if they hadn't earned it.

Nemity waded out of the water, her transparent shift clinging to every curve of her body. The glow of dusk lit up her body like an ethereal being emerging from the depths of sin and debauchery.

Bloody hell, he wanted to drag her back into the hot spring for another go.

Which told him volumes.

He wanted her. Again.

And that was never a good thing.

CHAPTER 11

Darkness was quickly descending and the moon was already casting silvery shards through the treetops. Slivers of light that then reflected off Callum's damp white lawn shirt next to her on the trail.

He carried his coat and waistcoat in his arm, his trousers still soaked and molded to his frame. Which showed off his tree trunks of legs and she had to admit she rather liked the current tightness of his trousers, how the fabric wrapped around his cock—a bulge she kept stealing glances at.

What they'd just done in the grotto had a mind of its own. Not that she'd wanted to stop it.

Moreover, she wanted to repeat it. And take it further. For if his shaft felt like that in her hand, pressed against her folds...

She had to swallow hard at the thought, ignoring the tingling along the crux of her that was driving her mind into things she knew she should avoid. For the reality was, Callum wasn't just a dalliance. He was with her for a reason —to protect her—and he was Charley's friend along with Thomas's hired brute force.

So many ways this could go wrong.

She was far from a virgin at this point. But she'd been fairly particular about the three men she'd had in bed. Clean. No attachments. Plenty of wealth, if not status, so she hadn't needed to worry about a money-grub trying to trap her.

They had been quick affairs where both parties had scratched an itch and then ways were parted with friendships intact.

She glanced at Callum, dread spreading in her chest.

So, so, so many ways this could go wrong.

At the moment, Callum looked disconcerted. His stare set straight ahead on the trail, his jaw rigid.

Like what they just did was a mistake. A mistake he didn't intend to ever make again.

Which would be a bloody shame.

She leaned into him with her shoulder as she hopped over a tree root bulging into the trail. "Seriously, Callum, do you mind that I took advantage of you?"

He barked out a laugh and looked down at her, a smile on his face. "You were taking advantage of me?"

Her shoulders lifted with a grin. "It kind of seemed that way to me."

He stopped in the middle of the trail.

It took her two more steps before she halted and turned around to him.

He moved to her, closing in on her space as he grabbed her shoulders and leaned over her.

His lips close to hers. Very close. "If you took advantage of me, then I sure as hell took advantage of you."

She let out a soundless chuckle. "You did nothing of the kind. Have you not learned that I am quite famous, at least in my own mind, for doing what I want? I wanted you in the grotto. I wanted more of you than I got, frankly."

His nostrils flared.

"Yes. More of you. All of you." Her hand slipped up along his neck. "But not if this is about to get messy. Not if you are going to browbeat yourself over a choice you don't think I made. Don't misread where I was back there in the water. I wanted you and I have no expectations of you past this moment in time. We can both walk away whenever we need to."

His grip on her tightened as his lips descended onto hers. Raw and hungry he attacked, and she knew in that instant he wanted her just the same.

Her body leaned into his, falling into the kiss wholeheartedly.

Foolish, as he made no promises to walk away. Quite the contrary with the heat of his kiss. But he'd already told her his time here was short-lived. Honest from the start.

Though he could just be one of those men with morals so thick that he would never admit to himself he was about to have a tawdry affair with a spinster, even if that was exactly where this was headed.

He pulled up, his steely eyes devouring her for a long moment before he straightened, looking over her head. "We should get back before we are searched for."

She nodded, spinning around, and they crossed the road and started on the last stretch of the trail to the manor in silence.

"I was scared, you should know."

He looked down at her with concern etched into his brow. "Scared when? Why?"

"I was scared when those men stole me from the gardens and tossed me into that wagon. So scared I could barely breathe, could barely move. My body just...froze. I didn't even try to fight them off."

He slipped an arm along her shoulders, pulling her into his warmth. "Understandable."

"But I don't think you can understand. You are here because Thomas believes you to be a man of action. I am not a woman of action. And I think you look down upon that."

He paused for a long moment. Considering his words. Considering them for so long she didn't think she could trust anything coming out of his mouth.

He glanced down at her. "I have been around a lot of women of action in my day. And yes, I do respect the hell out of them. But if you think that because you froze after having been abducted that you are weak, then you are sorely mistaken."

"You are rationalizing my weakness."

"Am I? A bag was tossed over your head, Nemity. You were grabbed—none too gently, I imagine, and they bound your hands, and then you were tossed into a wagon. How often does that happen to you?"

She glanced up at him sharply. "That was the first time."

"Exactly." He didn't say anything for a few steps, then sighed. "I shouldn't even tell you this for what you'll think of me, but the first time a knife was pulled on me—I froze."

"You did?"

"Yes. And I would have been gutted if a friend hadn't barreled into the man and crushed him to the ground. Someone had my back that day, and that was the most important thing. You had Mr. Youngstrom covering your back when you were abducted—late to the party though he was."

"And look what that got him."

"He did what was right—you've surrounded yourself with loyalty, so don't put his injury onto yourself—I have seen how Mr. Youngstrom wears his broken arm like a hard-won badge." His hand on her shoulder squeezed her. "But now that he has a broken arm, you need someone else to have your back—at least until the men that attacked you are found. You need to let me have your back, Nemity."

She looked up at him. "We've returned to that, then?"

"Yes, we have. I'm here to protect you, so let me protect you. I am not a shroud of drudgery meant to spoil your days. I think I just proved that back in the grotto. That I can watch over the front side of you, just as well as the back."

She blinked, staring at him for a long moment.

He couldn't have possibly said those words with a straight face.

But he did.

She burst out laughing, leaning into him with her hand on his chest. His arm curled right along with her, holding her into his chest for a long moment as they walked.

Her laughter easing, she pulled away to walk next to his side once more, looking up at him. "You have some surprises of your own, don't you, Cal?"

"It seems you've underestimated me from the start."

"Maybe I did do that." She nodded. "But I also apologized for it."

"You did."

They stepped past the edge of the woods and he dropped his hold on her, veering a step away as he walked alongside of her so that there was ample space between them. "I imagine you don't want staff to know of this."

"It would be easier if that were the case." Her brows lifted. "Do you take offense at that? I don't mean it as a reflection on your person. It is just easier..."

"No. Walk away. No attachments. That is what you wanted, yes?"

She nodded.

"Then that is what I will give you."

They hadn't made it fully across the great lawn that lined the east side of the estate when the side door to the manor opened and Mrs. Jorge came running from the house toward them, her creaky legs working hard but not making much distance.

That couldn't mean anything good.

Nemity's feet sped until she was in a full run to reach Mrs. Jorge.

"What? What is it?"

Out of breath, Mrs. Jorge held up the sealed letter in her hand. "This, child—this came an hour ago by special messenger with the express request it get to you with no delay. It is an emergency, he said."

Her heart dropped into her gut and she grabbed the letter from Mrs. Jorge, tearing through the wax seal and tilting the paper toward the torches that were lit along the gravel pathway to the side door.

She read it. Read it again.

Didn't even realize she was shaking until Callum's hands grabbed onto her shoulders and she felt herself knocking against his steady hold.

"What is it, Nemity?"

Breathless words crept from her mouth. "It's Susannah. She's, she's…"

Mrs. Jorge gasped, her hands going to her face. "What?"

"She's dying. Says she's dying. It's not even her handwriting."

"Where is she?" Mrs. Jorge asked.

"L-London."

A choked sob came from Mrs. Jorge and she spun toward the house as she whispered, "I'll go pack your things."

Callum rounded to the front of Nemity, but made sure to keep his grip on her shoulders. Without his hold, she surely would have crumpled to the ground.

"Who is Susannah?"

"She is…she is one of my dearest friends. My oldest friend."

She started to sway, black dots filling her eyes.

Her head dropped forward, her eyes closing.

No. No time for that. She had to stay steady.

Steady and get to London.

Posthaste.

Her look whipped up to Callum. "I have to leave. Tonight. Now. Can you please rouse Mr. Youngstrom? Have him saddle me a horse. I can take the route until I can match up with the timing of a mail coach."

"A mail coach?"

"Yes—anything to get to London with the utmost urgency. It will be the fastest. Even if I rode a horse at top speed, I'd fall off dead tired before I got to London. The mail coach will get me there in days."

He nodded. "Then I'm coming with you."

She didn't argue, didn't refuse.

That he offered shook her down to her bones in relief.

For she knew she was safe with him.

Knew he would get her to London, come hell or high water.

He was just that stubborn.

CHAPTER 12

Nemity bowed her head, forcing a breath through the impossibly large lump in her throat. Attempting with all her might to hold the tears at bay.

She didn't want to do this. Didn't want to face another person dying in front of her. The tortured breaths. Wheezed words.

She'd been in here for three hours now, and knew that Susannah had been hanging on until Nemity had appeared. And now that she had, Susannah could give up the ghost.

Another piece of Nemity's heart being ripped out and set to flames.

She forced a smile onto her face, squeezing Susannah's limp hand in between her palms as she lifted her look to her dearest friend. The one she'd played knight and damsel with at Springfell in the gardens. The one that she couldn't wait to report her first kiss to. The one that had suffered with her through all the dancing lessons by old Miss Fewnhall, who'd slapped their heads with a riding crop each time they stepped out of turn.

Their friendship was forged in youth, bonding them for

life by the hours spent laughing at the absurdity of the world they lived in.

Susannah had found her match during their first season together, and had loved her husband more than anything. Then he died a year ago in a carriage accident.

Since then, the doctor had said Susannah was suffering from consumption. Nemity knew it was a broken heart that was tearing her friend away to the grave.

"You can still live through this." A plea from Nemity's lips, even if she knew it was futile.

"Hush." Susannah's gravelly voice croaked out with a breath that came from her throat, not her lungs. "Promise me…" Six labored breaths, a rattle coming with each one, made her sallow cheeks press in and out. Such beauty reduced to this. Skin and bones and lungs that didn't work. "You didn't promise me."

"But their Aunt Agnes will never allow it."

"Promise me." The sudden barked shout from Susannah made Nemity jump. With more strength than should have been possible, Susannah's voice came harsh. "Lady Agnes is a vicious hag—you know it. Promise me you will find a way."

Nemity nodded. "I will. I will find a way. I swear it."

Susannah nodded, her head bobbing up and down on the pillow. "Thank you."

The last word drifted off, and her eyes closed.

She got the promise she needed from Nemity, and she was done.

Gone from this earth.

Nemity sat there in the room, still holding her friend's hand for long minutes, letting the tears come silently. Come in a torrent of grief.

For what was to come, it would be the only moments of heartbreak she would be allowed to feel, so she sank into the purgatory of it, letting it swallow her from head to toe.

Every year, her life seemed to get lonelier and lonelier.

Perhaps that was the price of living as she did. No compromises meant loneliness.

She wasn't sure in that moment if it was all worth it. Or maybe it was, for she would leave no one behind that would grieve her. And truly, that would be a gift in itself.

Her tears finally ceased and she took several more minutes to dry her face. She could do nothing about the soaked collar of her dress, but it was dark so didn't show wetness and would dry on its own time.

Her limbs and her mind numb, she peeled her fingers away from Susannah's hand.

Now was the hardest part.

Each step vibrating a shockwave through her chest, she made it down the stairs of Susannah's London townhouse.

There.

Voices. Not hushed like every word the servants said in this home.

She moved to the drawing room, pausing at the entrance.

Callum had brought her here, insisting he would stay until she was ready to go.

He had to be exhausted.

Days it had taken to get to London. Time and again, she'd fallen asleep on his shoulder or against his chest when he'd curled his arm around her. Every time she'd woken up, he was awake, alert, ever ready to deflect danger coming her way. Even though in the mail coach there had only been two old widows that were sisters and an older gentleman that looked like a mill worker, for how mangled his hands were with chips of stone embedded under the skin. None of them a threat to her or Callum, even if he did doze off.

She'd hoped he would take this time to nap. There wasn't any danger here in Susannah's house.

But no.

He was sitting on the floor, chatting with Susannah's two young children, two and four years old.

Nemity watched them from her angle at the doorway where she could see the children but Callum couldn't see her.

Even though he had to be dead tired, he was the epitome of patience with them, his attention full on them every time one of them was talking. Animated in his responses and questions, never mind that the younger one, Jacob, talked in two-word sentences at most.

As Jacob hung off Callum's shoulder, Georgette, the four-year-old, was showing Callum a drawing she had made, pointing out all the animals she'd seen at the menagerie. The drawing full of squiggles and lines and curves with very little likeness to them, but every time she would point to a blob of lines and name an animal, Callum would exclaim with much enthusiasm, "Yes, I can see it quite clearly. That is a fine drawing."

Nemity wondered who had taken them to the menagerie. Susannah had been churning through nannies monthly this past year, ever since her husband had died last summer and she had fallen ill.

Probably Miss Brooks, Susannah's housekeeper. A salty woman, she'd worked for Susannah's family for years.

Nemity stepped into the drawing room, setting a smile on her face. "I see you two sprites have found the big squishable bear I have brought you."

Both Jacob and Georgette looked up from Callum to her. Squeals erupted from both of them as they scrambled off of Callum and rushed to her skirts.

She'd spent so much time with these two in the past year, she'd been more their mother than Susannah was able to be.

She bent down as their little feet thudded across the floor and they threw themselves into her arms. She tumbled over backward onto the floor as they laughed, landing on top of her.

Laughter shook her and her stomach muscles strained as she sat up with the weight of both of them on her chest.

She looked up to Callum who had stood. "Thank you for entertaining them. You may just be a soft one after all."

He bristled, but the slightest smile quirked the edges of his lips. "We've been through this. I have no soft side."

"I beg to differ."

Before he could argue more, she looked down at the children leaning into her.

She gave them each a big kiss and a tight squeeze. "It is so good to see you, my darlings. Tell me, are you well? You have been paying mind to Miss Brooks like I asked you to?"

Georgette nodded, her face suddenly serious. "Yes, we have. Jacob was being naughty, but I told him not to be."

Nemity gave her comment the solemnity it required. "That is very responsible of you. I am proud of you."

She set both of them off her lap and moved to her feet, but her legs stayed bent as she balanced on her heels so she was still close to eye level with them.

"Do you two remember what I told you about your mama?"

Georgette stilled for a moment, her brown eyes going huge, and then she nodded. Jacob just stared at Nemity, his eyes perplexed like he was supposed to be doing something but he didn't know what.

Nemity rubbed her palm along the side of Georgette's deep brown curls. "It is time to go see her." She stood and held her hands down to each of them. "Come with me?"

They both took a hand and she turned toward the doorway, walking out into the hallway.

She couldn't look at Callum. Not when merely seeing his

face and the pity in his eyes would undo her. She couldn't afford to crumble in front of the children.

This next half hour had to happen.

The next days had to happen.

And she was the only one that could see it through.

Her legs numb, knowing on their own where she needed to go, she trudged up the stairs, clutching two tiny hands. Numb legs delivering her to more heartache.

It was painful, the whole of it.

Pain she wouldn't allow herself to feel. Instead, letting the numbness in her legs surge upward, filling her body until the whole of her was just going through the motions.

Jacob didn't want to go into the room. He stood by the door, turned away. Georgette moved in with Nemity at her side and leaned over the bed to her mama, touched her cheek, then rubbed it.

When Susannah didn't awaken, Georgette stepped back with a gasp and turned into Nemity's skirts, hiding her face deep in the folds.

It was enough that they knew. Enough that they saw Susannah one last time.

She stood with them in the room for some minutes, no one moving. Tears slipping down cheeks.

But what was the appropriate time to stand over the dead? To stand over someone that had a piece of your heart? To stand over one's mother that was no longer alive to mother? Five minutes? Five hours?

Jacob started twisting in place and Nemity guessed that was the clue she needed. If she could have remembered her own father dying when she was three, she would have experience to draw upon for how deeply a child would feel something like this. Experience with what she needed to do to help them.

As it was, she was walking through this blind.

She ushered the two of them out of Susannah's room and back down to the drawing room where Callum stood at the window, staring out into the street below. She sat and then pulled both of them onto her lap.

"I have a question for you two."

Two identical sets of brown eyes looked up at her, blinking, silent.

"Do you want to sleep in your beds tonight or do you want to come home to my house and sleep in my bed with me?"

"Can we come with you, Auntie Nemmy?" Georgette asked right away. Jacob glanced to his sister and then nodded his head, looking to Nemity.

"Of course, darling. You come with me and we will all snuggle under the covers together and be sad together. How does that sound?"

Georgette nodded, tears welling once more in her eyes.

Nemity's heart shattered all over again.

In reality, Georgette was young enough that she would likely never remember much of her mother. Days would pass. Then years. And she would know the fact that her mother died, but she wouldn't truly remember her.

Still, it hurt like a flaming arrow going straight through her chest to see both of these cherub faces looking up at her like their world had just collapsed.

Which it had.

She would do anything to take their pain away. And that meant not shedding one tear in front of them.

"Good." She hugged both of them. "Then you will come with me. That is how it will be."

She looked up to see Callum staring at her. His head angled ever so slightly to the side as he did when he was concentrating.

Wary curiosity palpitated in his silver-grey eyes.

"Will you please tell Miss Brooks to gather some of the children's things so they can come with me? I imagine she is below in the kitchens."

Callum's lips pursed for a second as though he was about to say something, but then he nodded and disappeared out of the room.

Thank the heavens.

Because with the way he was staring at her, she was in no mood to answer any of his questions.

Of which, she was sure there were plenty.

CHAPTER 13

"You earned it." Callum held out a tumbler filled to the brim with brandy to her.

She'd only just left the children sleeping in her bed and collapsed onto the sofa down here in the library of her London townhouse when he'd appeared with the drink.

Always knowing where she was.

Taking his job seriously, whether in Scotland or in London. She should have known.

She glanced up at him and then took the glass, grateful.

Taking a sip, she closed her eyes and took a deep breath as the brandy fired a path down her throat, chest and into her belly. Feeling again. A shot through the numbness.

One more sip and the brandy did an admirable job of clearing the lump that had been wedged in her throat for the last five hours.

Her eyes opened and she stared at the flickering flames in the fireplace for a long moment and then glanced up at Callum.

He hadn't moved from the spot where he stood, staring down at her.

"You're staring."

"I am." His finger flicked toward the drink she clutched between her hands. "That help?"

"Yes. Thank you."

He didn't move.

"You are staring down at me for a reason, aren't you?" She took another sip of the brandy, then leaned to the side to set it on a small round table next to the sofa. She tucked her bare feet up on the cushions under the skirts of her wrap and night rail as she leaned on the side arm.

"Maybe."

"Well, don't dance about it." Her hand flicked in the air. "Say whatever you are going to say."

"Georgette and Jacob—you are planning something."

She inhaled a deep breath and looked up at him. She could avoid this for a while, but Callum would find out soon enough. And when he found out, she imagined Charley and Thomas would be told posthaste.

May as well push it right along with a splash of fortitude.

"I am."

"What?"

"Georgette and Jacob, they have lost both of their parents. The only other living relative they have is their great-aunt, who is a bitter skinflint that has a mean streak like a badger."

"And?"

"And I cannot let them go to live in her household." Her hand went to the lapel of her wrap, scratching at the slope of her bare chest. "Susannah already suffered that fate. Their aunt doesn't want them, doesn't like them, and I cannot bear to think of them under her care."

"I am sure their aunt will hire a governess."

"Yes, but what sort of a governess? One exactly like the

one that raised Susannah? I have heard the horror stories she told of her governesses, and the governesses were preferable to the aunt."

His brows lifted as he stared at her, clearly thinking she exaggerated. "How bad could one old woman be?"

Her eyes narrowed at him. "A demon with a cane she isn't afraid to swing is bad at any age."

He exhaled a sigh, his head angling to the side. "Yet, what can you do?"

Her chin tilted up. "I promised her—promised Susannah I wouldn't let what happened to her, happen to them."

He let out a long sigh. "So you intend to take them? Steal them away?"

"What?" Her head snapped back. "Take them? What do you think of me?"

"I frankly don't know what you're thinking, Nem."

The line of her lips tightened as she glared up at him. "I am not foolish enough to steal them away. I intend to convince their aunt to let me have them."

He nodded, more to himself than to her, and moved to the table next to the sofa. He picked up the drink he'd handed her and took a large swallow.

Good. Maybe that would calm his wild ideas of what he thought she was capable of.

The glass in his hand, he moved to sit down next to her on the sofa. "You don't think she will easily let you have them? It doesn't sound as though she would want anything to do with them."

Nemity nodded, a deep frown setting onto her face. "One would think that of her. But Lady Agnes is a paragon of society. I fear she will never allow it."

"Why not?"

She scoffed a chuckle. "One, I am a spinster. Two, the scandals of my youth."

"What are the scandals of your youth?"

"You want the whole list or the most grievous ones in this instance?"

"Give me the grievous ones."

"Charley never told you?" She eyed him. "Thomas didn't tell you?"

"Tell me what?" He seemed to brace himself, then lifted the glass to his lips to take a swallow.

"I was nearly married twice. I have two broken engagements haunting me. Unwanted goods to anyone paying attention."

He jerked the glass away from his lips, choking slightly on the brandy. He looked to her. "Two?" He could barely get the word out for the brandy caught in his throat.

"Yes. Two. One broken engagement I could survive the scandal of—my inheritance alone gave me a pass on the first one. But two…two was one too many."

He stared at her, nodded, looked away as he took another swallow of the brandy, then turned to her, his silver-grey eyes settling on her face. "What happened?"

"Do you truly care enough to know?" Usually if men in society approached her without prior knowledge of her exploits, the moment they found out about her broken engagements was always the moment of stuttered excuses and impolite exits from her company.

Yet Callum was still sitting here. His attention fully on her.

"I do, actually," he said.

She stared at him, trying to judge his sincerity. She grabbed the glass from his hand and took another sip. Good thing he'd filled it full.

"With both of them, everything was set. The engagement, banns—people in the church on one of them."

He winced. "In the church?"

She nodded. "I was walking by a little cubby at the side of the church—out of sight—as everyone arrived and got settled. I was chatting with Charley when I heard my fiancé talking with the vicar." Holding the drink to her ribcage, her head fell back, her look on the delicate wisteria garland painted on the ceiling. "I believe my fiancé's exact words were, 'Horses and donkeys must be beaten and bridled—and so must wives.'"

Callum grunted. "Ass."

"Yes. At that, he was. Fooled once." She lifted her head, tipping the glass up to her lips, her tongue rolling the liquid about in her mouth.

"And the second?"

"The second one didn't make it to the church, thank the heavens." Her head shook slightly. "Though I did rather adore my second fiancé. A week before the wedding I walked into his study unannounced and found him…engaged with another person." Her look dipped down to the drink in her hand and she swirled it, watching the rings in the amber liquid. "That person was not a woman."

Callum seethed in a breath. "Harsh."

"Yes, it was that. I actually thought that I could really love him and he could love me, but he was clearly settling when his heart was committed elsewhere. Fooled twice."

"No wonder you have chosen the path of a spinster."

"It has been the best option—suffering each of those scandals was utterly exhausting. So I have not regretted it. Not until this moment."

"Because of Lady Agnes?"

"Yes." She groaned, her head flopping back onto the sofa.

"Yet why would she not overlook all of that? Does she actually want them?"

"Heavens no. But she does know how it will look to society, abandoning her kin. And her reputation is all to her—she would never abandon them. She never abandoned Susannah, even though Susannah begged time again to be set free from her aunt's vicious claws. Susannah would have lived on the London streets if that's what it took—she even ran away three times, only to be found and brought back to her aunt. It wasn't until she married that her aunt stopped controlling every bit of her life."

"Yet you say she is an old lady now, probably mellowed with time?" He slipped the glass from her hand and took a swallow. Probably trying to stop her from getting foxed. His size alone meant he could handle liquor better than her.

She shook her head. "Evil like that does not mellow. It is the last thing to sink to the grave."

His stare set hard on her, willing her to take heed. "Yet this is not your place to interfere, Nemity. Not in your situation. Do not be rash."

Her head snapped straight up, glaring at him. "My situation?" The words seethed out, the blood in her veins turning to fire.

He didn't think she should do this. Didn't believe she *could* do this.

Ass.

What the hell did he know?

Nemity stood up from the sofa, stomping from the room.

She didn't need his damn permission to do what she must.

Let him—let society—think what they will.

She wasn't letting those children fall to that witch.

CHAPTER 14

The very air around Nemity smelled of musty decay. Thick with it.

And this was the room that saw the most people in and out, so one would think fresh air would come in with visitors.

It did not. And the weight of the stench was starting to make her dizzy.

Or it could be that she hadn't been able to stomach food since Susannah died.

She wouldn't be able to eat properly until she knew Georgette and Jacob were hers. For they would be hers. She couldn't leave them to this monstrous temple of spite and damnation that was rotting from the inside out.

Standing, Nemity glanced around Lady Agnes's drawing room, trying to stifle her breathing to low, shallow breaths. As it was, she knew the stench would linger in her hair for days if she didn't wash it out when she got to her townhouse.

The heavy thunk of the cane Lady Agnes insisted on using—far too heavy for her slight frame—clunked in the hallway outside the drawing room.

Nemity straightened her shoulders, pulled her chin up and plastered her most serene smile on her face.

Lady Agnes made her way into the room, her small frame covered in layers of black clothing. Black dress, black shawl, black cap with a black veil. The woman did love a good mourning period. All the better to exclaim her piousness to the world.

Lady Agnes ignored her presence, so Nemity waited until Lady Agnes had sat on a wingback chair by the fire and settled herself before speaking.

"Lady Agnes, it was kind of you to see me during this difficult time."

Her shriveled top lip lifted in a snarl. "Susannah has died. What could you possibly need to speak with me about?"

Nothing to do now but get into it. Nemity drew a deep breath into her lungs. "My apologies in bothering you. I am sure you are in deep mourning. I know I am."

Her shrewd eyes cut into Nemity. "Be quick about it, Miss Wheldon, as you know I do not care for your sort, nor ever cared for your corrupting influence upon Susannah. What is it you want with me?"

"I would like to ask you to give Georgette and Jacob to me. I—"

"What? No. Absolutely unthinkable."

"Please, Lady Agnes, please listen to my offer. The children will always be yours, of course, but I would like to raise them. I will bring them to you anytime you wish to see them. Susannah wished this as well."

"No. It is preposterous." She lifted her cane and cracked it onto the floor. "You are a single woman. Why would I ever let you take those children? You? An aging spinster with one scandal after another trailing her. Absurd you would even think to come here and ask me such nonsense."

Well, hell. She was truly, to her ashen bones, against this.

Still, Nemity maintained her composure, nodding and not letting her smile falter as she took in all the barbs Lady Agnes threw at her. "Except I have changed. I have asked for forgiveness for all my sins, and have forsaken all my wicked ways."

"That will get you nowhere, begging for forgiveness. I will never allow those children to even be near a strumpet like yourself."

The old witch really was against her very existence. Panic set into her chest and she glanced about the room, looking for something—anything—to save this conversation from the complete disaster it was.

Her eye caught sight of Callum's back outside the window of the drawing room, standing at the front gate to Lady Agnes's townhouse.

Heaven strike her down, it was worth the chance.

"I am sorry, Lady Agnes." Her hands clasped together in front of her. "In my haste to speak about the children, I have not been clear."

"Clear how?"

"That I now strive for nothing more than to be a good, obedient wife."

"Hah." She squawked out a laugh. "Good obedient wife—you do no such thing. You did not marry, did you?"

"No. But I am engaged. My fiancé is waiting for me outside."

"Outside? Why in the world wouldn't he accompany you in?"

"I asked him not to. You do not know him and I didn't want to introduce a new person to you. I remember how you do not like new people."

Her ancient eyes going to thin slits, she jammed her cane into the wooden floor and stood, moving to the window. She stopped in front of it, looking out the glass to where Callum was standing alongside the front gate, waiting with his hands clasped behind his back.

Lady Agnes's look swung to Nemity, her crooked forefinger pointing out the window. "That one is yours? He is a beast."

Nemity kept her serene smile in place. "Not so much a beast, as a large man that has found a way to control me."

"Control you?" She scoffed another laugh. "I know that is not possible. I remember how many torrid scandals you nearly brought Susannah in upon."

Nemity took a step toward her. "Please, if you will just meet him, I imagine your opinion of the situation may change."

"You think you know me so well?" She lifted her cane in the air and jabbed it at Nemity. "You think you can control me so well? I am old, but I have not lost my mind yet."

She shook her head. "I would never think anything of the sort, Lady Agnes."

"Hmph." She turned to the window, a frown jutting up her thin lips. "I will make my own judgment on this man you intend to marry. Banns are posted?"

"No. We have been in Scotland, so intended to marry there."

Lady Agnes's face managed to wrinkle even more than it was. "Spits. A Scottish marriage is not appropriate by any means."

"Of course, as I remember. The Scotland wedding was merely because of our location and that we wanted the marriage to happen soon. Either way, we intended to post banns and marry here in England once we were in town. But after I found out about Susannah's failing health, we travelled immediately to London as I have only been concerned about her and the children, so we have not had the opportunity to move forth with our plans to marry."

"Hmph." Her weathered hand waved in the air. "Fine. Bring him in."

With a quick nod, Nemity spun and hurried out of the townhouse and to the front gate. "Callum, I need you."

He looked down at her, his right eyebrow lifting. "Need me for what?"

"I need you to come inside and go along with whatever I say. Please." She slipped her hand around his and squeezed it, trying to infuse the desperation of her current situation through her grip. "Lady Agnes is watching. Judging at this very moment. Please just do this for me."

To his credit, the second she said the old bat was watching, Callum forced the warmest smile onto his face as he looked at her, like he was a lovestruck gentleman under her spell.

So quick it took her a second to catch up with him. It was unnerving, how he could react so fast and know the exact face to put forth.

She just hoped he could continue the façade for the next several minutes—enough to convince Lady Agnes she was telling the truth.

"Whatever you need." He lifted his fingers to touch her cheek in the softest way, then tucked her hand into the crook of his arm and they walked up the steps to the townhouse.

Moving into the drawing room, Nemity drew her hand away from his arm and stepped toward Lady Agnes.

"Callum, allow me to introduce you to Lady Agnes Dierten. Lady Agnes, this is Mr. Lonstrick."

Lady Agnes moved past Nemity, her nose high as she inspected Callum at close proximity. Her eyes ran him up and down. "He is large. But pleasant enough to look upon. But I imagine you needed a large man."

"I am pleased to make your acquaintance, Lady Agnes."

Callum bowed deeply—obnoxiously deep—but it seemed to tickle Lady Agnes's sensibilities and she smirked.

Nemity had never seen the woman smile, much less smirk.

Nemity shuffled next to Callum, slipping her hand under his left arm and pulling herself tight to his side as she looked up at him. "Before she invited you in, I was telling Lady Agnes about our engagement. How we were set to marry in Scotland, but then news of Susannah reached us and we rushed posthaste to London to see her."

"You were?" He slid his right hand over her knuckles, his grip tightening on her hand.

His face still doted on her, while the pressure of his grip told her he didn't care for this.

Didn't care at all.

She could have warned him, yes, but then he wouldn't have come in.

She nodded, her face solemn. "Yes. I was telling her how I was saddened to see our wedding delayed, but that getting to London before Susannah passed was of utmost importance."

Lady Agnes tapped her cane on the floorboards for attention, her stare on Callum, suspicious. "Nemity has said you two intend to marry in England as well."

Callum looked to her, nodding. "As is only right. A Scottish wedding is not at all proper. We intended to do so as soon as banns could be posted and cleared."

Lady Agnes's lip turned into a sneer. "No special license?"

"It is not necessary. I am a man of rules and propriety and a special license screams of people with no control." He patted Nemity's hand. "I would wait as much time as needed to marry Nemity."

The squint on Lady Agnes's eyes tightened, then relaxed and her stare dropped to Nemity. "You have finally found your match then, silly girl?" Her gaze lifted to Callum. "She was always like this, a flighty dolt in the seasons, waiting for great love instead of being sensible and making a match with a well-heeled gentleman like Susannah did."

As much as it pained her to agree, Nemity nodded. "I did not have the fortune of fates that Susannah did early in the marriage mart. My choices were unfortunate, yes."

"Unfortunate?" Lady Nemity scoffed. "You were scandal after scandal, Miss Wheldon. Your mother made the worst mistake of making Lord Hedstrom your guardian—that man let you do whatever was flitting through that empty brain of yours, and he allowed all of those scandals to happen."

Callum cleared his throat, ready to say something, but Nemity leaned into him, cutting him off. "You will be pleased to know that Mr. Lonstrick has had the proper influence on me and I have left the chasing of scandals to the past."

Lady Agnes skewered Callum with her shrewd eyes.

Nemity stared up at him. "Dear Callum, can you please tell Lady Agnes how you strive to make sure I am at all times proper and obedient. How when I stray, you are quick to correct me and set me on the proper path."

Callum coughed and she knew, without a doubt, that he was going to ruin this for her. Ruin it because he thought she was raving mad, wanting to take on these children. Mad and entirely unsuitable for it.

He coughed into his hand once more, clearing his throat. "My apologies, Lady Agnes. The London air is a change for me. I prefer the countryside."

"Nonsense, I haven't been out of London in forty years and these lungs keep pushing air in and out," Lady Agnes spat out.

He inclined his head to Lady Agnes. "You are clearly made of sterner stuff than I, Lady Agnes. And yes, I do strive to keep Nemity in line. She can be brash and impulsive, but there has been nothing that a swat with a cane hasn't fixed." He looked down at Nemity and smiled lovingly.

Nemity almost blew up into a thousand pieces but managed to keep her mouth clamped shut. She had to for the children. Had to swallow every single nausea-inducing moment in this drawing room for them.

Lady Agnes, however, took like honey on a stick to this conversation and nodded with enthusiasm as she lifted her heavy cane and patted the side of it. "Spare the rod, ruin the child. A cane is truly the only way."

Callum inclined his head to the old bat. "We are in agreement on that score, my lady."

A little bit of bile slid up Nemity's throat.

She knew what Callum was doing, saying—he was doing it for her. But still. Just the words curdled her stomach. Especially knowing how much Susannah had suffered under Lady Agnes's cane.

The old woman's pinpricks of eyes centered on Callum, then slid to Nemity. "You will come to Vauxhall Gardens three days from now. A grand fireworks display is planned. I want Lady Gernstill and Lady Turgh to meet this gentleman as well. Then I will give you the decision on my niece and nephew."

"Yes, my lady." Nemity gave her a quick curtsy. "We won't take up any more of your time today. Thank you for seeing me." Nemity gave her a nod. "May I ask that Georgette and Jacob continue to stay with me for the next few days?"

"They are not at their townhouse?"

Nemity blinked, startled. "No. I thought it would be easier at Susannah's household to make arrangements for her burial without the children under foot."

"I see. That is fine." Lady Ameila flipped out her scraggly fingers. "Leave me."

With a quick smile, Nemity rounded Callum and they

walked out of the drawing room. Her grip on Callum's arm digging in, her fingernails near to cutting through his jacket.

The wicked old hag.

She didn't even know where the children were. Didn't care. Didn't care until it provided her the opportunity to have power over something. Over someone.

She just should have taken Georgette and Jacob up to Scotland and never said a word to Lady Agnes about doing so.

Lady Agnes probably wouldn't have even remembered she still had any relations left.

Vicious crone.

She may rue the day she got into the arrangement with Lady Agnes. But she would do it. Do it for the children. For Susannah.

She needed to save them from Lady Agnes if it was the last thing she did.

CHAPTER 15

"What in the bloody hell was that?"

Callum had managed to keep his mouth closed in the carriage ride back to Nemity's townhouse. He knew well enough not to talk in front of even the most loyal servants, and he had first-hand experience with how much a coachman could really hear drifting up from below. A lot.

So he'd ground his teeth as the coach had made its way through the slow London streets.

Sensing his fury, Nemity hadn't dared to say a word to him the entire ride.

But the moment they stepped in and closed the front door of the townhouse behind them, Callum grabbed Nemity's arm and swung her into the parlour—the closest room with a door for privacy.

He slammed the door closed and let her arm go, stepping past her, but then stopped, widening his stance with his arms folded over his chest as he turned back to her, blocking her from moving deeper into the room.

"What in the bloody hell was that?" The words hissed once more from his lips.

Her look darted up to him, then fell, her stare on his folded arms. "You didn't think you were getting engaged today, did you?"

"No." The words came out low, furious. "No, I did not."

She looked up at him, her eyes wide and pleading. "I am sorry. It was going terribly with Lady Agnes and then I caught sight of you from the window and the lie…it…it just slipped out of my mouth before I could think on it. The words came out and when I heard myself say them, it seemed the perfect solution. If Lady Agnes believes me to be married soon, she won't have any objections to letting me have Georgette and Jacob. And you played the exact part of a stern master for her. I think she herself fell in love with you and was wishing she was sixty years younger."

He glared at her.

He couldn't fault her reasoning, but he sure as hell faulted her for dragging him into this debacle.

She reached out, curling her fingers onto his folded arm. "Thank you for going along with it in front of her. I know you don't want to be in this situation, but I appreciate your help. If all goes well, very few people will know an engagement was even mentioned. I would never think to trap anyone into marriage this way, much less you."

He wasn't sure if that was a compliment or a barb. "Why not me?"

"Why not you?" Her brows drew together. "Well, you have made it very clear why you are in my life and that you will be gone as soon as the source of the danger is gone. You appeared fairly confident that you will find the assailants soon, and I have grown to trust your confidence on the matter. Should I not?"

He sighed, nodding. "You should."

"This is a fake engagement only." Her hand flipped up toward him. "And you yourself said you've played many parts in your day. This is no different—playing a stern but besotted fiancé may just be your finest performance."

"If I agree to do so."

"It is just for one night, Callum. Please. You have seen those children and how sweet they are. That was Susannah's doing. Please don't let that mean hag have at them. She will destroy them."

He recognized it, clear as the sun, the type of woman Lady Agnes was and how that would play out for the future of Georgette and Jacob.

That alone made him want to help Nemity.

But he didn't care for surprises, and Nemity and her damn impulsiveness had just thrust him into one hell of a disaster in the making.

Unthreading his arms, he took a step away from her, going to the sideboard and pouring himself two fingers of brandy. He swallowed it down in one gulp, set the glass down, and turned back toward her. She hadn't moved from where she stood in front of the door.

"I will consider helping you, but it will cost you."

"Cost me what?" Her hands went behind her, her fingers tracing about the doorknob like she was ready to bolt.

He took a step toward her. "What other secrets are you hiding?"

"What do you mean? Why do you think I'm hiding anything?"

His eyebrows lifted. She was going to be coy about it? Fine. He'd ask her point blank. "Susannah's children?"

Her eyes lifted upward to the bedroom she'd left them in with one of her London maids while they'd gone to talk with Lady Agnes. "What about them?"

"You are incredibly close to those children. It is clear you love them and you are going above and beyond to ensure you are the one to take care of them."

"And?" Her shoulders lifted. "I promised Susannah I would do so. Are you not bonded by your word? Why should my word hold so little consequence?"

"Do not try to spin this away from the question, Nemity."

"What exactly is the question, Callum?"

"Are one or both of them your children?"

Her head snapped back so hard and fast it hit the door behind her. "What?"

"You heard me."

"No—what—no." Her head flew back and forth. "What in the hell are you asking me? And why in the hell would you insinuate that I had not one, but *two* illegitimate children that I foisted onto my best friend and her husband?"

"Did you?"

She jabbed a step away from the door, her arms swinging up at her sides. "You think that little of my character that I would make a mistake like that not just once, but twice? Once could be forgiven, but *twice*? You must think me a tramp of the highest order for that. I may have had scandals in my seasons, and I may have enjoyed myself with a very few select men with the utmost discretion, but for you to accuse me of this? Of blatant promiscuity?"

She stopped her tirade, rubbing her hands across her eyes, and he could see the exhaustion playing out across her face.

She heaved a sigh. "No. No, Callum. Georgette and Jacob are not my children. I would never give up a child of mine, no matter the circumstances, no matter the scandal. I would live in exile up at Springfell without another thought if I had a child and I needed to shield him or her from the pernicious judgment of society hags like Lady Agnes." Her glare skewered him. "The judgement of people like you."

He clamped down on his tongue on her last words.

He was usually the last one to judge anyone on their actions.

But to imagine Nemity in another man's arms. To imagine her carrying another's babe. It struck a vicious chord deep within him.

Made him rear up against the very thought.

He had no right, but there it was.

He didn't want to think of her with another man. Not in the past. Not in the future.

He'd been an ass to even think she'd had illegitimate children.

She would never give up something she loved. He'd already deduced that about her. She was loyal to a fault. And she would love a child like it was her own heart beating.

Hell. In her mind, those two children upstairs were probably already hers. Probably had been since Susannah's health had begun to fade.

His look lifted to hers, his eyes earnest. "I am sorry. I should not have let my imagination run amok as it did."

"Why did it?"

"Because you yourself have admitted to affairs. And I don't like to imagine them. Don't like to imagine other men touching you."

Her shoulders fell, her body deflating of its anger at his words. She met his look, her eyes narrowing at him. "Why?"

"Because I like having my hands on you."

She shook her head, her eyes rolling to the ceiling, but a smile broke out across her lips as she let out a long sigh that turned into a groan.

He liked that he could do that—put a smile on her face and all it took was a little bit of honesty from him.

Her gaze dropped to him. "So will you do it? Be my betrothed until Lady Agnes is satisfied and allows me to have the children and bring them up to Scotland? If I get them north, I don't think she'll ever think on them again, much less ask for them. And she will die before they ever have to meet the atrocious woman. This can work, I know it can. Please say you'll do it?"

As much as he wanted to see her eyes light up when he said yes—for he'd already decided that he would help her do anything to keep those children away from that viper of an old crow—he wasn't quite done pressing this particular advantage over her. He stepped back to the sideboard and poured another swallow of the drink before looking to her.

"I'm not quite done poking my nose into your secrets."

Her shoulders lifted, exasperated. "What else could I possibly be hiding from you?"

"Lots, I imagine. You are very good at deflecting my numerous questions about your life." Holding the drink in his hand, he stepped to the middle of the room, dropping to sit on the arm of a wingback chair and stretching his legs out. At this level, they were almost eye to eye. "But I'm not asking for each and every one of your secrets, just the ones that might help me figure out who attacked you at Springfell."

She eyed him warily. "What is it you think I have secrets about?"

"It's quite clear you had a life here in London, Nem. A very full one. Friends that you adore. Susannah's children whom I think you adore even more."

"Yes. So?" She folded her arms over her ribcage.

His forefinger holding the tumbler flicked out to her. "So why were you up at Springfell Manor when all this was happening here in London?"

She turned away from him, walking across the room to look out the window of the parlour that faced the street. Carriages rolled past. Horses. People strolling along.

She was silent for a long moment. But she was considering. Finally considering telling him something of value.

She didn't turn around to him. "I had to take a break."

"A break, why?"

Her fingers reached out to softly drum on the glass in front of her. "There was an…incident."

Callum popped up from the arm of the chair and walked over to her, hovering behind her. "Another incident—as in someone else accosted you?"

"As in I was shoved into a carriage outside of the opera." She turned slightly to look at him over her shoulder. "Luckily, the heel of my slipper that night had a sharp edge to it, and I managed to kick off on the man that was inside of the carriage. Then I scrambled back down to the street before the carriage could make it down the block."

"You could have been grievously injured."

"But I wasn't."

He seethed out a livid breath. Why in the hell would she keep something like this from him? It made it damn hard to protect her. "I presume you saw who was inside of the carriage?"

Silence. She stared out the window.

He set his hand on her shoulder. "Tell me."

A sigh and she shook her head. "Lord Gwenton."

Gwenton? He searched his memory. He'd never heard the name.

"I don't know the name. Who is he?"

She turned toward him, leaning with her shoulder against the window as her arms had clasped in front of her once more. "He's German and he apparently does not know the basic customs in London society—simple things like how uncouth it is to shove a lady into a carriage to get her attention."

He grinned at that assessment. "Why did he need to get your attention?"

"Because he had it once and then he didn't anymore."

"Another broken heart?"

"Please, don't be silly." She waved her hand between them. "The man should not have been so careless with his heart if it was so easily broken. I attended several balls he was at and I talked to him at length—as long as one can at a ball—a grand total of three times. That was it. I thought him interesting, until his thick accent and overbearing manner began to wear upon me. I avoided him, and he didn't appreciate that—hence trying to get my attention outside of the opera."

"How would that have turned out for you if you hadn't been wearing sharp-heeled slippers that night?"

"I don't even bother to think on it."

His look hardened on her. "Yet you think enough on it to have kept the information from me."

"It was inconsequential."

"So inconsequential you needed to escape to Springfell?"

Her glare shot back at him. "I took a break from society. That is all. Lord Gwenton has left London, I was assured of it."

"Left London for where?"

"No." Her head leaned to the side, shaking. "You cannot seriously think he was the one behind my abduction at Springfell?"

"He tried to steal you away once, so I don't know what to think. But a detail like this—it is a fairly damn important detail, Nemity." He heaved a sigh, running his hand through his hair. "And I think you believe in people far too generously, while you don't think enough about how you affect them."

"How I affect them?" Her brows lifted high. "Three times. Three times I talked to the man."

"Yes, and how many times did I talk to you before I was imagining kissing you? Touching you?"

Her jaw dropped with a quick intake of breath.

"Exactly. You may not ask for the attention, but it finds its way to you. So you need to be damn well aware of what that could mean and how you need to be protecting yourself. Men are not kind. Men are not nice. Men are sick, randy, rutting bastards to a one if they can be, and it gives them far too much entitlement to take what they want. Men aren't to be trusted. Ever."

Her stare cut into him. "Do all those things apply to you?"

"Whether they do or not is a moot point."

"Oh, I think it a very valid point." Her hands shifted to rest at her waist. "Are you different or are you a contemptible bastard like the rest?"

"I am who I am. I have blood on my hands, so yes, to some, that does mean I am a contemptible bastard. And to others I conduct myself with a code of honor that allows me to sleep at night."

"And which man are you with me?" The blue of her irises sparked with fire, the violet rings around the edges deepening.

"I think you already know the answer to that."

She took a step closer, craning her neck so she could stare up at him. "What if I want to hear it?"

His jaw shifted back and forth as he met her stare. "If you need to hear that I want to wring your neck when you drive me to bedlam with your obstinate subterfuge and your willful ignorance—yes, you do."

Her lips tightened.

He leaned in over her before she could say a word. "You also drive me to bedlam with your damn smiles and your laughter that makes me think I wandered into a dreamy field of poppies and sunshine. You drive me to the brink of madness when my fingers are roving over your body, your skin, and making you scream under my touch. Those are the moments I would sell my soul for. But do I adhere to a code with you?" His look sank into her. "Yes. I have to. I am here to do a job, and I have to respect that."

She stared up at him, the heat in her blue eyes now unmistakable. "You're not only soft under your growl, you're actually a gentleman, aren't you?"

"If I am, no one but you has ever managed to see it in me."

She nodded, licking her lips, her voice a husky whisper. "But I do. I do see it in you. I see what you can be—at least to me."

With those words she reached up and wrapped her hands around his neck, pulling herself upward to meet his lips.

He shook his head as he slid his hand behind her. "The window."

She looked over her shoulder at the window they could be seen through from the street, then yelped as he lifted her up, and curled over her, laying her onto the floor.

For a timeless moment, he hovered over her, staring at her face, falling prey to the lust palpitating in her eyes. Lust for him.

Her mouth parted as her hands lifted up, curling around his neck and her fingernails dug into his skin.

He descended on her slowly, the touch of her lips under his like the sweetest honey. But as slow as he wanted to go, that first taste of her sent every nerve in his body into mayhem.

The kiss turned rabid, her hands going savage at his clothes, tearing off his coat and waistcoat, then ripping up his lawn shirt.

It wasn't until he was bare from the waist up did she slow, pulling away from the kiss for a moment as her eyes dipped down his body, her fingers trailing down his chest.

Then in a sudden rush, her hands dropped to his trousers, pulling open his fall front.

He cock wasn't complaining, but he stilled himself for a moment, smoothing hair away from her face. "We don't have to do this. I'll help you no matter what."

A wanton smile curled onto her lips. "That is exactly why I do want this—want you." Her hand wrapped around his shaft, sliding up the thick length of it. "And I want all of you this time. You deep inside of me."

He swallowed, having to catch his breath. Nemity did what she wanted, and she was always honest about it.

That she wanted him—all of him—it ripped open a part of him he didn't know existed. Something from the bowels of his soul that wanted—needed to make sure she felt this as he did. This unmanageable fire between the two of them that looked to scorch him at every turn.

His head dropped, and he kissed her, imprinting himself deep with every swipe of his tongue, every mewled sigh of hers that gave him breath.

Balancing on his right hand, he reached down with his left and dragged up her skirts, baring her legs.

Her right leg bent upward, and he traced the bare skin up from her ankle, to her knee, and he shifted inward, trailing his fingers along her inner thigh until he reached her folds. His middle finger slid inward, finding her already slick with want, and he swiped along her folds, finding her nub. Her body jerked with the touch, arching, and he circled the center of her pleasure until she was pulling herself up on him, her lips on his chest, gasping with every stroke.

He switched to circling her nub with his thumb and thrust one finger into her channel. Pumping. Two fingers and her legs went wide, welcoming him. A third finger filling her and a silent scream shook her, near to coming.

Her hand pushed up on his left arm, her voice breathless. "I want you. You, deep inside of me."

His mouth dropped to hers, searing a kiss on hers. He pulled up just enough to get words out, his lips brushing against her. "Hell, Nem, are you sure?"

She nodded, lifting her head to kiss him with even more fire.

Her hand shifted between them, grabbing his shaft, and she guided the tip of it to her entrance. Both of her hands came up and she wrapped them under his trousers, spreading across his butt.

Finding her lips once more, he drove into her in one solid thrust.

Her hips bucked, a carnal rasp vibrating from her.

Damn, she was tight. So damn tight clenched around his cock. It was all he could do not to come at first contact.

Her hips swiveled under him, demanding friction, and he withdrew, driving down into her again. Several more slow thrusts, and the pressure of her nails on his backside told him she was ready for more.

He increased the pace, slamming into her, a breath away from savage, and all she did was prod him faster. Wrap her legs around him. Arch her back to meet him with every thrust.

Until she was shaking, desperate for release as her nails scratched along his back, begging whispers flooding his ears.

Slipping his arm beneath her lower back for better leverage, he lifted her hips and drove into her with desperate intention. Raw. Three massive thrusts where his cock ravaged that sensitive spot deep within her, and she screamed, her body splintering.

Her inner channel constricting hard against his cock, he barely managed to pull it free before he fractured, his seed spilling onto her inner thighs.

She reached down, pumping him, drawing every last bit of his cum out of him, before her arm fell around his neck and she dragged him down to her face.

He picked her up, spinning them on the floor so he was on his back and she was on top before their lips could meet.

Her body still quivering, he kissed her, breathless, gentle, for she was a delicate prism of glass he didn't want to break. No matter that he'd just ravaged her body, punishing it in ways that he should have taken more care with.

Her body long atop his, it felt like an angel had landed on him, wanting to meld into him for warmth, for protection, for forever.

This.

In this moment. He could be another person. Live another life. A life he could actually enjoy. Embrace.

He could feel it in his chest, a living, breathing thing that begged to be set free.

Even if it could never actually be.

She moved, nuzzling her nose into his chest. Inhaling. Satisfied.

The moment slipped from him without warning, ashes scattering to a freezing wind.

He lifted his hand to the back of her hair, burying it in the lush thickness of the waves. "How many more secrets are you hiding from me, Nemity?"

Her head shifted, her cheek landing on his chest as her fingers traced down from his neck to circle the tattoo inked above his heart. "Not nearly as many as you obviously are."

He closed his mouth, inhaling.

She'd never mentioned that she thought he was hiding anything. But she was far cannier than he'd first given her credit for.

She saw the details of the world around her, the horror

and the deceptions, but she chose again and again to rise above it, to choose optimism, to choose happiness.

That wasn't idiocy. It was its own kind of intelligence.

A survival skill like no other.

It made her look strong, if not flighty. When it was really her fooling everyone around her into thinking everything was fine.

Even when it wasn't.

The strong didn't get devoured. The weak did.

A basic of survival.

Nemity was more of a match to him than he'd ever imagined.

Not that he could allow more to this than what it was. A tryst. That was all it would ever be. Could ever be.

And he'd better start wrapping his head around that reality, no matter how these fleeting moments felt.

CHAPTER 16

"Charley? What are you doing here?" Nemity didn't bother to hold in her squeal as she ran across the area in front of the Chinese Pavilions at Vauxhall Gardens.

The musicians in the upper open level of the orchestra had just broken from their last set of music, and her squeal rang out above the crowd, but she didn't care. Charley was here.

She crashed into him, her hands gripping onto his upper arms as he swept her into a hug.

He leaned down to her ear. "I convinced Thomas that I needed to get to London once we heard the news that Susannah was failing. I knew you would need me, Pip."

Her breath hiccupped and she nodded, burying her face into his shoulder for a long moment. "I do. Thank you for coming."

A hand touched her shoulder and Callum's low voice rumbled into her ear. "I'll go get us drinks."

She twisted in Charley's hug to look at Callum and nodded. He turned away and she watched him walking toward the closest bar, the boulder width of his frame moving through the crowd, causing people to jump out of his way.

Damn. He was a magnificent specimen of a man. Especially becoming in the crisp dark tailcoat that fit his frame to perfection. His waistcoat embroidered with the finest silk and his cravat knotted to perfection. He'd had his clothes delivered to her townhouse from his house on Seymour Street two days ago, and he'd dressed for her benefit tonight —dressed to impress Lady Agnes. Proving his prowess at becoming exactly what she wanted—needed—all without her even asking.

Charley squeezed her hard. "Of course we came. Once we arrived in town, I learned that Susannah had already died. You must be devastated." He pulled back from the hug to look at her. "We stopped by your townhouse to see you, but we were told you were here tonight."

"We?" She released her hold on his arms and straightened.

"Thomas and I."

"Thomas came down as well?"

"He did." Charley flipped his long fingers in the air. "I did not think he even knew who Susannah was."

"He did, actually." She nodded. "Don't you remember? When we were younger. Before Thomas left. That summer when we would all spend time together at the country parties in Norfolk? But that was in the before times."

Charley's eyes rolled up, a sigh exhaling from his lips. No one knew better than Charley how his brother had changed during his time away. "Now that was a different time, a different world."

She smiled, memories of those years flooding her mind. "It was. There was so much laughter and just…freedom. Riding in the fields. The games. Swimming. We were all rather innocent and carefree then, weren't we?"

Charley nodded, sadness twinging the outer edges of his

hazel eyes that matched Thomas's. He cleared his throat and looked around at the gaiety surrounding them. Hundreds of people in their best dresses milling about, chatting, listening to the music the orchestra had restarted, some dancing. "I am surprised you have come out tonight."

She nodded, looking around and trying to avoid his eyes.

She never could lie to Charley very well, but she couldn't tell him what she was really doing here with Callum.

If Charley decided to get involved with her convincing Lady Agnes that she and Callum were engaged, the plan could very well go to a steaming pile of rubbish. Charley loved a good scheme. And he was loyal to her and would want to help, but when he had too many drinks in him, he lacked a proper filter on his mouth.

She could already smell the Burgundy on his breath.

She couldn't risk him slipping up and saying the wrong thing at the wrong time. Lady Agnes already had her doubts about what Nemity had told her about her engagement, or she never would have asked for this second meeting with her and Callum.

No. As much as she would like him by her side, she needed Charley firmly out of the way tonight.

She gave him a sad smile. "I didn't think there was any better way to honor Susannah than to show up for fireworks here at the gardens. She always loved them, and she always loved an extravagant party. She would be disappointed with me if she knew I was sitting in the house, crying and moping about."

Charley nodded, his face serious for once. "She would hate that for you."

Nemity glanced about. "Did Thomas come with you?"

"No."

Thank the heavens. Only one of her cousins to get rid of.

"My brother stayed at our townhouse." His attention

waning, Charley looked around them, his gaze suddenly captured by a group of ladies standing near the far end of the Pavilions. "You know he doesn't come out to events like these. Much less know how to have fun at one. Is that Lady Prosswan?"

Nemity squinted, searching under the light of the lanterns at the group of ladies Charley hadn't stopped looking at. "I am not sure. I think so." Her lips pulled to the side and she looked to Charley. "Didn't your association with her flame out in the most dramatic way a few years ago?"

"Yes." He didn't look at her, his stare directly on Lady Prosswan who was laughing, setting her gloved hand on a friend's forearm, completely oblivious to Charley stripping her naked with his eyes from across the way. "But that was one marriage and one dead husband ago. She's had plenty of time to recover from our scandal."

"The same scandal that drove her into the baron's bed?"

"She never liked the man, much less loved him." He shrugged. "Besides, I don't hold grudges. She shouldn't either."

Callum appeared in front of them, balancing three glasses of wine in his hands—claret it looked, by the deep red hue. He also consciously or unconsciously blocked their view to the group of ladies. He'd been quick. Though he probably was quite good at getting a waiter's attention.

Callum held out the claret to them.

"Thank you, my good man." Charley took the glass and gave Nemity a slight bow. "I am off to see how scalded she still is by my presence."

Nemity scoffed a laugh as she grabbed her glass of wine from Callum. "Good luck with that."

Charley moved off, weaving his way through the crowd to Lady Prosswan.

Thank the heavens.

With any luck, Nemity wouldn't see Charley the rest of the night. Something she would usually be miffed about, but tonight, she needed Callum by her side and no one else.

She glanced at Callum and then turned her attention to Lady Prosswan and her friends. "Charley's chances are slim to none with Lady Prosswan, but she looks surrounded by plenty of beautiful friends, which is probably what my dear cousin is truly after."

Callum took a sip of his wine. "He does love flinging up skirts."

She chuckled and looked to him, pressing the edge of the glass to her lips. "And you haven't? Not in all the time you've spent around him?"

His face scrunched, offended. "I have far more discerning taste in the company I keep." He looked down at her and winked.

The wink looked so out of place within the hard lines of his face that she burst out laughing and started to choke on the wine. He lightly thwapped her back between her shoulders a few times.

Throat cleared, she looked up at him. "I don't know that you should wink. It is an odd juxtaposition to your usual grumpy façade."

"Grumpy men cannot wink?"

"They can if they want to make me laugh." She leaned into him, grabbing his upper arm with her hand. "I am sorry. It was entirely adorable. It was just unexpected."

His face scrunched up even more. *"Adorable?"*

Clearly that was the most egregious word she could ever utter about him.

"Winsome?"

He looked like he was about to crack her head in two.

She giggled. "Fetching?"

His nostrils flared.

"Charming?"

He stilled, glaring at her for the longest moment, and then gave a curt nod, though his words were begrudging. "Charming is acceptable."

She laughed, and it felt good. Felt real.

The night air on her bare arms with Callum next to her and she couldn't remember when she had last felt this calm. This relaxed. Her mind not scattering about from one worry to the next while she kept a smile on her face and witty comments on her lips.

Keeping her hand on his arm, she moved a step in front of him to face him fully. "Good. Charming it is. So charming it makes me want to lead you on a merry chase deep into the dark walks of the gardens."

The top of her head motioned to the right, aimed at the allée that led to the unlit lanes and alcoves of the gardens. "I daresay that seeing you in proper attire would have been reason enough for me to escape into the darkness, but your willingness to help me in this endeavor makes me want to disappear into the night with you all the more." She held his look for a long breath, wanting to just dissolve into the moment, even as she knew it had to end.

His eyes closed as his chest lifted in deep breath, then an exhale that looked like it existed merely to gain control of himself seeped from his lips. "While I would gladly take you up on that chase, I saw Lady Agnes in her supper box. Unfortunately, there is the actual purpose of us being here to deal with."

She dropped her hand from his arm and looked toward the row of supper boxes. "We should do this now while Charley is entertained and before Lady Agnes is foxed."

"Foxed at her advanced age?"

"How do you think she got so mean? I don't think I have

ever seen her not foxed, her beady little eyes spewing all the hatred she brews in that cesspool of a heart."

He chuckled. "Tell me what you truly think of her." He held out his arm for her to take and she set her gloved hand into the crook of his elbow.

She glanced up at him with a half smile. "Let us do this and be done with it. You remember all we talked about?"

"I do."

She trusted that. Trusted that he had listened to every word she'd said since they'd come up with this plan and that he was taking this as seriously as she was.

She had begun to think Callum wanted Georgette and Jacob out of Lady Agnes's clutches just as much as she did. He liked the children. During the last few days, he'd had the patience of a saint with them. He'd tossed rocks for hours with Jacob into the Serpentine when they had brought them to the park. Listened to Georgette explain in great detail every little line she drew of her animals. Had even suggested they go to the menagerie the next day so Georgette could get a good image in her head of what the lion looked like.

He had disappeared a few times to take care of some "matters" as he put it—leaving her at her townhouse with the children and the four guards he'd hired to watch the front and back of the townhouse at all times.

He didn't tell her where he was going. She didn't ask. She had too much on her mind to pepper him with questions she didn't imagine she'd get answers to anyway.

Dreading the upcoming encounter, they walked toward the row of supper boxes, and as heavy as her steps were, Callum kept propelling her forward. As if to match her mood, the skies opened up as they walked and started spitting drizzle onto them.

Callum leaned slightly toward her as they walked through

the crowd. "Remember, Lady Agnes cannot know how much you want this, want those children. She sees that, and she will wield that power over you out of sheer spite. She will take the children away from you just because she can. Because that is what evil people do. Take things away for no rhyme or reason."

He said the words with such an edge that she glanced up at him. His jaw was set hard, the muscles along it twitching. His eyes haunted. What he had just said meant something more to him than he'd ever let on.

Yet it was clear. He knew the exact type of person Lady Agnes was. And if she were to guess, somewhere in his years he'd suffered under the exact type of person as Lady Agnes.

Not that he'd ever so much as hinted to her anything about it. He dodged most questions about his past. And she had never demanded to know anything about him.

But this. The way he said it, it made her heart hurt for him in some odd way. Silly, and probably just her imagination taking a hold of her.

"Cal—"

"We're almost there." He nodded forward.

Her look shifted forward and she attempted to compose herself. "I'm going to be sick."

This moment, what they did in the next minutes was everything—*everything.*

"I doubt it. You are going to take a sip of your wine, set that smile on your face that would bore through granite it is so solid, and we are going to convince the old bat we are the perfect home for those children."

She looked up at him, at the determination on his face, and it was enough to convince her that she could do this. His belief in her made her believe it the same as he did.

He knew how much this meant to her, and he made sure she didn't falter in her steps, even when Lady Agnes moved into view. Her face wrinkled as she pointed at them, saying something to her companion on her left and the two of them hackled. The sound ringing cruel over the general din around them.

Evil, bitter woman.

Callum propelled her forward until they came to a stop across the table from Lady Agnes, sitting on a throne of her own making, passing pernicious judgement over the masses.

Is this what happened to loveless old spinsters? They turned into this?

Nemity set a bright smile on her face. "Lady Agnes, thank you for seeing us again. Have you made a decision about your great-niece and nephew?"

"Hmph." Lady Agnes grunted and made a show of pulling up her cane and cracking it onto the table. The glasses of wine sitting atop rattled, one of them nearly tipping over. "Whether or not I have made a decision? That is the first thing you think to say to me? What you want out of me? A fishmonger has more manners than you, you little hoyden."

Nemity almost shattered the glass in her fingers, but Callum's arm tightened around her hand, his bicep pressing into her knuckles.

The slightest movement and something only she would notice, but it was enough. Her fingers on her wine glass relaxed.

Callum stepped slightly forward, his face stern. "I apologize for my betrothed, Lady Agnes. Miss Wheldon does not always remember her place and that was ill-mannered. A habit I am working hard to break her of."

Lady Agnes stared up at Callum, her mouth twisting into a tiny circle, making her lips look like the end of an orange.

"Fine." She lifted her cane off the table. "As long as you are willing to break her of these bad habits. I will not have my kin sullied by the devilry of a wild Pict."

Callum inclined his head to Lady Agnes, his look grave. "That is the last thing I will allow in my household."

Poking the end of her cane onto the floor next to her, Lady Agnes stared up at him. "Sitting with me is Lady Gernstill and Lady Turgh. I will not introduce you because there is no need for them to ever commit you to memory. But I have asked them if they know of you, sir, and neither one has ever heard your name. You are not of society."

Nemity jumped in. "He is—"

"Nemity, cease." Callum set his hand on her shoulder. "The question was addressed to me. I will answer it."

Nemity clamped her mouth closed, ice slipping down her spine.

This was scary, how easily Callum slipped into this role and how brutally *real* he made it seem. Like every word he spoke was actually truth and this was really how little he thought of her.

Callum looked directly to both the ladies flanking Lady Agnes at the table, then settled his gaze on the wretched woman. "It does not surprise me that they have not heard of me. I have never lived in London, and it was only happenstance that I met Miss Wheldon in Edinburgh. She was at the Royal Museum at the university looking for the Chamber of Rarities and had found herself lost in the geological records. I walked her to the correct area."

Lady Agnes's ancient, colorless eyes squinted at Callum. "What were you doing in the geological area of the library?"

"I was doing research for an investment that I was to make in a mine in Cheshire."

"I see." Her withered lips tightened. "I may be old, but do not try to outwit me, Mr. Lonstrick. That does not answer the question I asked and my gout will not take long to ache with the drizzle that has started. Hurry with what you need to say, sir."

He inclined his head to her. "My apologies, Lady Agnes. Quite directly, my great-great-great-grandfather was the Earl of Groum."

Lady Gernstill, the elderly woman to the left of Lady Agnes sat straighter, leaning to Lady Agnes's ear. "That was the earl with eight daughters, three sons."

Callum looked to her and nodded. "Yes, and my lineage comes from the sixth daughter, and had subsequently branched off from daughter, after daughter, so I am quite removed from the family. I doubt the current earl even has a handle on who in England is currently related to him at this point."

Lady Gernstill leaned forward onto the table, her look shrewd on Callum. "Which daughter? I do remember my mother talking of the family."

He nodded to her. "Abigail. Sixth daughter, as I said. She married a vicar in Derbyshire."

Lady Gernstill paused, seeming to think for a long moment, and then she looked to Lady Agnes and nodded.

Nemity exhaled a slight sigh of relief. If there was one thing Lady Agnes and her crones did well, it was to know the hierarchy of everyone that had ever stepped foot in London.

"Blood enough, I suppose for Miss Wheldon. Her father was only a baron and Lord Hedstrom has not done his duty to see the chit wed well, as he should have." Lady Agnes shifted her glare to Nemity. "It is good that you have me to help look out for you, Miss Wheldon."

Nemity didn't reply right away and Callum swiveled the tip of his boot until it kicked into her ankle.

She blinked, her mouth opening.

She couldn't do it. Couldn't thank this woman for anything.

Callum pressed down with the toe of his boot, stepping on her foot with just enough pressure to sting.

An instant smile flashed onto her face and she nodded to Lady Agnes. "I am fortunate. Thank you for your generosity."

Lady Agnes's eyes narrowed to slits as she stared at Nemity.

Nemity held her gaze, a smile that couldn't be broken frozen on her face.

Lady Agnes lifted her cane and slammed it down onto the table again. "Very well." She shifted her stare to Callum, addressing him. "I have observed you two from afar tonight, and from up close. It appears as though you have genuine affection for each other, even though I never would have believed Miss Wheldon would choose a man as strict as yourself."

Callum nodded. "I believe that is an honest assessment of the situation. I do not adhere to the nonsense of poetry, but I believe that sometimes the heart knows what one actually needs, instead of wants. And Nemity needs a strong hand at her back. It was fortunate she realized it."

"Yes. Fortunate indeed." Lady Agnes's left, wiry eyebrow lifted. "Lord Hedstrom has approved the marriage?"

"He has," Callum said.

Lady Agnes seethed out an exhale, looking to Nemity. "You may take Georgette and Jacob and raise them. I give my permission."

Thank the heavens.

Everything within her turned to jelly and she lost all feeling of her muscles holding her upright. Sensing her imminent collapse, Callum shifter closer to her, setting his glass of wine down on the table, then taking hers from her hand and placing it down as he grabbed her upper arm with his right hand. Propping her up with the strength emanating from his hand alone.

Tears filling her eyes, her head started bobbing. "Thank you, Lady Agnes. Thank you."

"Lady Agnes does not need to witness your show of emotions, Nemity." Callum hissed out, then sighed in disgust as he moved in front of her, turning her away from Lady Agnes as he did. "My apologies, ladies. Miss Wheldon still has improvement to be made in regards to her overly emotional state."

"Indeed she does." Lady Agnes leaned to the side to see Nemity behind Callum and wrinkled her nose, looking her up and down in pity. "See that you take care of that Mr. Lonstrick."

"I endeavor to do so."

Lady Agnes grunted approval. "Before you take your leave, please note that I would rather do without any visits from the children. A letter every year reporting on their well-being will be sufficient."

"I will see it done." Callum nodded in turn to each of the ladies at the table while simultaneously hiding and propping Nemity up. "Good eve to all of you."

He turned and wrapped his arm around Nemity's waist, picking her up in front of him so her toes only brushed the ground as he walked away from the supper box. Into the drizzle that hadn't dampened the revelry happening about them, he quickly lost them into the crowd and away from Lady Agnes's eyes.

It wasn't until he was on the opposite side of the orchestra and next to the lavishly painted boards on this side of the structure that Callum stopped and set her onto her own two feet.

Her balance solid about her, she spun to him, her breathing rapid and out of control.

He saw it on her face instantly. "Nemity, what is wrong?"

CHAPTER 17

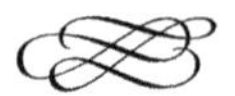

She had to swallow three separate gulps of air before she could force words out to answer Callum. "Tell me one thing."

"Yes?" His brow furrowed.

"Was that the real you back there with Lady Agnes?"

His head snapped back. "You have to ask me that? That was exactly what we talked about me doing—being a pious, controlling ass."

Her eyes closed, her breathing slipping even more out of control.

He grabbed her shoulders, probably to steady her, but it just sent her heart thudding hard in her chest, her entire body near to being out of control.

"Hell, Nem, look at me."

She couldn't do it.

His fingers tightened into the back of her shoulders. "Look at me."

She forced her eyes open.

"I scared you?"

She nodded. She didn't want to admit to it.

But he did.

He was the exact reminder of how horrible of a mistake one could make in a partner. How close she had come not once, but twice. Everyone could be a wolf in sheep's clothing. Everyone *was* a wolf in sheep's clothing.

How Callum had acted in front of Lady Agnes was a stark reminder of that.

He grabbed both of her arms, making her face him, waiting until her look crept up to him.

Her body froze, petrified stiff, as he slowly leaned down to her, his face only a breath away from hers.

"Look in my eyes, Nemity. What do you see?"

She forced her look into his, only to find the silver in his irises were sparkling, cutting into her.

Her lips parted, her words a whisper. "I see…I see the light from the torches."

"You think that light would reflect in my eyes if I was truly as soulless as I appeared back there? That light is for you. So you know I am in here. I am still the Callum you know."

He shook his head, closing his eyes as he drew in a deep breath. He opened his eyes, his look still sparkling with intensity. "That was not the real me back there with Lady Agnes. That was me channeling the ghost of someone well gone from this earth. It is not who I am, and not who I'll ever be. If you are ever, *ever,* wondering who I am, you look for the light in my eyes. It will guide you right back to the real me."

Her breath caught in her throat.

Heaven help her, she believed him.

It may be the stupidest thing she'd ever done in her life, to trust him. But she did.

He just gave her the one thing she needed in life—Georgette and Jacob safe—and he did it at apparent cost to himself dredging up his past.

Not that he would ever actually tell her of his past.

She exhaled, collapsing against him, and he wrapped his arms around her, holding her in the cocoon of him for long seconds. His chin rested on the top of her head.

So long, she began to wonder if it was more for his benefit than for hers.

His chin shifted against her head. "Lady Agnes just left her supper box and is making her way toward the main entrance. Her gout must have worsened with the drizzle." He pulled back slightly from her to see her face, then glanced around at the frivolity surrounding them. "Would you like to leave?"

She caught his eye, and a mischievous smile touched her lips. "No, Susannah would like this. I wasn't lying earlier. She would like that I am here. She would scold me for not living life to the fullest if she saw me sulking home now. So this—this festivity about us—this is how I need to honor her."

He smiled, genuine, and nodded.

She glanced to her left. "Do you know what Susannah liked to do best here at Vauxhall?"

"No."

"She liked to lead a merry chase through the dark gardens." With a laugh, she ducked out of his arms and ran down the closest allée, turning left at the first corridor of hedges before she took another right.

Callum's footsteps thundered behind her, along with a "blasted woman" muttering from his lips after every turn she took.

Turning to the right, she yanked herself to a stop. This alcove she knew, and luckily enough, it was empty. She scampered into it, spinning back toward the tight entrance, the gravel under her feet crunching.

Under an arbor of vines at the entrance to the alcove,

Callum stood heaving in the dark, the outline of him only visible from the light cast far in the distance by the thousands of hanging lanterns.

In here, with the overcast skies, it was dark and perfect.

He took one step in. Two. Three.

All she needed, and she rushed him, her lips meeting his as her arms wrapped around his neck.

His hand slid in along her jawline, adjusting the angle of her head so he could deepen the kiss, and she sank into the overwhelming air of him.

It was like this each and every time he kissed her.

Overwhelming and mind numbing. She lost each and every thought in her brain, except for the crushing urge to rip off his clothes and crawl onto him. And then to let everything she was smother into his being.

She backed up, pulling him with her until her shoulder blades brushed against the shrubbery.

There. Far enough into the alcove that one could only see the back of him if they stumbled by the opening.

One would know without a doubt what he was doing, but there was no telling who he was doing it with, or even who he was.

The perfect spot and she was going to utilize it to its full possibilities.

He pulled up slightly. "I don't want you to ever be scared of me, Nem."

"I'm not. I see—I see the you that would never hurt me, never put me at risk. I see that, who you are underneath this brawn that people don't like to look beneath."

His breath hitched. "Hell, you're destroying me right now."

She chuckled. "Let me help you out and make that complete destruction."

She popped free the buttons on his fall front, his shaft spilling into her hands.

Damn, he was so big. So big and hard she'd been sure he was going to split her in two that first time he sank deep into her.

To her utter surprise, his shaft had slid flawlessly into her, like the best fitting glove, every nook and cranny filled to perfection. The man had stamina beyond anything she'd experienced—able to control himself until she was writhing, coming violently on his cock.

His lips captured hers and he kissed her, his tongue diving deep until he pulled back, biting her lower lip. She exhaled a shuddered breath. He knew she loved that. That he didn't treat her like delicate China that could break.

He demanded things of her body, pushed her to the edges of pain and pleasure and she loved every second of it, more than happy to oblige him in however he wanted to contort her body.

And in this moment, she was frenzied, looking to get devoured like she never had in these gardens.

She wrapped her hands around his neck and his fingers went down to her thighs, dragging at her dress, making quick work of finding his way beneath her skirts.

His hands gripping the back of her thighs, he lifted her, setting the tip of his shaft at her entrance. Her legs wrapped around him and she captured his face in her hands, staring down at him as he impaled her on his cock without preamble.

Her head fell back, her eyes closing as he filled her deep, pressure hitting her from the inside out in all the right spots.

He lifted her, his cock sliding smoothly out of her, before slamming back into her depths.

Again and again and again.

A frantic pace that ground across her hardened nub,

making every second he filled her to the hilt its own moment of ecstasy. Over and over until she was panting into his neck, mewls she couldn't control starting. He grabbed her by the back of her hair, pulling her head back so he could lock his mouth over hers, swallowing all of the sounds she made.

A growl vibrated from his throat into her, and he lifted her, then plunged up into her in a definitive thrust. Her body shattered in that second, and just as the explosion overtook her, she could feel his cock expanding within her, pulsing, his hot seed filling her before he could pull out.

What should send a spike of fear into her chest only sent her orgasm into a level she didn't know existed, her inner walls clenching brutally hard on him, waves of pleasure searing through her body.

His mouth pulled away from hers as his arms wrapped around her, locking her onto his body with his chest heaving, warring with her for space.

His face buried into her hair, his voice low and raw. "I don't know how you wreck me like this every time we're together, but it's only getting worse."

Her face buried in his chest, she sucked in a deep breath.

She knew exactly what he was talking about, because it was the same for her.

A slippery slope for both of them, and damned if she wasn't sliding down that hill head first.

CHAPTER 18

Magical.

In all of the times she had been at Vauxhall Gardens, she'd always loved the fun of it, but it had never been magical. Not until tonight.

Not until Callum.

Her legs still woozy from being thoroughly wrecked by him in the alcove, she leaned against his arm as they worked their way through the crowds in the gardens. Most people were already turned toward the river to where a few errant fireworks had started popping behind them, announcing the show was imminent.

Contrary to the crowds surging toward the river, they were working against the flow of people.

She wanted to get home to make sure Georgette and Jacob were settled and to tell them the good news, that they would be coming back to Scotland with her.

The full fireworks show started with five loud bangs and she jumped, looking up at Callum with a laugh at her lips. "They scare me every time."

Callum grinned and set his arm around her, wrapping his

hand around her waist.

"Oh. Charley." She stopped, looking around. "I completely forgot he was here. Should we find him to tell him we're leaving?"

Callum scanned the crowd around them. With his height, he would be able to find Charley far faster than she could. "I can make a quick swoop around the pavilion, but I imagine he is ensconced in a dark corner of the gardens by now."

She shrugged. "That will have to do—then we can at least say we tried to find him, rather than us completely abandoning him."

Callum nodded. "I'll meet you by the entrance next to the proprietor's house." His hand dropped away from her and he moved to the left into the crowd.

Nemity continued on, bumping into people as she made her way toward the main entrance gate of the garden.

"Nemity—Nemity—Nemity."

In between the cracks of the fireworks, she heard her name and spun, looking for the source.

"Nemity." Vanessa Haldren, Countess of Cladwell, ran up to her from the side of the orchestra. Her old friend. One in the group of women she and Susannah had danced through the seasons with when they were younger.

"Vanessa." Nemity grabbed Vanessa's arms and pulled her into a hug with a laugh. She hadn't seen Vanessa in two years.

"Nemity, I'm so glad I caught you—so glad I saw you with Lady Agnes. I waited until you were done talking with her—because who wants to get near that old bat? But then I looked away and you were gone." The booms of the fireworks peppered every third word she spoke.

Nemity waved the fact that she'd disappeared away, Vanessa knew full well where she'd disappeared to. "It is so good to see you. When did you get into town? You must have so much to report on your travels as you've been gone for so long. How was the continent?"

"Grand, and I will delight in telling you all about it, but that's not why I wanted to grab you." Vanessa looked around the crowd. Most people about them had their gazes focused on the bright lights flashing in the sky.

Nemity paused as a cluster of fireworks cracked into the air. "No? Why? You look like something is amiss?"

"There is." Her look jumped from the surrounding crowd to Nemity, and Vanessa leaned close, talking into Nemity's ear. "That man I saw with you earlier—the one talking with you to Lady Agnes."

Nemity's brow furrowed as she looked at her friend. "Yes? Mr. Lonstrick?"

Vanessa's nose wrinkled. "Lonstrick, is that what he is calling himself now?"

Nemity stilled, staring at her friend. "What are you talking about?"

"That man you are here with, I don't know where or how you met him, but do you remember that summer when we were twenty and I had a short affair with our gardener and then he disappeared on me? His name was John."

Nemity's eyes narrowed at her friend. Vanessa was a mess that summer, but that fall was when she'd met her husband.

"Yes, I recall." The words came from her mouth slowly, hesitancy thick in her voice.

"That gardener is your Mr. Lonstrick. The man you were with. I would know him anywhere. He had a beard back then, and not now, but I would recognize him anywhere." Vanessa grabbed her arm. "He's a glib-tonged, fortune-hunting charlatan, that one, Nemity. And he's dangerous."

"What? No. How do you even know that?"

"Days after I had relations with him, that was when my uncle disappeared." Vanessa's words sped as she tried to get them in between the pops of fireworks. "My father never said anything about it, but I know John was arguing with my uncle in the carriage house right before my uncle disappeared, never to be seen again. John disappeared the same day."

Nemity's head started to shake. There had to be a mistake. "No, you cannot possibly think Mr. Lonstrick was your gardener."

"I don't just think, I know." Vanessa's words grew pitched. "I even asked my father once about what happened to John and he just said John had been relieved of his duties with us."

"But that doesn't prove anything—that doesn't even prove that your John is Mr. Lonstrick."

Vanessa muttered something incomprehensible under the booms of fireworks and she grabbed Nemity by both arms, her look panicked. "I am not lying—I have no reason to lie. Please Nemity, just be careful. Whoever he said he was, that man is not. How can I make you believe…"

Vanessa's head dropped, shaking for a long second, then her look whipped up to Nemity. "Does he have a tattoo on his chest? A round one that looks like an emblem or something akin to it?"

Nemity's gut dropped.

No. No. No.

It couldn't possibly be.

Vanessa shook Nemity. "Is he marked like that on his chest?"

The world around her imploding on her, everyone and everything seemed to suddenly move slower. Crawling along.

She had to get out of here. Away.

She yanked her arms out of Vanessa's grip. "You must be mistaken. Mistaken."

Ignoring Vanessa's concerned face and her reaching to

stop her, Nemity turned and ran, immediately bumping into a man behind her. The impact bounced her backward, but her feet kept moving forward. Fast. As fast as she could make them when they felt like they'd been encased in solid stone.

There. The entrance.

But hell.

That was where Callum was going to meet her.

Her feet slowed. The lights of the lanterns around her swirling.

Charley. She had to find Charley. He could get her home.

She stopped, spinning in a circle, trying to find direction in the crowd.

Charley.

How was she going to find Charley in this crush?

Hands landed on her shoulders. "Nemity." Callum's voice in her ear. "I couldn't find Charley. Are you ready?"

Her arm swung up to knock his hands away from her shoulders as she spun around to him. "What are you?"

His head snapped back, his face instantly concerned. "What? What are you talking about?"

She stepped into him, her voice a manic growl. "What are you? Are you a gardener? John? Do you remember my friend Vanessa? For she certainly remembers you."

His head whipped up, searching around them. "Va—"

He stopped himself, looking back down at her, but in that one little movement, she had her answer.

He knew Vanessa. Looked for her.

A layer of panic he was trying to hide simmered in his eyes.

"You lying, rotten, despicable ass. Don't you dare come near me again."

"Nem." His hands lifted to grab her, to stop her, but she jumped to the side, escaping his grasp and broke into a full run, weaving around people in the crowd.

There. Vanessa.

Vanessa and her husband could get her home.

Get her home so she could gather up Georgette and Jacob before Callum could get to them.

They were her only concern now.

CHAPTER 19

Dammit.

A roar at his lips, Callum scrambled after Nemity in the crowd, but she was slight and fast, and no matter how many people he pushed out of his way, she was just out of his reach.

And then there.

Fucking hell.

Valerie—no, Vanessa. Vanessa was her name.

Nemity screeched to a halt in front of Vanessa, grabbing her wrist. Vanessa wrapped her arms around Nemity. Nemity's shoulders shook. Sobs.

Vanessa.

Vanessa.

A stupid, stupid transgression when he was on a job for her father, investigating stolen funds from his accounts and if they were tied to his younger brother, who he was sure was plotting something with his mistress.

Vanessa had been a welcome dalliance in the middle of the months' long drudgery of that mission.

The damn fireworks boomed harder in the sky and filled

his head like a blacksmith setting hammer to anvil had crawled into his skull.

His chest tight, he started pushing his way through the crowd.

Nemity. He had to get to her.

Had to explain.

He just had to explain.

Except she was so damn far away.

He shoved a man on his left, making him fall, but he didn't even look back.

He wasn't going to let his past take this from him. Take *her* from him.

Vanessa turned and said something to the tall man next to her. The man's look came up, scanning the crowd as he sidled to the other side of Nemity and the three of them moved through the crush, headed toward the river entrance to the gardens.

Bloody fucking hell.

He wasn't getting near her now.

The tightness in his chest spun into a full-out storm that he was having a hard time controlling.

He turned and ran toward the main entrance to the gardens.

He had to get to her townhouse before her.

CHAPTER 20

The crying next to Nemity didn't even register in her ears.

It was foggy, distanced, barely echoing in her head.

Probably because it was in rhythm with the tears she was sobbing deep in her chest where no one could see them or hear them.

To Georgette and Jacob, Nemity gave them nothing but smiles and as much cheer as she could muster.

Even though they'd been dreadfully sad the entire trip north.

Like they now realized it was real—their mother dying, never to be touched, to be seen again.

After she'd run from Callum at Vauxhall Gardens, she'd gathered the children and went straight to the Hedstrom townhouse to find Thomas. It had been dreadfully late, and he had been all sorts of furious at her intrusion with two children in tow, but she had somehow managed to convince Thomas to take her back north post haste when the sun rose.

She wasn't about to risk even a day where Callum could show up at her London doorstep.

For the hard truth of the matter was that she didn't know Callum.

Didn't even know if Callum was his real name.

Didn't know if anything about the man was real.

She'd hoped Charley would have appeared at the Hedstrom townhouse before they left so she could talk to him about Callum. So she could manage to at least set into her mind how someone so devious had made it that close to her.

But Charley hadn't appeared at the townhouse before they left. Most likely asleep in Lady Prosswan's bed, knowing Charley.

She'd just have to interrogate Charley about Callum the next time he made it north.

Thomas, for his part, hadn't questioned her too deeply on any of it. She'd told him she and Callum had grown close, but that he'd betrayed her most grievously.

That was all Thomas had needed to hear to get him to agree to take her and the children away from London. Like he already knew all the details and didn't want to hear them from her mouth.

He was the one that had sent Callum to her doorstep, after all. Forced him into her life. She didn't imagine her cousin capable of guilt, but in this, Thomas had looked sheepish, almost apologetic.

He'd trusted the wrong man just as she had.

Or maybe Thomas was just exhausted with her and this was the path of least resistance.

Day three of the journey north to Scotland was not going well.

None of them—she, Thomas, Georgette and Jacob—had gotten enough sleep at the coaching inns along the route. It had been hot—far too hot this far north, making the days in the carriage quite miserable. The windows had been open, but that had just made the dry dust of the road kick up and coat them in dirt.

And now both the children were arguing about which hand of hers they were holding—Jacob had dissolved into tears, which had made Georgette start wailing even louder.

She could only sit in the middle of the mess of everything around her, numb.

"Nemity. Nemity. Nemity!"

Jerking her out of her reverie, her look snapped to Thomas sitting across from her and the children in the carriage.

She blinked slowly at him, not sure how many times he'd barked out her name.

His face red in anger, his glare sliced into her. "You need to shut the mouths on these two brats. They've both been caterwauling for the last hour." His voice vicious, it made her breath catch in her throat.

An hour? Surely that was an exaggeration.

But she hadn't heard any of it. She'd just been sitting in a fog. A fog of her own making. Her own, stupid, foolish making.

Two times, she'd been duped by men nearly to the altar.

And just when she'd thought she'd found something different, something real with Callum, it was ripped away from her in the most brutal way. Because the cruel reality of it was that *she* was the problem. There was no other option. *She* was the one that set herself up for this heartache again and again and again.

So very stupid.

"Nemity! Shut them the hell up!"

She jerked, her eyes opening wide at Thomas, suddenly understanding the wrath that was aimed at them from across the carriage.

Thomas had been mean in the last years, yes—but mean to two innocent children?

This was a new low, even for him.

Her protective instincts surged and she threw an arm around each of the children. "You could find it in your heart to be kinder to them, Thomas."

"Could I? I just tramped all the way to London for you because Charley insisted. And now I am tramping all the way back north to Scotland with hardly a full twenty-four hours in London, and you're asking me to be *kinder* to children you have insisted on taking on as your own?"

Her grip on Jacob and Georgette tightened. "You don't get a say in that. I promised Susannah I would take them."

His fingers tore at his dark hair as his voice took on an even harder edge. "I should, if I was performing my duty as your guardian like I should be. They're not yours. They shouldn't be yours. I should have told you that three nights ago when you showed up at my door with them in tow."

Her jaw dropped, her words low. "If you feel this strongly about it why didn't you say anything?"

"Because I was tired and I was trying not to react to another one of your doltish ideas about how you should run your own life when it's quite clear you need someone to run it for you."

Her head snapped back, thudding against the hard shell of the carriage behind her. "I think I run my life perfectly fine."

"Of course you do. You're not responsible to anyone for anything, and now you think you can suddenly be responsible for these two." He waved his hand at Georgette and Jacob on either side of her. "You haven't ever been responsible enough to even catch a husband, so why in the world would I think you can do this?"

Her lip snarled. "Just because I did not marry does not mean I cannot be a mother to them."

"Doesn't it? You couldn't do the simplest thing, Nemity. It wasn't that hard—marry someone—anyone. My father did a shit job of marrying you off and of all the things I've had to clean up after him, you are the most troublesome. And now you're adding these brats into the mix."

"I never asked to have you in my life, Thomas. Do us both a favor and sign over the stewardship of my estate to Charley —to anyone else."

He scoffed a laugh. "Charley would blow through your entire fortune in a year."

Her eyes went wide in shock. "He couldn't do that—not with my money."

"You don't think he'd find a way? Don't tell me you're that ignorant, Nemity."

Her head felt as though it was about to explode for the rage pounding inside of it. She glared at him, no longer caring how or why he'd turned into this vile creature.

Words seethed in a scream from her tight lips. "How in the world did you become such a vicious viper?"

"A viper?"

Georgette gave a sudden scream at the yelling and tried to shrink herself back into the cushions.

Thomas leaned forward. "I told you to shut those brats up."

Her arms flung out, shielding both of the children from him the best she could. "Leave them be."

He leaned forward even farther, almost off his bench, his words pelting into her. "Here's the reality, Nemity—you can't take on these children."

"Why not?" She tried to control her voice, merely to not frighten the children any further.

"Because you cannot do whatever you damn well please. You've lived a bloody charmed life where everything has always gone your way and you know nothing of hardship or what it takes to actually survive. You'll never be married now —not with these two in tow."

"That is what you are worried about?" Her voice had started to shake for the rage blistering her words. "Still trying to marry me off? No—I don't care about that. This is what Susannah wanted. She wanted me to raise them."

"Why? You? What could have possibly possessed her to pick the likes of you?"

A blade right to her belly and she had to choke her words out. "Because I can love them like no one else can. I can take care of them."

"You spoiled little brat. You can't even take care of yourself." His hands gripping his knees tightened, his knuckles turning white. "Everyone around you, for your entire life has made everything right for you." His teeth gritted, baring in a tight line. "You are an ignorant twit that knows nothing of what the real world consists of."

She seethed out a breath, leaning forward, shoving her face into his to put all his attention on her instead of the children for she really didn't know what he would do next.

Hit them? Hit her?

She'd never seen him with this much rage and viciousness storming around him.

Still, whatever was happening to him, she was going to take the brunt of it—not the children.

"I know a hell of a lot more than you think I do." Her voice pitched high. "You talk about spoiled? You've become a bitter, vicious ass that no one wants to be around, when you once had the whole world at your fingertips. But now you choose this—you choose this wretched existence for yourself and now you're trying to make everyone around you just as miserable as you are because you are a small, poisonous, wicked man who I don't even recognize as my cousin."

"Is that so?" His words ground out, the veins in his forehead looking ready to pop. In the instant when she thought he was about to leap across the carriage and choke her, Thomas suddenly shoved himself backward, hitting the cushions hard.

His hand flew up, his fist pounding on the roof of the carriage, a roar filling the air. "Stop the coach."

The horses slowed and the carriage rolled to a stop.

Her breath thundering, she stared at him, not moving. Afraid to move.

His glare cleaved into her, his voice deadly low. "Nemity. Get out."

"What?" Her hands tightened on Georgette and Jacob, silently willing them to quiet their sobs even though she knew it was impossible for their young minds to comprehend what all this screaming was about.

His lip snarled. "Get out. Right now. Get out of the carriage. Get you and these two squealing brats out of the carriage."

She glanced out the open window. Having pulled off the main thoroughfare early this morning, they were now in the middle of the longest barren stretch of road.

Her look swung back to Thomas. "What? Thomas, you cannot be serious."

"Get out before I shove you out. Get out and find out exactly what sort of world you've been living in. Find out how you think you can survive, because you can't. You're worthless. Worthless to me. Worthless to those children. And the sooner you figure that out, the better."

Each word, a tiny dagger though her chest.

She knew Thomas was different now than he once was, but still, she couldn't help but remember him from when he was younger. A different person. Someone she liked. Admired. Respected. Loved like a big brother.

But this…this was hateful.

And it was real.

Thomas thought she was a steaming pile of rubbish.

A burden he didn't want to shoulder anymore.

For as vicious as his words were, she still had a shred of tattered dignity left beating within her.

She peeled her hand away from Georgette's grip and grabbed the door handle, opening it. Jumping down to the ground without the aid of the steps—Thomas's driver had been waiting for instructions, not thinking she was actually going to exit. She turned to the children and they quickly scrambled past Thomas and into her arms, and she set them on the road next to her.

She grabbed each of their hands, taking a step back away from the carriage so they weren't near the wheels.

Without looking at her, Thomas reached out and grabbed the door, slamming it closed. He banged on the roof of the carriage. "Go on."

His face in shock, Thomas's driver looked over his shoulder at her, not sure what to do in the moment.

Thomas knocked again, screaming at the man. The driver glanced down at the back of the carriage, looked at her, mouthed something at her that she didn't quite understand, then spun away from her. He clicked the horses onward.

She stood there at the side of the road, holding onto the children's hands, watching the carriage disappear.

Watching.

Watching.

Watching.

Watching until it was long gone from sight.

It didn't come back.

Fingers tugged at her fore and middle finger. "Auntie Nemmy?"

She looked down at the cherub face of Georgette. Confused. Not scared.

Not scared because she didn't know she should be.

Nemity knew this stretch of road. It was barren, not a farm or a village for miles. Thomas would have to come back, wouldn't he?

He didn't.

She waited for an hour, probably more, on the side of the road.

No Thomas, and no other passersby.

The sun beating down on them.

Georgette and Jacob moved onto the side of the road to sit in the grass where it was at least cool.

Her stomach started to rumble and the children asked for food. Again and again and again.

Until, finally, she looked around.

She'd spent the last three days wallowing in self-pity, and that had to stop. Now.

She had to figure out something.

Waiting here would do them no good.

Trees. Trees. Road. Trees. Field of stone and scrubby grasses that rolled up a craggy hill.

She knew this area. Sometimes there were sheep in that field.

Not now, but if sheep were sometimes in the area, they had to come from somewhere.

She rustled the children from the spot they had found on the side of the road and they traversed up the field onto the top of the hill.

Nemity spun about, looking in all directions. Nothing.

More fields. Trees. More fields of nothing.

Wait. Something brown sticking up from the landscape.

It would have to do.

She dropped down to her knees, pulling both of the children in front of her. "Do you two remember the beautiful tapestries we saw at the museum, the ones with knights and princesses and unicorns?"

Georgette's eyes lit up and she clapped her hands. "I do, Auntie Nemmy."

She smiled wide, forcing enthusiasm into her eyes. "Good, I do too. And do you remember how we talked about what grand adventures the knights must have had, travelling the land?"

Jacob grinned, nodding his head. He loved the wooden sword that was still sitting in his room at Susannah's town-house—she hoped the staff packed it in the trunks for them they were to send to Springfell.

She squeezed him and he giggled. "Well, guess what? We get to go on our own knightly adventure, travelling the land for our next fair. Doesn't that sound fun?"

Both of the children laughed, nodding.

She stood up, determination in her voice as she pointed across the field. "Lucky for us, we have just become knights of old on a quest across the land. We need to get to that cottage by nightfall."

"Which one, Auntie Nemmy?" Georgette squinted, trying to find where she pointed to.

"Right there." Nemity dropped her arm to set it next to Georgette's temple, pointing. "Do you see it?"

"I do." Georgette nodded vigorously, her brown curls bobbing up and down atop her shoulders.

"Good. Off we go." She picked up Jacob, propping him on her hip, and she grabbed Georgette's hand. Her head down, she started to walk.

Two hours later, with dusk settling about them, and the muscles in her arms screaming from carrying both of the children, she kicked open the half askew door that had rotted on ancient hinges.

The brown structure wasn't a cottage, it was an abandoned barn.

But with darkness settling in, it would have to do.

She tiptoed into the stale air inside the barn, and birds on rafters above tweeted, their peace disturbed.

Dirty hay. But a mostly intact roof over their heads.

It would have to do.

She went to the far end of the barn where a pile of hay looked cleaner in the dim light.

Ignoring the stench, she shuffled the hay back and forth with the toe of her boot, trying to find a halfway clean patch.

Jacob didn't wait for her, and he crawled onto the pile of hay, clutching the stick he'd found along the way that he was using as a sword.

Exhausted, she realized the futility of looking for clean hay and she grabbed Georgette's hand, pulling her next to her as she sat down.

Lying down in the hay, she huddled the children close into her on either side.

They had stopped complaining of hunger an hour ago, their little bodies falling to sleep almost instantly.

It wasn't until their eyes closed, their breathing slow and even, that the tears came, streaming down her face. Panic and exhaustion whipping her into a silent frenzy.

What had she done?

She hadn't even thought to grab her reticule as she'd gotten out of the carriage.

Hadn't thought at all.

She had nothing. *Nothing.*

And she had two hungry mouths that she knew would wake up crying, waiting for her to feed them.

What in the hell had she done?

CHAPTER 21

Callum walked into the tavern on the main floor of the coaching inn, his fists already curled as he searched the darkened nooks of the large room.

There. A private back area, set apart with a thick stone wall.

That's exactly where the bastard would be.

He stomped past the tables of travelers laughing and drinking, the blood red haze in his eyes blurring the world, but also helping him to focus specifically on his target.

He moved past the stone wall that led to the smaller area —where there was space for ten or so people around a long rectangular table. But there was only one person in the room, sitting by the fireplace, his bleary eyes staring at the drink in front of him as he poured the last drops of a bottle of brandy into the glass.

He dared to get drunk now?

Double the bastard.

"Thomas." His voice a low roar, Callum didn't want to draw attention to the room when he was about to kill the man.

Thomas set the empty brandy bottle down, his clumsy fingers knocking the bottle to the table.

Enough of a distraction that Callum didn't see Thomas lunging at him with his fist flying through the air.

Knuckles slammed into Callum's chin and it actually stung, stumbling him back a step.

Callum was bigger, but Thomas wasn't slight—he was nearly as tall and had plenty of muscle on his frame.

Thomas's feet shifted to swing another blow at him. "What the hell did you do to her?" He swung.

Callum dodged the blow and stood straight, his eyes wide in indignant surprise, his words spitting out through gritted teeth. "Do to her? I didn't do a damn thing to Nemity."

Thomas's missed blow sent him half splayed onto the table, scratching for stability as his look jerked to Callum. "You fucking well did, man." Thomas's words slurred, fast and jumbled together. "The way she came to me—came to me in the middle of the fucking night because of you. I was paying you to protect her—not play with her."

Thomas found his footing and shoved off from the table, his fist pulling back for another blow. Callum wasn't about to let it land on him and he sprang forward, wrapping his hand around Thomas's throat as he shoved him backward until his body slammed into the stone wall. "I wasn't playing with her." His fingers tightened around Thomas's throat. "Where in the hell is she?"

Thomas deflated in front of him, all fight in him evaporated. His look went to the low ceiling as words croaked out of his throat. "She's not here."

Callum yanked him off the wall and slammed him back into it. "I fucking bloody well know that. The stableboy said you were the only one in the carriage when you got into town. But you left London with her and the children, so I ask you again"—he shoved his face into Thomas's, a deadly roar growling from his throat—"where in the hell is she?"

Silent, Thomas's eyes squinted closed, like he was trying to change the past—or not face it.

Real, visceral terror shot through Callum's chest. He tried to remain calm in situations like this—when he didn't know what the hell was happening. But Thomas's silence pointed in only one direction. Nemity was dead.

Somehow, between London and here, she'd died.

Everything within him dissolved into a black void with that thought.

But no. He wouldn't accept it. Didn't know it.

He dragged Thomas from the wall by his throat and slammed him back into it again, this time with more force. "Where is she?"

Thomas clawed at his hand around his throat, searching for breath. Breath he needed to talk.

Callum relaxed his grip enough for a trickle of air to make it into Thomas's lungs.

Thomas wheezed a breath. "I—I sent my driver back for her. I got here and I sent the driver. He should have been back with her by now. He should have."

Callum sucked in a breath. She was alive. He was ready to throttle the life out of Thomas's eyes, but that wouldn't get him anywhere nearer to finding Nemity.

One of the hardest things he ever had to do, he dropped his grip from Thomas's neck and took a step back. "Explain."

Thomas spewed out a brandy-soaked cough, still trying to catch his breath. "I couldn't be in the same coach with her. Not with her and those children. The children were crying and I—I..." Thomas lifted a hand and smacked the heel of his palm against his own temple. Hard. So hard Thomas stumbled to the side. "Something snapped in my head and I couldn't control it and all I could see was red and black and rage and I couldn't find my way out of it. I tried to stay calm, but then Nemity started arguing with me." His eyes closed as he collapsed back against the stone wall.

"So you fucking kicked her out of the carriage?"

"In the middle of nowhere." Thomas's eyes stayed closed, his head shaking, his dark hair falling in front of his eyes. "Not my finest moment."

Callum couldn't keep his voice steady, the fury seizing him making him choke out every word. "What the hell are you thinking, man?"

Thomas opened his bloodshot eyes and his look lifted, haunted, to Callum. "I'm thinking I didn't want to hurt her. Didn't want to hurt those children." His eyes closed and his chin dropped down, his voice a whisper. "They should have been back by now. They should already be here. It was an hour back and I sent my driver right away. He dropped me off and he went back. They should be here. They should..."

Callum slammed his fist into a stone next to Thomas's head. His knuckles split, bloody. But better his skin than Thomas's skull. He didn't have time to murder the bastard right now. "You fucking asshole. If any one of them is hurt in the slightest way I am going to hunt you down and flay you alive."

Not willing to split his opposite knuckles with another punch at the rocks, Callum settled for kicking a fat stone low on the wall. The pain vibrating up his leg was worth it.

He turned to stomp out of the private dining room.

"You're fired, Callum." Thomas's voice cut weakly into the air behind him.

Callum stopped at the entrance and looked back to Thomas. "No. I quit. Find someone else to save your ass."

He stormed out of the coaching inn and grabbed his horse's reins from the stableboy who he'd had water his horse for him.

An hour back.

He mounted and set the horse on a quick pace, his mind frantic.

It had been near dark, but he hadn't seen anything on the entire length of that barren stretch of road. Though he had been pushing his horse hard.

Nor had he seen Thomas's carriage and driver. That, he would have noticed, for he'd been searching for it since he'd convinced the scullery maid at the Hedstrom townhouse to tell him that Thomas had left abruptly with Miss Wheldon and two children days ago.

The only place they would be going was back to Springfell Manor or Ravenstone Castle, both of which veered off of this stretch of road another half day north.

Dusk had settled and he was fuming, not able to see what he needed to along the roadside in order to find Nemity and the children.

And there was nothing, not another soul on the road until twenty minutes had gone by.

Lanterns on a coach. A coach moving slowly.

Callum kicked his heels into his horse and sped to meet the coach. Thomas's coach—he already recognized it in the distance.

The carriage slowed as he approached, and he came to a stop next to it. The curtain in the carriage was drawn.

"Perry, tell me you found them," Callum said, looking up at Thomas's driver.

Perry heaved out a sigh. "No, sir. No, I did not. I dinnae ken where they would go. I even went down the stretch on the three roads that branched, but I couldnae find them. I'm sorry, sir. I never should have left them."

"No, you damn well shouldn't have. How in the hell do you lose a woman with two wee ones in tow?"

"I'm sorry, sir, I tried to stop three times to go back but

his lordship widnae have it—said he'd drive the rig himself and leave me as well—then I'd be no help to anyone."

Callum ran his hand down his face, growling to himself. "It wasn't your fault. Keep looking. I'll double back."

"Yes, sir."

"If you find them, deliver them to the coaching inn, get them in a room, and tell them not to step one foot outside that room until I'm there—no, hell"—he shook his head to himself, realizing Nemity would never stay in a coaching inn waiting for him, of all people—"tell her not to leave there until Charley comes for them. Tell Miss Wheldon that Charley is coming. She'll stay in one place if she thinks he's coming. Tell her that and then come and get me. I'll get them safely home."

Perry nodded, tipping his hat. "Yes, sir."

"Wait—where exactly did you leave them?"

"That area with the forest on the southern side and the sheep pastures opposite. There is that hill, the tallest in the area—it was near there."

His gut sinking as the chill air around him settled in with darkness, Callum nodded and flicked his reins, taking off into the darkness.

His eyes had better adjust to the darkness soon, for he needed to find her.

Had to find her.

CHAPTER 22

loody hell.

No.

Impossible.

Two days.

Two days he'd been scouring the countryside. Working in concentric circles outward from the exact spot Thomas had kicked Nemity and the children from the carriage.

He'd found some hay in an abandoned barn that had looked recently ruffled. It could have possibly been the three of them. Or it could have been a wild animal. Beyond that, no obvious tracks, no random strips of cloth on the roadside. Nothing.

This was when he needed Rory from the Guardians. Rory could track anything, anyone with the slightest imprint on the grass. Could see things others couldn't.

But to fetch Rory from wherever he was currently trying to track down Nemity's abductors, by the time they got back, all trace of Nemity would be gone.

Not that he had any trail at all.

So he'd been working in ever expanding circles, looking

at every divot in the ground, stopping at every cottage or farm in the area.

No one had seen Nemity or the children.

How had some sort of otherworld sorcery made it possible for a lady in all her finery with two children in tow manage to disappear?

He heaved a sigh from atop his horse.

Apparently, he was looking at that very sorcery.

Or maybe he was seeing things. A mirage.

A hallucination of Nemity standing outside a cottage nestled in a crook between two hills, throwing a wet sheet over a long line of rope to dry it. The top half of her dark red hair was pulled back, the rest of the locks long on her shoulders and lifting in the breeze. Her cheeks were pink, her eyes alert and alive, like she'd been running. The sleeves of her elegant but now rumpled dark blue travelling dress were rolled up to her elbows, and she had a simple white apron wrapped around the front of her.

No. Not real.

He was so exhausted, he had to be hallucinating. The wild machinations of his desperate imagination.

Then the mirage of Nemity turned to an older lady next to her. The older woman laughed, shaking her head, and started rearranging the sheet on the line.

A fucking hallucination.

It had to be.

He alighted his horse and grabbed the reins, walking the distance from the overgrown lane he'd found branching off from the side road. The pathway to the cottage cut between the hills, barely wide enough for a wagon.

Closer. Closer still. And the ghost of Nemity didn't disappear.

Nemity and the woman next to her continued to pull out sheets and clothing and hang them on a line stretched between the cottage and a gnarled old oak tree that only had half of its branches producing leaves.

As the older woman moved away from the drying line, toward the thatched-roof cottage, Nemity turned to where he couldn't see the angle of her face and bent to rummage in the large basket by her feet.

He kept his stare trained on Nemity as he moved in, waiting for her to somehow transform into a stranger he'd mistaken for Nemity in his exhaustion. A woman he was about to scare half to death.

"Stop right there, good sir."

Callum looked to his left to the see the older woman standing in front of the cottage, a Baker rifle propped against her shoulder and aimed directly at him.

He froze, instinct taking over.

One never knew how shaky a finger on a trigger was.

Nemity yelped in surprise and though Callum stayed still, his eyes shifted to her.

Her blue eyes wide, her jaw had dropped, the white towel in her hands sinking to a sopping pile on the ground next to her feet.

"Smart man. Ye have no business here, sir." The older woman took two steps away from the cottage, advancing on him. The scratch of age tinged her voice, but her words were hard steel. She wasn't just dallying about at shooting him. "I encourage ye to be on yer way."

His gaze locked solely on the threat, Callum's fingers spread wide and he slowly raised his hands in the air, the reins of the horse looped in around his thumb.

"Mable—no—no." Nemity ran toward the older woman, her hand raised. "No. He's not a threat. I know him." She grabbed the end of the barrel and pushed it downward.

The older woman looked to her, her left grey eyebrow lifting high. "Do ye, now?"

"I do. He's..." Nemity's head swiveled, her look landing on him. "He's... He's... I don't actually know who he is."

"Nemity—"

The older woman snorted a grumble and looked to him, her look laced with pure disgust. If he was ten steps closer to her, he was pretty sure she would have spit on him. "He's the one, then? The liar?"

"Yes." Nemity looked directly at him, scorn vibrating in her eyes. "He's the one."

The woman lifted the rifle back up, and Callum was now fully convinced it was actually loaded and that her aim would be spot on.

"I don't think that's necessary, Mable." Nemity's voice had gone hard, her stare on him turning to disgust. "I am positive this man is leaving right now."

Callum exhaled a breath. "Nemity, please, you need to let me—"

"She will shoot you, I have no doubt. So you best be gone." Nemity's glare cut a flaming arrow right through his gut. "Leave. Leave!" The last word erupted, the full venom of her anger unleashing.

His stare stayed on Nemity, ignoring the older woman looking for the slightest reason to shoot him. "Please, Nemity. You need to let me explain. Please."

"Explain what? That you're a liar?" She stepped toward him, her arm swinging in the air. "That you did everything you could to try to get at my money? That you faked everything?"

"No. I didn't fake everything." His look sliced into her. "Not by far."

"Tell it to someone who will believe you."

This was going to rubbish far too quickly.

He nodded, trying to calm her. "You are right. I am not what you think I am. But my name, Callum, that is exactly who I am. I have never lied to you on that score."

She scoffed a forced chuckle. "You think that is supposed to make anything better? When you lied about everything else? Your name means nothing to me when the rest of you is a sniveling, spurious liar not worth the bottom of my boot."

"Nemity…I…" His words dissolved as he glanced at the older woman, then looked back to Nemity. He didn't want to do this in front of an audience. It wasn't in his nature, groveling. But he'd do what he had to, to get her to listen to him.

He notched his voice down, slowing his words, for each one of them had to make an impact on her in order to cut through the lies he'd laid at her door. "Yes, I am a liar. Yes, there are things I never told you—I couldn't tell you. But you—me—I never lied about one second of that. I never faked one second of that. Never faked one look. Never faked one touch. That—that was real. When I was with you—every one of the moments, that was me, that was truth."

She shook her head, her look going up to the grey sky and then dropping to him. "Do you even know what real is?"

"No. Probably not." He heaved a sigh. "Because I haven't been real in a very, very long time. But I am risking my life with the barrel of that rifle pointed at me to stand this ground and tell you that I have been looking for you nonstop since Thomas kicked you out of his carriage. I haven't slept, I haven't eaten, and I'm damn well convinced I might be in a nightmare of my own making right now, but I am here. This seems pretty damn real and I'm asking you just to give me five minutes. Just five minutes."

Her glare cut into him. "Why did you even bother to come look for me? I have nothing for you."

His arms lifted at his sides. "Because it is you, Nemity. It is you. I just needed to know you were safe."

Her eyes closed with a pained exhale.

Heaven above, please let this be the moment, the moment she broke just a little bit. That was all he needed. The slightest crack.

Her blue eyes opened to him, staring at him, and he wasn't sure what he saw in them.

Her head turned from him as she looked to the older woman next to her. "Mable, it is fine. I will talk to him. The rifle can go down. Five minutes and then you can blast a hole in his gut. Will you check on Georgette and Jacob for me, please?"

Thank the heavens.

Mable's eyes narrowed at Callum, the side of her mouth pulling back in a tight line. She dropped the rifle to her side and looked to Nemity. "I will check on them, make sure they are still asleep, then I'll be waiting on the bench." She motioned with her head toward a roughhewn bench sitting to the left of the door of the cottage.

Nemity nodded. "Thank you."

Callum waited until Mable disappeared into the cottage.

Avoiding Nemity's stare, he walked his horse over to the gnarled tree and looped the reins onto a dead, but sturdy branch. Buying time as he tried to gather all his thoughts through the muddle of exhaustion in his brain.

He had to make the next minutes count—count like nothing else ever had in his life.

Nemity followed him part of the way, stopping a healthy distance away from him. Her arms threaded tight against her ribcage. "You look like hell."

He turned to her, finally allowing himself to look at her.

He didn't know how to do this. Didn't know how to not screw this up even more grievously than it already was. He needed to do this right, but he had no idea what right was.

His hand ran through his hair, scuffing the back of his neck. "Well, if it's any consolation, I've been in hell, searching every last speck of this countryside for you." He paused, a breathless chuckle lifting from his chest as he looked to the sheet she'd hung to dry. "And you've been here all along? Doing wash?"

Her jaw shifted outward, her lips pulling tight. "This isn't about me. You said you wanted five minutes—you've already wasted one of them."

"Nemity, there are things I cannot tell you. You have to trust me on them."

Her head dipped down, her stare skewering him. "Except we went through this—I have no trust for you."

"Because some woman told you something about me at Vauxhall?"

"Because that woman is my friend. Someone I've known since I was nine years old. Someone I trust. Someone who wouldn't lie to me."

He nodded, scuffing the back of his neck again.

He had to do it.

He had to tell her.

He nodded more to himself than to her, his look meeting hers. "I'll tell you. I'll tell you everything."

Her glare eating into him hadn't softened. "Is it even worth my time?"

"I don't know." His shoulders lifted, because he truly didn't know. He'd never had to tell anyone about his life. Never had *wanted* to tell anyone about his life. "I don't know how you'll react. But what I tell you, it will be the truth. I swear my life upon it."

Her lips parted and a long sigh escaped. Her fingers flicked up at him. "Fine."

He nodded.

An awkward silence descended

He had her ear, but now where to start? His look dipped to the ground, searching for inspiration in the tufts of grass sprouting up from the worn dirt. Searching for something that would convince her this was the truth. Something he could point to that was real, not just words.

His gaze lifted to her. "I have to show you something."

"Then show me."

"It's on my person and I'd rather not have your friend advancing on me with that rifle if I half undress."

Her eyes ran up and down his body, her eyebrows jutting inward. "You need to half undress?"

"I do."

A strangled sigh erupted from her. She motioned past the half-dead tree. "We can go down to the brook." She looked over her shoulder to the cottage. Mable was already sitting a distance away on the simple wooden bench, her eyes skewering him, the rifle clutched in her right hand.

"Mable, we're going down to the brook," Nemity called out to her.

Mable's brow wrinkled. "Ye think that wise?"

"No, but I'm going to do it. I'll stay within earshot. He'll need his horse to get out of here, and if he comes over the ridge alone, you have my permission to shoot him."

"Does he ken I'm a good shot?"

"I am guessing that he has quickly come to that conclusion."

Mable nodded, eyeing him with a great deal of malice, as though she was already imagining the hole she'd blast through him. "I'll be ready."

With a nod to her, Nemity turned back to him and moved forward, walking past him without a word.

He followed, quickly falling in step beside her.

Past one of the hills surrounding the cottage, the land rolled downward to a pleasant brook where willow trees lined the edges of the bank.

They walked the distance in silence. Silence he was afraid to break.

She was next to him. Willing to listen to him.

He was afraid anything but the truth in this moment would sink him for good in her eyes.

But the truth itself could sink him just as well.

Between two willow trees, they reached the edge of the brook, pebbles crunching underfoot with the water bubbling by Nemity's boots. She turned to him, drawing her arms in to clasp them across her ribcage. "What is it you needed to show me?"

He peeled off his dark coat, then his waistcoat, dropping them down to the rocky bank of the brook. Before she could stop him, he pulled free his lawn shirt and tugged it off over his head.

Half naked in front of her, Nemity's gaze flickered across his chest, and her fingers twitched, a flash of craving in her eyes.

That had never been a problem between them, her enjoyment of his body. But that wouldn't make her listen to him.

Only the truth could turn this around now.

CHAPTER 23

Her look lifted to him, her blue eyes as hard as ever, disbelief vibrating in the purple that ringed her irises. “You are a silly man if you think I want to touch you right now.”

“I don’t want you to touch me, but I do want you to look.” He pointed to his tattoo, the only thing he’d ever bothered to mark himself with. “Look at the ink on my chest.”

Her eyes didn’t dip downward. “I’ve seen it.”

“Look at it again.”

She glared at him for a long moment, then her gaze dropped to his chest, to the intricate round emblem tattooed on the left side of his chest. “And?”

His forefinger touched the ink, just above his heart. “Look at this closely. You cannot see it with just a courtesy glance at the curves and swirls, but look closely on the middle ring of it. It is faded, but tell me what you see.”

Her lips pulled to the side as she stared at it. She glanced up at his face, and then took a step closer, leaning in toward his chest. Her eyes squinting slightly at the faded black design.

He stared down at the top of her head, his fingers curling and uncurling at his sides.

Heaven help him, he wanted to touch her. Wanted to feel her skin under his fingertips, wanted to feel her pulse thrumming along her neck.

She shuffled another step closer, studying the tattoo. Close enough that her breath wisped across his skin and he nearly broke, needing to grab her, needing to crush her into him after the last days he spent going mad looking for her, not knowing whether or not she was safe.

"This ring?" She reached out and touched his chest with the slightest brush of her forefinger drifting across the ink.

"Yes." His muscles straining, the word came out pained for all he wanted from her in the moment but knew he couldn't have.

"It—oh—there are letters in the ring."

"Yes."

Her forefinger dragged down around the circle, finding the first letter, then up around the circle, tracing the letters.

The softest exclamation vibrated from her throat before her finger made the circle around the emblem. He knew it was hard to make out, the letters so flourished it took concentration to decipher each one. But it was there.

She looked up at him, her brow furrowed. "Guardians of the Bones?"

His chest lifted in a heavy sigh, making the full of her palm touch onto his chest.

Her hand snapped away, but she didn't move backward, only stared up at him, waiting.

"Yes. Guardians of the Bones. It is what I am. I am a guardian for hire. It is what I have been since I was fourteen years old and I was big enough to be mistaken for a man."

Her brow furrowed, a frown setting on her lips. "But you said you were in the army. You said you were a spy."

"I never said I was a spy, that was your word. But I was in the army in all those roles I talked about. I was there protecting the sons of England's finest aristocracy from their own dreams of grandeur on the battlefields."

Her brow still perplexed, her head angled to the side. "So people hired you to protect them? Why is that such a secret?"

"It's a secret because we protect the people that don't need or believe they need protecting—the ones that would refuse it. Most often, the people who hire us don't want the people we're protecting to know who we are. So we are footman, or maids, or governesses, or drivers, or—"

"Gardeners."

He nodded. "That one was a bit different, because I was actually hired by Vanessa's father to sort out what his younger brother was scheming. The best way to dig into anybody's life is to be the person they don't give a second thought to. In that situation with Vanessa's family, a gardener was a good position to go in as. I had free access to anywhere on the grounds—no one questions anything of a man always walking around with shears in his hands and boxwood cuttings clinging to his shirt."

Her eyes went wide as her mouth parted with an intake of breath. "Vanessa said—she said her uncle disappeared at the same time that you did, never to be seen again. Does that mean..."

Her voice trailed off as a flash of fear flickered in her eyes.

Shit.

Fear he never wanted to see in her. Fear of him.

But he couldn't hold back the truth from her, not now.

His voice went grave. "I made him disappear. He was trying to kill his mistress's husband and leave the country with her and the money he stole from his older brother. I got there just as he was about to kill the husband, stopping him, but it turned ugly."

"Ugly for Vanessa's uncle?"

He nodded, his face solemn.

Her head dropped, a long breath exhaling from her and she took a step away, facing the brook, her arms curling around her middle.

He could only stand in silence, watching her mull over what he'd just told her. Watching her judge the weight of his soul.

Her stare on the lazy water drifting by, it took long moments before a choked whisper eked from her. "Am I safe around you?"

"You will always be safe because of me."

Her head turned, her gaze intense on him. "What does that mean?"

"It means that Thomas hired me to investigate some things for him. I am one of the best investigators in the Guardians. But then Thomas shifted my duties to you when you were abducted. The most important thing to him was to have me keep you safe. You were never supposed to know who I really was." He paused, rubbing his forehead. "No one is ever supposed to know who I really am, for everything I've been working on for Thomas for the last eight months would be at risk. Our identities are always kept secret for the safety of all the Guardians."

She nodded, taking in the information. "Do you make a lot of people…disappear?" Her voice shook, even as her gaze remained intense on him.

A slice deep into his soul, the monster that he was bleeding out with the cut.

He steeled himself, meeting her gaze. "I do what I have to when it is warranted to keep the people I have been hired to keep safe, safe. That is my job. That is what I am good at. That is what I am paid to do."

"A mercenary, then." She heaved a sigh, tilting her head

back and looking at the sky through the tree branches above. "You said eight months—so you are not really friends with Charley?"

Her gaze dropped to him and he shook his head.

"Does Charley know that?"

He shook his head.

"Why? What has Charley done that could possibly warrant Thomas hiring someone like…like…"

"Like me?"

She swallowed hard, nodding.

"That, you'll have to ask Thomas about. What I have even told you right now is beyond a betrayal to the job. A betrayal to the code all the guardians live by."

She heaved a sigh. "And that is what I am, just a job to you?"

"I wanted you to be just a job to me." He took a step toward her, his voice rough. "And I fought damn hard to stay within those lines. The whole of this would have been a lot simpler if you were just a job. But you're not. And I was an idiot to think you could be. Ever since I met you, all I have wanted was to keep you safe. And then all I wanted was you."

Her breath hitched, her stare digging into him.

He could see it in her, her mind warring with her heart, with her body, with her instinct.

She wanted to believe him, she just didn't know if she should. He couldn't blame her wariness with her history of abandoned engagements.

Her lips pursed. "All of this…all of what you're telling me. It could still be lies. Merely lies you're telling me."

"Then why in the hell would I be here?" His hands lifted at his sides. "Why would I have torn apart this earth trying to find you?"

"You don't want to lose your job with Thomas? With the Guardians?"

He shook his head. "Thomas was the one that dumped you in the middle of nowhere. And when I found him at the tavern in Stenton, I quit. I'm not working for him. Not anymore. Not after what he did to you. The ass can figure his own mess out."

Her jaw dropped. "You quit?"

"I did." He stepped in front of her, daring to set his hands on her shoulders as he centered his stare on her, intention in his voice. "When you left me in London—for one second I thought to let you leave. Thought that was the moment I should let it all go. Let it be the end of whatever this is between us."

"Why didn't you?"

"I imagined never looking at your face again." His fingers curled up onto her neck. "Never hearing your laugh. Never arguing with you. Never touching you. Never leaning in and having the scent of your citrus and honey hit my brain and send a surge to my groin. Never hearing your moans when I have your body twisting under my hands. Never watching ecstasy chase across your face when I make you come. Never feeling the frantic beat of your heart under my palm right after. Never seeing that soft smile on your face, when I know, for just that one moment in time, you are in complete and utter peace in my arms."

His head dropped, his forehead meeting hers.

This was what he got for living in lies for the past fifteen years. He had a hard time knowing what the truth actually was until it hit him like a shovel in the face. That was what he felt in the middle of Vauxhall watching her run from him.

Devastation.

True devastation, like he hadn't felt since he was seven.

His hand lifted, his thumb running along her cheek. "I imagined all of that and there was no question in what I was doing next. I wasn't about to let you go. I don't think I'll ever be able to, not unless I want to be half a man. A hollowed-out shell that moves throughout life without a beating heart. For that's exactly what I was before you. A carcass of a man, pretending to be everything I'm not."

"Callum…" Her hands lifted, settling onto his bare chest—the caress of an angel. Yet he could still see the doubt in her eyes.

"Nemity, this is the moment. This is the moment I need you to look for that light in my eyes and hear what I am telling you. For it is the truth. That I have even told you what I have of me could be a grave mistake."

Her countenance reflecting the seriousness of his words, she nodded. "Are you telling me all of this so I have power to wield over you?"

"You already have power over me that I would rather you not. And yes, this is even more, as much as it kills me to do so. I will give you all the power in the world over me if it will make you believe in this truth that is standing before you now. Even if it wrecks me. Even if you use it to destroy me."

She gasped a breath, her hands moving up his chest. "You know I would never use this to destroy you."

"I don't know that." His words cracked, rough. "But I damn well have to trust it."

With a soft mewl, she pulled herself up and kissed him. Kissed him hard and frantic and full of intention.

Hell. He needed her. Needed her more than anything in this moment.

The undeniable force between the two of them took over and while a snippet of his brain said they couldn't do this here, he couldn't bring himself to listen to it and he picked her up, walking toward the willow tree with its long branches.

Her legs wrapped around him as he set her back against

the tree, one hand supporting her while the other went in a flurry to her skirts, baring her legs, her sex to him.

Without breaking the kiss, her hands went just as ferocious to unbutton his trousers, freeing him.

No time for soft caresses or languid kisses, the raw, voracious need pushed both of them onward and he plunged his shaft into her.

He lost his breath. Damn.

She was already soaked for him and he pulled out, slick with her need. He lifted her slightly, adjusting his angle for his shaft to grind against her at just the right spot with every thrust, and he went feral. He drove into her relentlessly, dragging his cock against her folds with every stroke. Pulling shuddered moans from her lips even as his mouth stayed locked on hers.

He needed this. Every one of her breaths. Every one of her moans. Every one of the shudders ripping through her body.

He needed all of them because she was his, whether she knew or not. She was.

Her shuttered eyes opened to him, begging silently, and he took it for what it was. She was so damn close, yet she wanted to drag it out.

He held on admirably, until her leg muscles turned to iron around him and she curled toward him. He drove into her, deeper than he thought possible and a choked scream warbled from her mouth. Her body shook, her inner walls contracting hard along his cock as the release hit her.

Two more drives and he lost all control, devouring her as he erupted deep within her.

Shattering his body and all the last vestiges of control he pretended to have.

He collapsed against her. Unable to grasp onto any solid thought in his head, other than one pounding desire.

He'd found her.
Now he just had to keep her.

CHAPTER 24

Nemity buried her face in Callum's shoulder, gasping for breath, the heat pouring off of his skin making her wish she could strip down and set the full of her body against his.

Still holding her against the tree, he'd wrapped his arms around her, saving her back from digging into the bark. He was having just as much trouble as her in finding his breath.

This was how it was with them. Sudden explosions that wrecked them both fully and muddled her mind. Set her emotions raw and jagged. Left her completely vulnerable.

Made her want more than just these scattered, stolen moments with him.

But that wasn't the deal.

He'd made that clear. She'd made that clear.

Even if he sounded like he was quite possibly softening on his stance. Yet he didn't promise her anything, so she couldn't allow herself to want anything.

His head shifted above her as he set his lips onto the top of her head. "How did you end up here? I looked and looked and looked and couldn't find a trace of you and Georgette and Jacob."

She drew in a deep breath, locking the scent of his skin into her nose since she knew it would be stolen away from her in the next minutes.

She shifted, pulling back to look up at him. "We spent that first night in an abandoned barn near to where Thomas dumped us on the side of the road."

"Fuck." His lip curled, his look going up to the sky. "Damn Thomas."

"Yes...well...I agree."

"I saw that spot, saw the hay inside and thought it could have been you, but I wasn't sure. Georgette and Jacob, how did they fare?" He extracted her from his body and set her feet onto the ground, his hands gripping her arms in case her balance was off. It was. Legs full of jelly were the curse of a rabid coupling against a tree.

He smoothed down her skirts as she leaned against the tree for support, then left her to pick up his shirt, waistcoat and coat and started dragging them onto his frame. Her stare locked on him—he was a beautiful man to watch move, even doing the most mundane things. How had she ever, for even one second, considered him death?

Her fingers clutched onto the edges of her skirts as she shook out the wrinkles, even though her dress was now wrinkled beyond saving after the last two days. "Georgette and Jacob were fine once they realized they weren't getting any food—they complained plenty before that. I tried to make it an adventure for them—telling them we were knights of old on a quest across the land."

His head popped out the top of his lawn shirt and he looked at her. "That was smart."

She shrugged. "It was helpful, for I knew I couldn't get

very far walking with them—it kept them motivated to keep trudging along."

The sudden thought of that first night alone with them hit her hard and her breath caught in her throat.

His eyes studying her face, Callum moved back toward her, concern etched in his brow. "What? What happened?"

She had to catch her breath, swallowing a lump down her throat. She waved her right hand in the air. "It was nothing—nothing."

His look set hard on her. "It's something for the fear I just saw flash in your eyes."

"It was just…" She looked down, staring at the tips of his dark boots. "That first night, I was scared. Scared like I'd never been in my life. Scared not for me, but for them. For Georgette and Jacob. I was terrified that something would happen to them and I couldn't stand the thought. And it felt like I was failing them—truly failing them and I hadn't even had them for more than a week. Failing them, failing Susannah and how she trusted me with them. I shouldn't have argued with Thomas. I should have groveled so that he didn't kick us out of the carriage—didn't leave us. Anything."

"That wasn't your fault, Nemity." The fury firing in his eyes told her that Callum was already dreaming up ways to make Thomas pay for what he'd done.

"It wasn't not my fault—I pushed him." She shook her head. "I always push him. And that night when the children fell asleep next to me on the hay, clutching onto me, I'd just never been gutted like that—so hopeless. I didn't have any money, any food—nothing."

She drew a shaky breath. It did nothing to stop the quiver in her limbs.

He wrapped his arms around her, holding her tight to him. Just the small touch and the quiver flooding her veins abated.

"What did you do?" he asked.

She scoffed a laugh. "I cried myself to sleep, and when I woke up I was on a mission to get us to the closest village, no matter how long it took. We made it to the road, then walked along beside it deep into the tree line so I could judge whoever was on the road before approaching him. Mable was the third person we saw that day."

"You convinced her to stop?"

"I did. She was plenty suspicious though. It was her alone in her wagon and she had one hand on her rifle. For the first five minutes, I thought I'd made a terrible mistake."

He loosened his hold and looked down at her. "Yet you managed to convince her to help you?"

She nodded. "It took a roundabout way—I kept naming people I knew in the area, or who had come from this area, trying to convince her I was who I said I was and I could pay her for help. I'm sure she thought I was mad, babbling name after name as I did. But then I finally threw out the name of my governess when I was eight—it was what I needed. Mable is a second cousin of my old governess. Mable and I both attended her wedding, though I'd only been nine at the time and don't recall meeting Mable."

A crooked smile came to his lips. "You weren't wrong when you said luck does tend to find you."

She gave an embarrassed grin and shrugged. "Charmed, I guess. Undeservedly so, sometimes. I just knew—hoped—that if I blurted out enough names, we would eventually find a connection. Her husband, Lenard, is currently in Edinburgh, and he should be back within two days. Then she was going to have him bring me home."

He grinned, shaking his head as he stepped back to put his waistcoat on. "Bloody well lucky, you are."

Her lips pulled wide in a sheepish smile. "It helps that Georgette and Jacob are so wicked adorable with their big eyes. Mable is keen on them. And I've tried to help out where I could, so we aren't a burden on her. Georgette has taken a liking to gathering the eggs from the chickens."

"And I saw you hanging sheets to dry as I came in from the lane."

She chuckled. "You saw the mess I was making of them?"

He grinned. "I did."

"I was trying to learn. I washed them as well—I think. Mable did do some scrubbing of them after me. But I did do it. One never knows when one must trade laundry for food—or so Mable has told me."

He laughed, shoving his arms into his coat. He pointed at the hill they'd come down. "Let us see if I can throw a pouch of coins at her to borrow her wagon so I can get us back to Springfell."

She nodded and he wrapped a hand around her lower back as they walked up the hill toward the cottage.

Her steps slowed as she glanced up at him. She still had some questions she wanted answered outside of Mable's hearing. "Callum, before we get up there, I need you to tell me this, and don't shove it off under some 'code' that you live by in order not to answer."

His lips pulled to the side in a quirk and then he looked down at her. She wasn't sure if that meant he was getting ready to lie to her or if he was loathing the fact that he'd told her anything of his past in the first place. "Yes?"

"If you don't work for Thomas anymore, then it seems as though you should be able to tell me what he hired you to do for him—before he sent you to look after me."

He half nodded, noncommittal. "By that logic, yes. Except for the fact that guardians never talk about clients."

"No." Her feet stopped, forcing him to halt beside her. "If you want me to trust you, Callum, then you have to trust me."

He stared down at her for a long breath, waiting for her to break.

She held her own silence and he finally puffed out an exasperated breath.

"Fine, what do you want to know?"

"I want to know about Charley."

He winced. "What do you want to know?"

"I just want to get it straight in my mind. So you are not a friend of Charley's?"

"No—yes."

Her head cocked to the side. "Thomas had you befriend him for some reason—why?"

He looked around, possibly hoping for some sort of intervention that would allow him to escape from this. None came and he looked down to her, his voice dipping, serious. "He thinks Charley is out to kill him."

"What?" Her head shook, her eyes going wide. "Kill him, why?"

"There was a string of accidents at Ravenstone where Thomas could have easily been killed. One or two accidents is unfortunate. Three in a short amount of time points to foul play. We assume Charley wants the title, the land, the money."

"That is insanity." Her voice pitched up. "Charley doesn't want any of that. Charley loves his life of debauchery. His life of irresponsibility. The title would shackle him to everything he loathes."

His right eyebrow lifted. "You think? For Charley spent six years thinking he was inheriting it all."

Her head flew back and forth. "No. You're wrong. Charley wouldn't hurt anyone. I know that in my bones. Thomas is wrong. Wrong to ever think that of his brother."

"Is he?"

"Yes." She couldn't keep the growl out of her voice. "Even

with all the time you've spent with him, you clearly don't know Charley—he couldn't hurt a fly. And you know full well what Thomas just did to me."

"I appreciate your loyalty to Charley, Nemity. I do. But in this case, your loyalty may be clouding your view of him."

"I am loyal because he has always been there for me. My biggest supporter. My most loyal friend."

"Yet the fact remains that the accidents happened, and they were too suspicious." He lifted his shoulders. "It has been what I've been trying to sort for months now, until I was diverted to protect you and investigate who would have kidnapped you."

Her lips pursed, her look running over his face. "Thomas has turned you into his docile lapdog, hasn't he?"

His top lip lifted for a moment, the barb striking a nerve, but he held onto his composure. "Can we pause this discussion until I get you and the children home to Springfell?"

Her hand flew up at her side. "It's an argument, not a discussion, and I don't see why we need to pause it when you just need to see what is obvious in front of you."

Both of his eyebrows lifted high. "That you think Charley can do no wrong? I see that just fine. While I, myself, have witnessed plenty of suspect moments in my last eight months with him."

Her arms folded over her chest. "Then you are mistaking those moments. Charley is good."

His face went solemn, his head shaking. "I don't know if that is true or not."

Her stare pinned him. "Then I don't know if you are good or not."

He blew out a big sigh. "Please, Nem. Please, can we just get back to Springfell today? I swear we can argue this out to your heart's content when we are back at the manor in privacy."

"Fine." She motioned toward the hill and they started walking an arm's width apart.

Just over the crest of the hill, she saw Mable had continued on with hanging the laundry, her rifle propped onto the base of the tree the line was tied around.

Mable set the skirt that was in her hands back down into the basket and picked up her rifle, walking over to them once she noticed them coming over the hill.

Her stare ate into Callum, then she looked to Nemity. "You two work out whatever needed to be worked out?"

Nemity glanced up at Callum.

They had worked out some things and hadn't worked out others, so she wasn't sure how to respond to Mable.

Instead, she pointed at the laundry now hanging on the line. "You didn't interrupt us. You went back to the laundry when you should have let me finish it."

Mable chuckled. "Oh, I did come to interrupt, but once I crested the hill, I thought the better of it."

Nemity coughed out a strained laugh. "You watched?"

Mable shrugged. "Not for long. A minute or two." Her gaze shifted to Callum, looking him up and down. By the unabashed look on her face, she approved of Callum's performance.

"Mable." Nemity squealed her name, laughing.

Mable looked to her. "What? Lenard won't be home for another day or so. It'll get me through." She winked at Nemity.

Callum laughed, a low chuckle that vibrated across the land.

Mable waved her hand to them. "Come, I imagine the wee ones will be waking from their naps soon and I already hitched up the wagon for you. We'll get you on your way."

"You did?"

"Of course I did, dear. A lady like you doesn't have to wait long for someone to come and collect her, no matter what you think to the contrary."

Mable started walking toward the cottage.

She and Callum followed, Mable's generosity of spirit hitting her hard, sending a lump into her throat.

Mable had taken her in, fed her, gave her and the children somewhere to sleep, all without any expectation.

She'd be sending an even bigger sack of coins back with the wagon when it was returned, and it still wouldn't be enough to repay Mable for her kindness.

CHAPTER 25

Nemity smiled, watching Georgette line up the rocks on the flat stone edge of the grand pool at Springfell. Her tiny fingers had set the little pebbles from the walkway all in a perfectly neat line, which was exactly her personality.

She was only four, but already she was attempting to make everything perfect and in line for her younger brother. Entertaining him, watching over him, keeping him quiet. It'd been a heavy load for her tiny shoulders. And Jacob looked up to his sister for everything.

Living through the last year of Susannah's illness as they had was not kind.

Now, at least, she hoped Georgette could let go of the worry constantly in her eyes. Worry that belonged on someone sixty years her senior that had a lifetime of pain to show.

Nemity wanted nothing more than Georgette's lines of rocks to be curving and wild and going nowhere and it wouldn't matter. A year ago, Georgette had been a silly wild hoyden, just like her mama once was when she and Nemity and their band of friends had taken on the *ton*. Georgette had been destined to be just the same until her father died and Susannah fell ill.

Jacob, the complete opposite of his sister, was busy gleefully tossing handfuls of pebbles into the water like a hatter. Squealing and jumping up and down each time he sent a cascade of ripples across the water. He'd inherited his mama's wild way and his father's roguish handsomeness—something she could already recognize in his cherub face.

She exhaled a long sigh.

This was exactly what she'd needed for the past week—to get Georgette and Jacob here where she could surround them with security and love and fun and happiness.

Watching Callum with them on the ride to Springfell the day before had made her heart twist in a thousand good ways. How understanding he was with them—patient and funny—and he always had room in his lap for both of them, no matter that he was busy driving the wagon.

One night in their new rooms—well, Georgette's new room, because Jacob had wanted to sleep in his sister's bed—and Nemity was already seeing sparks in their eyes that hadn't been there before.

For as much as she was terrified after Thomas kicked them out of the carriage, they had thought all of the journey to the manor was a grand adventure.

"You didn't wake me up."

She smiled to herself and turned around from where she was sitting on the stone ledge of the grand pool. A distance away, Callum stepped off the bottom step of the wide stone stairs embedded into the slope that led up to the manor house. His boots crunched along the cream-colored pebbles lining the walkway as he strolled toward them.

"You looked peaceful."

He chuckled. "That, I don't believe—I haven't had peaceful sleep in...well...forever. If ever."

Her bottom lip jutted upward. "Your brow was furrowed, I suppose. Peaceful or not, you'd been awake for days because of me and I wasn't about to deprive you of a few hours of sleep. Plus, you earned a bit of relaxation after last night." Her look turned utterly carnal as she grinned up at him.

He had. Once they had gotten the children settled and asleep, he had dragged her into her room and stripped her down, twisting her body into all manner of positions that shouldn't have been possible. There was the extra benefit of the long stubble invading his face from the days searching for her—he'd dragged it against almost every inch of her skin, the wantonness of it driving her mad, and she discovered she wouldn't mind if he grew a beard.

And he hadn't slept outside her room in his usual spot.

This time he'd slept in her bed, the length of his body curling around her. Protecting her even in sleep.

He couldn't hide his grin in reply, and with the smooth skin from a fresh shave, it made his face look almost boyish.

"Uncle Cal, Uncle Cal." Jacob ran over to him, both of his fists still full of pebbles. Georgette was quick on his heels, wiping the dust on her hands off on her dress as she ran. Both of them latched onto one of his tree trunk legs, squeezing, and he ruffled their hair. "You both have been good this morning?"

"Oh yes, Uncle Cal." Georgette bobbed her head up and down. "Auntie Nemmy said our eyes are alive with...with..."

She looked over her shoulder to Nemity.

"Mischief," Nemity supplied.

"Mischief," Georgette repeated, nodding her head.

"You look like it, Sprite." He glanced to the side of the pond at her handiwork with the rocks. "That has to be the longest, straightest snake yet."

"It is, it is. And I'm going to make it even longer." With a hop, she ran back to the side of the pond, picking up more pebbles on the way. Jacob followed her back, tossing one of his fistfuls of pebbles into the water and laughing, then looking back at Callum.

Callum laughed. "Like musical droplets."

Nemity stared at him, slightly stunned.

He'd figured out Georgette was actually making a snake, which was obvious once he'd said it, for her love of animals. And Jacob loved anything that made musical sounds.

How he'd determined all of that about each of them in the short time he knew them stunned her. And scared her.

The children were quickly falling in love with him.

She drew in a steadying breath. One problem at a time.

She stood up, moving toward Callum like a cat after a mouse, stealth in her eyes. She didn't want to barrage him with this first thing in the morning, but she knew as well as he did what he was really distracting her from last night.

She lauded him for managing to avoid the argument, but he didn't realize her capacity for tenacity. Their difference of opinion on Charley had been a festering wound, itching at her since they'd first argued about it.

He was avoiding the topic while all she wanted to do was convince him he was wrong about Charley. She had to make him see that.

The best chance she had to force him to have this conversation again was in front of the children. Georgette and Jacob wouldn't know what they were talking about and Callum couldn't just strip her clothes off her to make her shut up on the matter.

She ran her fingertips up along the front line of his waistcoat. He hadn't bothered with a coat this morning, merely rolled up the sleeves of his lawn shirt. Her fingers stopped, thrumming on his chest through his shirt as she looked up at him. "We have to talk about Charley."

"Nemity—"

"No. I know exactly what you were doing last night, avoiding the topic in the best way you knew how."

He had enough sense to look rebuked. "You think me that devious? Can't I just want to enjoy your body?"

She grinned. "You can. Anytime. Just don't think it got you out of the conversation."

"Or we could just foist the children off onto Mrs. Jorge and I can drag you back into bed."

"See? Devious." Her forefinger tapped on his chest. "I am asking you to rethink all of the suspect thoughts you've had about Charley. You have been listening to Thomas and not to reality. Charley is not a threat to anyone."

His lips pulled tight, his chest lifting under her hand as he drew in a long breath. "You don't know that."

"Except I do. You have spent eight months in his presence—carousing with him and I imagine spying on him when you weren't in his company." She stopped, her eyes going huge. "Wait. Did you ever spy on Charlie when he was with me? In London? Months ago?"

He winced. "Maybe?" His shoulders lifted. "I am not sure. He talks to so many people when he is in the park, and I do remember him spending time one afternoon with a woman with two small children, six or seven months ago. But I couldn't say for certain if that was you or not." He looked past her to the children. "I was a distance away, but judging by the hair color of the children alone, yes, it was Georgette and Jacob. The woman had a bonnet on covering the whole of her hair and she never turned my way."

She nodded slowly, slightly unnerved. She still had to settle in her mind the fact that he'd been in Charley's life all this time, spying on him.

His fingers lifted, tracing down the side of her waist as his voice dipped. "You...you I would have remembered seeing with him."

Her look narrowed at him. He wasn't about to distract her again. "Fine. So you spied on him a lot. And in that time, have you ever—ever—even seen him angry? Much less so angry he would try to kill his own flesh and blood?"

Callum's mouth clamped closed, his nostrils flaring. "No."

She nodded. "He doesn't have it in him. So maybe, just maybe, you have it wrong. Thomas has it wrong. Just because Thomas hired you, it doesn't mean he's right—it doesn't mean that he isn't the one actually trying to hurt Charley."

His brow furrowed. "Why would you say that? That doesn't make any sense."

A splattering of pebbles tinkled into the water and she glanced over her shoulder to check on Jacob. A wild grin cut across his cherub face as he glanced to his sister. Georgette was still busy lining her little matching pebbles onto the end of her snake.

Nemity looked back to Callum. "Does it make any sense that Thomas kicked me out of his carriage with two defenseless children?"

His jaw tightened, flexing. "No."

"No." She shook her head. "Thomas has not been right since he came back. That is something I know. I also know that Charley has been my friend my entire life. He got me through two broken engagements and the scandal of them. He made me hold my head up high after the scandals, showed me how to move forward. You are wrong about him. Thomas is wrong about him. If someone was trying to hurt Thomas, you need to start looking elsewhere. There must be something else, someone else to start looking at. Or maybe all of this is in Thomas's head. Maybe your entire time working for him has been a waste."

The side of his mouth quirked up. "I wouldn't call it a complete waste, because it brought me to you."

She smiled. "It did do that. And while I may have regretted your initial intrusion into my life, I don't regret for one instant what it has turned into."

He stepped in closer to her, his hand moving up so he could slide his fingers into her upsweep. Her breath caught in her throat.

Holy sin. When he looked at her like that, her thighs had to clamp together just to remain standing.

"Miss Wheldon, Miss Wheldon." Mrs. Jorge called out to her from the wide stone steps that led down into the gardens from the main house. Mrs. Jorge was running—running when her crooked gait shouldn't allow her to do so.

Nemity stepped to the side of Callum and hurried toward her, if only to slow Mrs. Jorge down so she didn't trip on the stairs and crack her head wide open on the stones. "Mrs. Jorge, what is it?"

Her hand flat on her chest, Mrs. Jorge panted, slowing her steps as Nemity rushed toward her. "You have a visitor—an unexpected one and one you need to see right away."

Dread flooded her chest, flipping her stomach. "Who?"

"Lady Agnes, she—"

"Lady Agnes? What? Here?"

"Yes. Lady Agnes. She just arrived and she pushed her way into the house. Poor Mr. Flourin, she hit him with her cane when he opened the door. I heard the commotion and I intervened and I showed her to the Yellow drawing room. I told her I would get you directly."

Nemity's head fell, her eyes closing. It took her a long moment before she could even draw a breath, and when she did so, it was a long one meant to fortify, but it only made her stomach churn all the more.

She opened her eyes and looked at Mrs. Jorge. "The Yellow drawing room, you said?"

"Yes."

Nemity looked over her shoulder at Callum. He gave her a nod.

"Mrs. Jorge, can you please look after the children while we go in to greet Lady Agnes?"

"Yes, ma'am."

"Thank you. I promise I have already sent word to Lord Hedstrom's man that I will need to hire a governess as soon as possible for the children."

Mrs. Jorge's gaze shifted to Georgette and Jacob. "I do not mind, ma'am. I have always liked these two muffins."

"Thank you."

Turning from the children, Nemity clutched her skirts, and she and Callum moved quickly up the wide stairs on the slope and into the manor house.

Smoothing the front of her peach day dress outside of the drawing room, Nemity tried to calm herself. No matter how she spun it in her mind, Lady Agnes wouldn't be here for any good reason.

"No use putting it off, Nem." Callum's low voice whispered into her ear. "Avoiding it only shows weakness and you can bet Lady Agnes has been watching us come up from the gardens through the windows."

Nemity nodded and opened the door to the drawing room.

Sure enough, Lady Agnes was standing in front of the window that looked out upon the gardens.

She and Callum moved into the room. "Lady Agnes, what a pleasant surprise. I never would have imagined you would make the trip all the way north. Whatever you needed, you could have sent word and I would have come to you."

"Would you have? I doubt that, child." Lady Agnes's lips

pursed as she turned from the window and jabbed her cane into the wooden floorboards. "Nowhere is too far to go to protect the reputation of my kin."

"Reputation? What are talking about, Lady Agnes?" Nemity gestured toward the window. "As I am sure you can see, the children are well and happy."

"Hmmph. Playing with rocks is not becoming, but that is the least of my worries at the moment."

"Please, sit." Nemity motioned to the yellow silk damask chair next to Lady Agnes. She looked to the round rosewood table in the corner of the room. "Good, I see tea was brought in. May I pour?"

Lady Agnes shook her head, her mouth still pinched. "I will stand for the moment."

Nemity nodded, remaining standing. Lady Agnes was the most direct person she'd ever encountered, so she may as well dive into it with her. "What is your worry?"

"You left London abruptly with the children." Lady Agnes's nose turned up, shaming all the better at that angle. "I rather believed you were to stay in London until banns were posted and you were married before you travelled north."

"That..." Nemity nodded, clasping her hands in front of her belly. "Yes, my cousin, Lord Hedstrom, needed to leave London and he has the best travelling carriage with space for the children, so I thought it best that we travel with him."

"So you took the children and yet you are not married?" Her look flickered back and forth between Nemity and Callum.

"I did." Nemity inclined her head toward Callum. "I apologize. I have just been overwhelmed by Susannah's death, and then thinking of the children and that it would be best to get them settled as quickly as possible away from where their mother passed on."

"Is that so?" Her shrewd eyes locked onto Callum and she stared at him for a long moment. "Mr. Lonstrick, would you please excuse us? Nemity and I have some things to discuss in private."

Callum looked to Nemity and all she could offer him was weak smile and a nod.

"As you wish, Lady Agnes." He gave a quick bow to her and exited the room, closing the door behind him.

The click of the latch had barely echoed into the room and Lady Agnes advanced on her, her cane clunking into the floor with each step, her lips drawing into a tight line.

"A gardener, Miss Wheldon?" The words spit like little spikes of hot iron at Nemity. "A philandering gardener? That is who you think to marry?"

Dammit all to hell.

Her heart stopped in her chest. Lady Agnes was going to take Georgette and Jacob from her.

Frozen for a long second, she suddenly heard Callum's voice in her mind. *Avoidance equals weakness.*

Exactly what she needed to spur herself into motion. For weakness was something that Lady Agnes sniffed out and feasted upon.

Setting her countenance to indifferent regard, she smiled at Lady Agnes, unflustered. "You have spoken to my friend, Lady Cladwell, I presume?"

"That little minx tried to avoid me for days and then I cornered her at the opera house. Lady Turgh witnessed you at Vauxhall getting swooped away by Lord and Lady Cladwell. You left Mr. Lonstrick searching for you in the crowd. Lady Turgh said it did not amount to a happy couple looking forward to upcoming nuptials. And then you disappeared from London with my niece and nephew not but a day after. All that, and you think I would allow you to keep my niece and nephew?"

Her gut dropping, Nemity needed to sit, but her smile stayed serene, not widening, not dissolving. Fortitude. Fortitude in her spine if she was to get through this. "I would like some tea, Lady Agnes, are you sure you will not join me?"

"I will not. I am waiting for answers."

Nemity nodded, then moved to the teapot on the serving table at the side of the room. She took her time pouring, then dropping one teaspoon of sugar into the cup. Not that she liked sugar in her tea, she more just needed the extra time to stir.

Methodically, she stirred until the sugar dissolved, then moved to sit on the chaise lounge that faced Lady Agnes. She took a sip of the tea, then looked up at the elderly woman.

So righteous. So very righteous in every move she made, every edict she flung out to society. Holding on so tightly to her punctilious judgements because they were the only thing she had in life.

Georgette and Jacob were Nemity's insurance in not ending up like Lady Agnes. A family. A family so she didn't end up a shriveled old pernicious witch with nothing better to do than make everyone around her as miserable as she was.

She wasn't about to let this crone take Georgette and Jacob from her.

Setting the tea cup on the plate, she leaned forward and placed it on the low rosewood inlaid table in front of her and took her time smoothing her skirts as her look lifted to Lady Agnes.

"Lady Cladwell is correct. Mr. Lonstrick was a gardener, though his fortunes have changed since that time, years ago, when he was doing honest work for an upstanding member of society, Vanessa's father. Mr. Lonstrick was merely trying to make an honest way in the world and he was not lying about his lineage, of which you assessed and approved of. I think someone with your knowledge of society knows very well how far-flung members of nobility can come into poverty."

Lady Agnes jabbed a step forward, her wrinkled face stretching tight as her lips pursed to an even tighter hole. "And it is exactly that, the taint of poverty on the man you think to help raise these children. To discipline them. It is unthinkable."

"Yet it was that very discipline that allowed Mr. Lonstrick to pull himself out of poverty." Nemity paused, picking up her tea and taking another sip. "If anything, I believe it shows the true character of the man. That he is willing to look hardship directly in the eye and overcome it with a keen mind, hard work, and an unbending will. Those are traits that would be good to instill in any child, do you not agree?"

Lady Agnes's thin nostrils flared, yet she didn't argue the point. "Miss Wheldon, be that as it may, the fact remains that you fled north with the children before you were married."

Nemity nodded, the serene smile still plastered on her face. "Again, I wanted to see the children settled as soon as possible, instead of living in one home, then moving to another only weeks later. They have just lost their mother and I want to make this time as easy as possible for them. Indeed, it was Mr. Lonstrick that insisted my own desires to be wed quickly be overridden in order to make Georgette and Jacob feel secure in their new home. The delay would show a remarkable fortitude of restraint, I believe were his exact words. The wedding is still planned—though a Scottish one at that—as soon as we can arrange my cousins and the vicar to come here to the manor."

Lady Agnes's eyes narrowed on Nemity. "It will happen soon, then?"

"It will." Nemity set the tea cup and plate back onto the

table. Only by the grace of the heavens did the shake in her hands not transfer into the cup clinking on the plate.

"Good." Both of her withered hands grabbed the top of her cane and she clunked the tip of it into the carpet. "Then you will not mind me staying until the nuptials are complete."

Nemity's look snapped up to Lady Agnes. "Stay here at Springfell? It may be days. A week even before all the arrangements can be made."

"Then it is a good thing I have no pressing engagements in London." Lady Agnes's mouth pulled back in a straight line that may have been a smile, Nemity couldn't tell for sure.

"We are happy to have you here." Nemity swooped her hand into the air. "You are always welcome at Springfell, whether you are here for a wedding or to see the children."

Lady Agnes's hawk eyes cut into her, and then she harrumphed and moved to the settee by the fire and sat down. "You may serve me that tea, now."

Nemity nodded and stood, going to the teapot on the table. Her stare fixed out on the children by the pond, wondering what in the hell she'd just done.

And how in the hell she could make it out of this predicament.

CHAPTER 26

Where in the blasted world did Callum disappear to?

She'd spent far too much time listening to Lady Agnes drone on about her uncomfortable journey north, before she could excuse herself to check on the children.

She found them with Mrs. Jorge in the library, where they had fallen asleep on the couch while Mrs. Jorge read to them from *Frankenstein*. While she'd have to speak to her maid about her choice in reading material, the fact remained that Mrs. Jorge was a delight in helping her with Georgette and Jacob, when that was the last thing her job entailed.

Though Mrs. Jorge *had* taken to the role with aplomb. And it might be easier to find a new maid, than it would to find a suitable governess. Nemity could deal with a new, inept maid. What she didn't want was for the children to have to deal with a new, inept governess.

A possibility she would discuss with Mrs. Jorge once the children went to bed this eve.

The more pressing matter at the moment—in the long list of pressing matters—was to find Callum.

He'd disappeared from the house, which was odd because she knew he always liked to be within a hundred steps of her —within screaming distance—as his drive to protect her overrode everything else.

Except not at the moment.

After a quick sweep of the gardens, she made her way to the stables.

Callum was inside one of the stalls, his head bobbing up and down from view as he saddled his horse.

She walked down the length of the main corridor in the barn, her approach silent, for he didn't look up as she came to a stop in front of the stall. That, or he knew full well she was watching him and he was purposefully not looking in her direction.

"Ca—" She stopped, having to clear her throat. "Callum, where are you going?"

"Lady Agnes knows about my gardening assignment, I imagine." Not surprised at her presence at all, he glanced up at her, then went back to tightening a strap. He'd known full well the moment she'd entered the barn.

Nemity took a step forward, her hands wrapping over the top of the stall's half wall as she watched him continue to avoid her. "She does know you were a gardener, but I deflected that easily enough. She was more concerned about why I left London in such haste after leaving Vauxhall without you."

His head stayed bowed as he worked on the girth and he nodded to himself. "And what did you tell her?"

"You were already here, so it was easy enough to convince her we did not break things off and that I absconded with the children to hide that fact."

He nodded again. "If anyone could convince her of that, it would be you." He finished tightening all the saddle's straps and stood upright, moving to the half door and stepping out into the main walkway. His arms crossed over his chest as he leaned his hip on the half wall next to her. "That is all? She is satisfied?"

"No." Her jaw fell slightly and she took in a shaky breath. "I told her we are getting married. She is insisting on staying until she witnesses it with her own eyes."

His eyes went wide. "You what?"

"I am sorry." Her words rushed out. "It was the only way I could convince her to not take Georgette and Jacob. I didn't think she would insist on staying until the deed was done."

His head turned in the general direction of the manor house. "You think that old bat doesn't know every trick you have up your very loose sleeves?"

Her fingers went on his arm and she couldn't hide the tremble in her hand. She looked up at him, fear creeping into her voice that she didn't want to admit to. "Where are you going, Callum? Are you running from me?"

His mouth opened. Closed. Opened again and he shook his head. His fingers ran through his hair. "Hell, Nemity. No. Yes. No."

Her hand snapped away from him and she shuffled a step backward.

He was leaving. Leaving her.

She'd only said it because she didn't believe it. But then there, out of nowhere, he was leaving her.

Leaving.

Another step backward, her left hand landed on the top of the half wall so she wouldn't lose her balance as dizziness set in.

He was leaving.

After everything. He was leaving her.

And that would mean Georgette and Jacob would be leaving her as well.

Everyone...gone.

Her stomach started to twist, bile chasing up her throat.

"Nemity, you have to understand." He took a step forward, his hand going out to seemingly catch her upper arm before she lost her balance, but she jerked another step backward and out of his reach before he could grab her.

Her look went vicious on him. "Understand what? You'd thought to be quicker in abandoning me? Already gone? Direct in your exit?"

"Nem...no, I don't know what I'm doing down here."

Her left hand flew up, swinging toward his saddled horse. "You're leaving, that much is obvious."

"No." His head tilted back, his look on the rafters above as a growl rumbled from his throat. "No, I'm confused, and that is a state I am never in. I'm thinking one thing and then you appear in front of me and I'm thinking another, and I don't know where my mind is at."

She sucked in a breath, attempting to keep calm when she was about to lose everything. "Confused about what?"

His stare still on the rafters above, he shook his head. Like he expected all the answers he needed to just come raining down from above and they weren't. "I don't tell you much about me—I know that. And you don't ask, you don't push because that is who you are and I adore that about you."

His stare dropped to her, his look carving deep into her with want and madness and restraint, making her heartbeat thunder out of control. "I've nearly died multiple times in my life, Nem."

"Callum—"

His hand flew up between them. "Stop. What you need to hear about is the first time I almost died."

She swayed slightly, but then her grip on the half wall tightened, refusing to let her fall even if the bones of her knuckles popped out of her skin.

She nodded, her voice soft. "Tell me."

He stared at her for a long moment, and she could see the torment in his eyes. The torment he was unleashing to the light of day for her.

His head dipped, his stare centering on the hay-strewn floor between them. "They came at night...Boney's forces."

He heaved a deep breath and lifted his gaze to her. "Even though he lived in England for much of his life, my father was Prussian, and at that, loyal to his homeland. My mother was the daughter of a wealthy London merchant. When I was six, my father brought us all to Prussia—with Austria close to falling to France, he was well aware of what the future held. My grandfather—my mother's father—fought him, tried to convince him to let me and my mother stay behind in England, but my father would not hear of it. The night before we left, they fought again, my grandfather's last stand. But in the middle of it, my grandfather dropped dead. I do not know the circumstances, only that my mother was destroyed by her father's death. And she was my world...my very happy world."

He swallowed hard. "So we moved to Prussia, and my father bought us a beautiful manor outside of Berlin. It was grand and ostentatious, but it had beautiful gardens my mother and I played in every day. Father was gone much of the time in service to the army, and for that, I was glad. He was not a kind man. An exacting bastard, if I were to judge him."

"That was who you were channeling at Vauxhall?"

"Mostly." His shoulders lifted. "But we held those days high, those days when it was just me and my mother. There was laughter and sweets and warmth and learning—she was intelligent and taught me so much in my early years. French, German, some Latin. Mathematics and philosophy—topics that were far beyond my years, but she never dumbed any of it down for my age. She expected me to learn and I did."

Her heart constricted, for it was easy to see how much he adored his mother.

"And when my father would arrive for short visits, she would trot me out and I would recite all I learned. I realized many years later, all of that was about pleasing my father, living up to his high standards in his wife, in his son. If we didn't perform to his exact specifications, my mother felt the back of his hand."

An intake of breath, and her fingers lifted to her lips.

"It wasn't long before Prussia entered the coalition, and not long after that, my father led a contingent in the Battle of Jena–Auerstedt. He escaped with his life and returned home, but it wasn't for long. Boney's forces were on his trail."

He paused, pinching the bridge of his nose for a long breath. "They came in a swarm that night. All these men with rifles with bayonets, flooding the house. My father rushed me and my mother up the servants' stairs and he shoved us into a far-flung room to hide, but they found us. My father fought them, fought to save us, fought them from coming into the room—the one admirable thing I remember about him. He was trying to give my mother and me time enough to escape.

"Our driver, Hector, was on the ground outside of the window and my mother didn't hesitate, didn't say a word, she just pushed me out the window. Hector caught me—broke my fall as I was just skin and bones at that age. He set me down and waited for my mother to follow, but halfway out the window, she stopped, then slumped onto the windowsill. He saw that and he picked me up and ran with me over his shoulder. The last time I saw my mother was when I was hanging over Hector's shoulder, and she was half splayed out of that window, blood dripping from her face. Even in the dark, I could see it so clearly with the light from the torches below. The blood splattering out onto her cheek.

She didn't even get a chance to say goodbye to me. Didn't get a chance to kiss my forehead like she did—long—like she was imprinting herself onto me every time she did so."

Tears brimming in her eyes, Nemity couldn't help them from spilling over.

At that, Callum's eyes closed, wincing as the memory took a hold of him.

Nemity's hand crumpled, her knuckles pressing into her lips as the pain in him palpitated in the air around her and made her own heart crack in two for him.

His head turned to the side, his eyes still closed as he started talking again. "The man that saved me—Hector—he took me in. Raised me. Any family I had in Prussia or in England was dead." He opened his eyes and expelled a deep breath. "Then, years later, I found out what Hector really was."

Her brow furrowed as she tried to force words past the lump in her throat. "What was he?"

"He was the first Guardian of the Bones. Before he died, before we left England, my grandfather had at great expense employed Hector to protect us—my mother and me—without us or my father knowing. My father never would have stood for his father-in-law's interference. Hector looked the average man on every account, but he was deadly, one of the deadliest people I've ever known. He killed two men while carrying me that night we escaped from Berlin. And his breath never even quickened, he was that efficient."

Her hand dropped to her side. "He came with you from England?"

"He did. He was the first Guardian. My grandfather's surname was Bones, hence, he deemed them the Guardians of the Bones."

"Them?"

"There was another as well. Hector and a maid in our

household, who wasn't truly a maid, but a guardian as well. Miss Bannerson. Those two brought me back to England, kept me fed, gave me a home to live in while they built the Guardians of the Bones. It was during the Continental wars and the need for people like them was great. Ones that would protect the people in harm's way that needed protecting. Both of them were gone much of the time. And then I grew tall and strong—earlier than most boys—and Hector asked me to become a Guardian. He'd already taught me everything he knew, and I owed my life to him, so I said yes."

"How old were you?"

"Thirteen, nearly fourteen."

She gasped, her hand covering her mouth. Her fingers slowly fell away as she shook her head. "And you've been paying back that debt ever since."

He shrugged. "This job—it was what I was meant to do."

She nodded, her look sinking to the ground, studying stands of hay as the breath stole out of her chest. She knew what he was saying. He was telling her he was always going to be a guardian. That he was leaving because he would never be anything more than a guardian. Never be anything to her other than a stray dalliance.

No.

Clarity slammed into her.

She didn't want him to go. Didn't want him to be a guardian. Didn't want him to be her protector. She wanted him.

Him.

As a husband. As the one that she knew to her bones would never hurt her—would move the sun and stars for her if it made her happy. She wanted him as the father that Georgette and Jacob needed. She wanted him because of his intelligence and his wit and that undeniable energy between them that drew her to him, a moth to flame.

She wanted *him.*

Heaven above, she was in love with him. Deeply so. Irrevocably so.

So much so that the pains in her chest at the thought of him leaving her now were close to making her collapse onto the ground.

She'd been alone for so long, accustomed to it. Thrived on it. And now this. An upheaval of her whole life.

An upheaval she was going to have to fight for.

Her look crept up to him, her voice cracking with the weight of all that was running rampant through her mind. "And are you meant to be a guardian for the rest of your life?"

"All I know is that I've been doing what fate has handed me."

Her stare sank into him, willing him with everything she was to hear her, to feel this like she was feeling it. "Callum, fate handed you me."

He paused, a breath of air puffing out.

His eyes locked on hers, the silver that reflected the world around it sparking in a way she'd never seen before.

Possibility. He was seeing it. Imagining it.

His look snapped away, and he shook his head, running a hand through his hair. "What you're asking of me, Nem… you're asking me to give up everything I've ever known."

"Except you've also known what a family is. You had that with your mother. You know that a family can be your whole world."

His voice dipped into a heart-wrenching growl. "And that is the worst of it."

"How can you not want to choose me?" She took a step toward him, closing in on the space between them. "Choose a family with me?"

"My mother was everything, Nemity." His growl turned

into thunder. "Everything. And she was ripped away—skewered in front of me. I wanted to be there with her. Dead. That was where I wanted to be."

She heaved a frustrated breath. "So you'll not risk having a family again only to lose it? That is ridiculous, Callum. You risk your life all the time with the Guardians."

"Yes, but that is just me. If I die, I die. I am responsible to only me."

"So you're choosing the coward's way?" Her voice turned desperate and she hated it, but damned if she wasn't going to fight this down to the last tooth. "You're willing to take yourself away from me? When I think you are everything? Everything I always wanted but never got?"

"Nemity..."

"Stay." She reached out and grabbed his forearm. "Stay with me. Please. Please st—"

"No. Stop." He yanked his arm out from her grip.

"What?"

He stepped back. "No. This isn't right." Another step away. "I have to go talk to Thomas."

Three more steps and he moved into the stall and grabbed the reins of his horse, then led Pharaoh out, his feet not slowing as he walked past her. "I can't do this right now, Nemity. Wait. Just please, wait. Don't do a thing until I'm back."

"But..."

Without another word, he disappeared out into the daylight, leaving her in the shadows.

He didn't want her.

CHAPTER 27

"I saw your man leave." Lady Agnes's scratchy voice grated into her ears. "He tore across the front lane like the devil himself was on his back."

Closing her eyes, Nemity stopped in the foyer as Lady Agnes came out of the front drawing room.

Of course she saw. Lady Agnes saw every damn thing there was to see.

Without responding, Nemity moved past her, not even looking at the woman.

She had to go hide. Be in silence with herself and get her mind straight before she set herself in front of the children. For she refused to let them see any worry in her eyes. Not now. Not ever.

Lady Agnes's sharp voice cut into her retreat. "I assume the wedding has been canceled."

Nemity spun around to her, a forced smile on her face. "On the contrary, he will be back soon enough. He is making the arrangements—he has to talk to Thomas."

A lie.

She had no doubt Lady Agnes saw straight through her deceit.

Lady Agnes harrumphed. "About your fortune, no doubt."

Nemity kept walking away, even though the words were a blow straight to her gut, making her slightly double over.

It was always the source of her worth in the *ton*. Her fortune. Her status. Her burden.

Yet this was where she was.

If she had to buy a husband in order for her to keep Georgette and Jacob, she would do it.

She would offer up to Callum everything she had. Give him everything so he would trade away the rest of his life being shackled to her.

It was the only way, really. Her last chance.

No matter her pride. No matter that Callum didn't want her.

The one good man she'd truly wanted to marry, and he didn't want her.

Even if he didn't want her, he would be honor bound to be the best father he could to Georgette and Jacob. She knew that without a doubt of him.

So she would grovel, give up anything for him to marry her. If that was what it took, then those would be the first words out of her mouth when he returned.

Her feet trudging up the stairs, she looked out the window high above the front door of Springwell. Heavy clouds were rolling in, a blanket of rain nearly to the manor. Perfect for her mood. As if her emotions controlled the weather.

At least the skies could cry, even if she could not.

It rained the entire night and into the next day.

Such a heavy downpour that she would at least have an excuse for Callum not showing up in the next day, as the roads would be soup at this point.

She'd spent the day entertaining the children in the library. She'd had her old doll house brought down from storage, and Georgette had delighted is setting everything into its proper place. Jacob had taken to the miniature wooden horses that had been stored with the doll house, and spent an inordinate amount of time setting up a siege on the doll house.

Throughout all the play, she'd started teaching them some of the songs she remembered from her childhood. She was an awful singer, but lucky for her, children were rarely judgmental about her voice. In the middle of singing "Oranges and Lemons" with the children, she hadn't heard the knock on the front door and jumped when Charley's voice cut into the air behind her. "What is all this caterwauling I hear in here?"

Both of the children looked up, smiles lighting up their faces when they spied Charley at the door of the library.

"Charley," Georgette squealed and ran toward him, wrapping her arms around his leg.

"Hello, Cherub." He tousled her hair and bent down to sweep Jacob into his arms as Jacob's little legs nearly lost balance they were running so hard. "And hello to you, little sir. I heard you both travelled here with Auntie Nemmy."

Both of the children knew and loved Charley, for he would sometimes join Nemity when she brought the children to Hyde Park every other day earlier in the year. He always had time for them and would pick flowers with Georgette, letting her tuck them into his hair.

Nemity stood from the carpet where they were playing and moved toward him.

"Charley, what on earth are you doing here? You are soaking wet—oh, no—and now you're soaking the children." Laughing, Nemity rushed forward, pulling Jacob from his arms, only to realize the transfer of moisture had already happened onto Jacob's clothes, and she immediately set him down.

She shook her head as she peeled Georgette away from Charley's wet trousers. "Georgette, you as well? Ugh."

Grabbing both of the children's hands, she walked them to the door of the library and out into the hallway. "Mrs. Jorge? Are you nearby?" she called out.

She heard the footsteps walking from the connecting hallway before Mrs. Jorge appeared. "Yes, ma'am?"

"Would you please take Georgette and Jacob up for a change of clothes? They are soaked."

Mrs. Jorge's forehead furrowed. "Wet? How did that come to be?"

"Charley is here and Charley is soaked through. That didn't stop these two from hugging him." She bent down and tickled their ribcages.

They tried to wiggle away from her as squeals of laughter echoed down the corridor.

"Ah, I thought I saw someone coming up from the stables, but I assumed it was Mr. Lonstrick."

That sobered Nemity.

She shook her head. "Just Charley." She smiled. "You take them and I'll go see to Charley."

Mrs. Jorge nodded and took the children's hands.

Nemity returned to the library. Charley had moved toward the window, watching the rain pelting down against the pane. At least he hadn't taken a seat with his wet clothes.

"Is it as atrocious out there as it looks?" she asked, looking past him out the window.

"It is starting to ease." He leaned forward to look up out the window, searching the sky. "Or at least it was."

"Why were you even travelling in this weather?"

"I didn't really have a choice. I came up straight from London." Charley turned to her. "Is Callum here?"

"Callum?" Her brows drew together. "No. He went to Ravenstone."

He looked her over, puffing out a long breath. "You cannot do it—tell me you didn't already do it, Nemity."

Her eyebrows drew together. "Do what?"

"Marry Callum."

"Oh." Her face fell. "You know about that?"

Charley's voice pitched as he leaned closer to her, almost manic. "Did you marry him?"

"No, no."

He exhaled a relieved sigh, smiling and nodding as he stood straight. "Good."

He left her by the window and went to the sideboard, pouring himself a full drink of Scotch whisky. He took several sips that appeared to calm him and he looked to her.

"Why did you think I was about to marry Callum?"

"Because one of Lady Agnes's biddies that was at Vauxhall that night has spread it all over London that you two plan to marry—you know those women cannot keep their traps shut." He shook his head, taking another swallow. "But hell, Nemity, I talked to Vanessa after I heard the news and couldn't find you and she told me Callum is a bloody gardener. You were about to marry a *gardener*."

She rushed to the door of the library, closing the door for privacy. Walking across the library to him, she kept her voice low. "Lady Agnes is here, so we will need to speak quietly."

His eyebrows shot up. "The old bat is here?"

"Yes."

"Why? Because of Georgette and Jacob?" he asked.

Her head bobbed back and forth. "It takes some explanation."

He lifted his drink to her. "I'm all ears, as long as you're not marrying Callum."

Her look cut into him. "I don't understand your urgency,

or why you would even care if I was marrying him—I thought Callum was your good friend."

Charley sobered, shaking his head. "He's not. The man is a user, just like you thought him to be. After the rumors of you marrying started, I cornered Vanessa and she told me who he really was years ago—a common workman, for pity's sake. He had me fooled." His eyes narrowed, irate. "The bastard used me to get to you. He must have had you marked for a very long time. And when he came upon me, he must have known our connection and jumped at the chance to get close to you."

"Charley, no. I don't want you to think that Callum is not your friend. I am sure he is." She knew she couldn't explain everything to him, but she also didn't want Charley to think he'd been duped.

"No, I won't hear it, Pip. Anyone who would dare to hurt you, to lie to you, isn't my friend. He lied to all of us about his past—to you, to me. A bloody gardener, of all things." He set his drink down and grabbed her shoulders. "Tell me you're not about to marry him. Tell me he hasn't convinced you he is innocent. He is rotten, Nemity, rotten."

She dropped her right shoulder, turning away from his hold on her. She took a step to the sideboard and poured herself a splash of brandy. "Except, what if he isn't?"

"Hell. No." His voice dipped in disbelief. "You are actually considering it, aren't you? No—you cannot. I cannot express this enough to you—you cannot think to go through with it. It would be a scandal beyond all others, marrying a low-class gardener—a ruthless scandal that would close all doors to you."

She swallowed the brandy, staring at the black marble counter of the sideboard. "I don't care about open doors."

"You may not, but do you care about doors being open for Georgette and Jacob—do you think that will fly?

Everyone knowing you married a fortune-hunting scoundrel? Those two innocent children will have no future —none." His look went to the ceiling. "I'm sure Vanessa has already told most of the *ton* that you were duped by the man."

She shook her head. "No, Vanessa wouldn't do that. She is discreet. She told me about Callum and that is the end of it."

"She already told Lady Agnes. Why else would the old bat be up here other than to rip those children away from you?"

"No. I am working out an arrangement with Lady Agnes. And Vanessa wouldn't do anything that would harm the children or me. The rumors will die away. I'm sure Vanessa will stay quiet about what she knows."

"No. You're miscalculating, Nemity. You don't know Vanessa now. She's changed. She couldn't wait to tell me what happened at Vauxhall. She's not your friend like you think she is."

Her head snapped back. "But she is—"

"No, I am." He set his right hand on her shoulder, his fingers pressing in with vehemence. "I am the only one that is going to tell you the truth about what will happen if you marry Callum. And that is that you will ruin any future Susannah's children will have. The only other alternative is to leave them under the care of Lady Agnes."

Her left arm wrapped around her belly, her right elbow propping on it as she sent her clasped fingers to her lips. "That, I cannot allow."

"How about this—you and the children come back to Ravenstone with me. We'll figure all of this out. You'll at least be protected there."

"No. Not Ravenstone." Her head shook. "I don't want to see Thomas."

"Why not?"

"You don't know—don't know what he did to me?" She

let out an exasperated sigh. "You don't know what he did to the children?"

Charley stilled, his look going dead serious for a change. "No. What did he do?"

She met his stare. "Thomas kicked me and the children out of the carriage on the road to Stenton. In the middle of nowhere."

"He what?" His eyes went wide, his lip snarling. "That bastard."

"Exactly."

"How did you get back here?"

"Callum found us."

Charley's knuckles tightened and he jammed his fist into the marble top of the sideboard. "So you think Callum is your damn savior now?"

"No. He found us and brought us back here, yes, but I would have gotten us here on my own even if he hadn't."

"You have a hell of a lot more explaining to do, it seems. But whatever Callum did for you, don't believe it, Nemity. Don't believe him. You cannot marry him. He's a liar. There is no doubt about that." He paused, giving an exasperated exhale. "What happened with him? You need to tell me."

Biting her tongue, Nemity turned and took a step away from him. "No—not now. I need…" She looked out the window. The rain had dropped to a mist. "I have—I have to think. I have to get out of here."

Charley glanced out the window. "I understand. But Thomas wouldn't want you out there on your own. We still don't know who abducted you, and without a guard here, you're vulnerable."

"Good thing Thomas isn't here, then, as I have to get out of this house. You don't need to worry on me—what happened was weeks ago, and there hasn't been the slightest indication of any other threat to me. I'm sure whoever was responsible is now on the other side of England. Everyone has overreacted." She moved toward the door. "Will you please stay in the house, watch Georgette and Jacob? I just need to get out of here for a few minutes. I need to think in silence."

"Fine." He nodded. "At least tell me where you'll be. The pool?"

She shrugged. "I don't know, maybe. Or maybe I'll just wander."

His lips pursed, scolding. "Again, Thomas would say you shouldn't be out wandering by yourself."

She looked back to him, smiling sweetly. "Yes, well, you're not Thomas, are you?"

He chuckled. "That I am not—I'm glad you realize it."

She hopped back across the room to him and kissed him on the cheek. "Thank you for being you. Tell Georgette and Jacob I'll be back in an hour. Earlier if the rain picks up again."

He nodded and she was out the door.

That was the thing about Charley. He always had her back. Thinking of long-term ramifications instead of what was in front of her.

He wasn't wrong about all the doors in society clamping shut to Georgette and Jacob if she married Callum and raised them.

Not that it would matter anyway, since it appeared that Callum had already left her. He said he'd be back, but she didn't hold out much hope for that.

One problem on top of another.

The most pressing one she needed to figure out was a way to convince Lady Agnes not to take the children away.

She had to salvage what little she could of the family she'd been so close to having.

CHAPTER 28

She'd wrapped a shawl around her shoulders to cut the chill that had set into the air with the rain, and the brim of her hat kept the drizzle off her face, so her body wasn't as miserable as her mind currently was.

Nemity had come out into the silence of the woods so that she could think, but with every step she took, her mind just grew more muddled.

No way out.

She had to marry Callum to keep Georgette and Jacob. That was, if she could even convince Callum to marry her when he came back.

If he came back.

But if she married him, Charley was right—scandal would ensue and she would ruin Georgette and Jacob's futures. Charley had spoken the cold truth on that accord.

Either way, Georgette and Jacob were at risk.

But still, she couldn't let the children go with Lady Agnes. Her heart ached even considering the thought of those two beautiful souls being ground to dust under Lady Agnes's watch.

She puffed out a big sigh, looking up at the dark wet leaves above her, droplets cascading from them, and let the mist cover her face. She'd been out for a half hour, on the path to the hot spring, and she was no closer to reconciling anything in her mind than she had been in the library.

Answers.

She needed answers, a direction forward. Any little crumb that she had missed that would lead her down the right path.

Searching so hard for that little crumb, she didn't hear the twigs snapping behind her. Not until it was too late.

Not until a hand wrapped over her mouth, stuffing a wretched rag between her teeth and deep into her throat, making her gag.

Cutting her air.

Arms locked around her torso, clamping her elbows to her body.

Someone grabbing her feet. Picking her up. Two people.

She struggled against them, twisting and wiggling with all her might.

A burlap sack yanked down around her head, cutting off her sight.

Hell.

Not again.

CHAPTER 29

A torrent of rain whipped into his face as Callum glared at the castle.

He'd had two other stops before this, now here, the last destination in the line.

All of that had taken far too long—travel slow in the downpour.

His first stop had been to arrange for a clergyman to come to Springfell. His second to check in with his men in Haddington that he had scouring the area in search of Nemity's abductors—a wasted stop, for they were nowhere to be found and he'd ended up having to spend the night at a coaching inn after leaving them explicit instructions to make way to Springfell to protect Nemity until he returned.

Now he faced Ravenstone Castle.

Soaked to the bone and cold, his fury had been building with every step his horse took to the castle. It loomed ahead, a grey monolith jutting up high into the wicked grey skies.

Knowing he was coming here to face Thomas, Callum had been trying to rein in the pummeling that his fists still wanted to dole out to the ass.

Putting not only Nemity, but also Georgette and Jacob in danger like that—it was unforgivable. The man hadn't yet suffered nearly enough under Callum's fists for what he did.

Fifteen minutes later, Callum had dismounted and was leading his horse into the main stable at Ravenstone when he glanced down the center aisle, only to see Thomas's head pop up in a horse's stall, then dip back down.

All the fury Callum had been trying to control exploded in his veins and he tied his horse to the nearest post, his steps thundering deep into the barn.

He was on Thomas in seconds, gripping the back of his shirt and yanking him upright, his fist landing on his jaw before Thomas knew what was happening.

The hoof pick in Thomas's hand went flying as he thudded into a wall, the horse he was tending to snorting and stomping in place.

Thomas caught himself, blood cutting from his lip as he found his footing, and he turned to Callum heaving at the entrance of the stall, ready to attack him again.

Thomas pushed off from the wall, his thumb wiping at the blood alongside his mouth as he advanced on Callum. "What in the fucking hell do you think you're doing?"

"Resisting beating you into a bloody pulp for what you did to Nemity." Callum crossed his arms over his chest, staring Thomas down. He wanted to destroy the man, but at the moment, he needed him alive and able to sign papers.

Thomas stilled, his face ashen. "Nemity—is she all right? The children? My coachman hasn't returned yet—I had him looking for them."

"They are fine, no thanks to you, you fucking ass."

To hell with it.

Callum pulled free his arms and yanked back his right elbow, advancing on Thomas, ready to sink another blow on the bastard's face.

Thomas held his hand up. "You might want to rethink that—I have one of the kidnappers—your men from the Guardians, they brought him here."

Callum stopped, his fist dropping from the air. "What?"

"One of the kidnappers. One of the men that abducted Nemity weeks ago. He's in a cell in the undercrofts."

Callum slammed the side of his fist into the wooden slat wall next to him, his voice a roar. "Bloody hell, why weren't those the first words out of your mouth?"

"You were punching me," Thomas thundered back.

The horse in the stall jumped again, snorting with the noise.

Thomas pointed out of the stall and Callum stepped out of it, Thomas following. He latched the gate and then turned to Callum, his chest heaving.

Callum didn't give him even a second to catch his breath. This was why his men were gone when he'd stopped at their base in Haddington to talk with them. He'd just figured they were out combing the surrounding villages and towns, as they had been since arriving in the area. "You get anything out of the man?"

Thomas shook his head. "Not yet. Your men just delivered him early today, but I wasn't in the right frame of mind after dealing with Charley all morning."

"Charley?" Callum's brows shot up. "Charley came up from London?"

"He did." Thomas lifted his arm, wiping the sleeve of his rolled-up lawn shirt against his mouth to clear the blood. The red streak on the white cloth was immediate and long. He glanced down at it, shaking his head, then sent a glare at Callum. "And my brother was on a tear—railing at me for letting you anywhere near Nemity."

Callum exhaled a seething sigh.

Thomas took a step toward him, his voice going deadly.

"And this is where I punch you the fuck out for not staying in your position."

Callum's teeth gritted. "And just what is my position?"

"It certainly isn't to ruin someone under your protection."

Callum shook his head. "You don't know that. You don't know anything about what has happened."

Thomas took a step toward him, getting into his face. "You think I'm blind? I spent two days in a carriage with Nemity moping about you."

"Moping?"

"Yes. Fucking moping."

Thank the angels. That was the best thing he could possibly hear.

He gave Thomas a curt nod. "That's why I'm here. I'm going to marry Nemity."

"You're what?" Thomas's head snapped back. "No—I won't allow it."

Callum eyed him coolly. "I think we both know Nemity will do the exact opposite of anything you say just to spite you. Any sway you had with her was destroyed the moment you tossed her and the children out of your carriage."

Thomas's eyes closed and he spun away from Callum, collapsing back against a wall between horse stalls. His fingers ran over his face, the butts of his palms digging into his eyes. "I—I'm sorry." His hands dropped away from his face and he looked to Callum. "Does she know how sorry I am?"

Callum could see the torment in his eyes—true remorse. So much so that all the fury in him dissipated. What he was looking at wasn't an evil ass. It was a broken man.

Broken by what, he didn't know. But he sure as hell recognized someone walking around blindly in the shell of a body.

Callum's voice tempered. "What in the hell were you thinking, Thomas?"

"I wasn't—I don't even remember doing it. Don't know how to describe it."

"Try."

He shook his head, and then clunked it back onto the wooden slat behind him, his vacant stare going on the open rafters above. "I was watching the children cry—they'd been crying off and on for two days, and Nemity was just sitting there, her eyes glazed over, not even hearing them, and something snapped in my brain and I…I…I blacked out. Coming out of it, it was like a dream, like I had vague snippets of Jacob wailing. Nemity spitting out words at me. Of anger. Uncontrollable anger to the point I didn't know my own mind. And then they were no longer in the carriage with me."

His look dropped to Callum. "You don't know how I want to take those minutes back. How I want to go through that again, only under control. Which I wasn't."

Callum heaved a sigh. He'd never been one to hold a drowning man's head under water. He met Thomas's look. "I don't know if she's going to want to hear it from you, but you need to tell her that."

Thomas's head dropped forward, his stare on the ground. "I will. I will." His look snapped up to Callum. "But don't think I'm giving you my blessing to marry her."

The snarl came back to Callum's voice. "Again, I don't give a damn what you bless or don't. I'm marrying her. But I'm not doing it before I talk to you about her fortune."

At that, Thomas shoved himself from the wall, his fists pulling back. "I'm going to break every fucking tooth in your mouth."

He swung. Hard. Callum only barely caught his fist in the

air before shouting into Thomas's face. "I don't want her bloody fortune."

Thomas stilled, his eyes wide. "What?"

"I don't want it. I want you to put it in a trust that she can access any time she wants on her own terms."

Thomas yanked his fist from Callum's hold, taking a step back, his brow furrowed. "What are you talking about?"

"Her fortune. You can still oversee it, but I want her to have control over it, so it's not a dangling carrot that you hold over her anytime you want to get her to do something."

"I don't do that."

"Really? For you sure as hell threaten it a lot."

"I do?" Thomas frowned.

"Yes." Callum sighed. "It'll be easier if you arrange it from the start before we're married. But if you don't do so, then mark my words, as her husband, I will come after every penny of it, take it from you, and put it in a trust for her myself. But I really want it done beforehand, so she doesn't wonder on it."

"Well, hell." Thomas rubbed his jaw, staring at him. "You really mean it, don't you?"

"I do."

Thomas nodded. "Aye. I can arrange it."

"Good." Callum nodded. "Now can we go deal with this bastard that thought to put his hands on Nemity? My fists still need to hit something."

Thomas flicked his hand forward and they trudged side by side up to the castle and down into the bowels of the stones.

"They bloodied the man fairly well when they caught him." Thomas opened the ancient wooden door to the small storage room, and they both ducked under the low curved stones to step into the room.

The bastard lay in the middle of the cell, chained to the

floor by a shackle around his ankle, his clothes torn and bloodied.

Callum peeled off his overcoat and coat, rolling up the sleeves of his lawn shirt as Thomas walked to the man and kicked him in the ribcage.

The man grunted, curling into himself as he rolled onto his back, staring up at Thomas with burning malice in his eyes. "I already told them other grunts I dinnae ken where they're gonna take her."

Callum rushed over to the heap on the floor, glaring down at him. "What? What did you just say?"

"I said I swear I dinnae ken where they'll take her."

He leaned down, wrapping his hand under the man's jaw and crushing it inward. "Who is taking her?"

"Oh, fuck." The man's eyes flickered back and forth from Callum to Thomas, his body starting to flop, searching for something to push off from to get away from Callum.

Callum stuck his thumb under his jawbone, digging it in for maximum pain, his voice a roar. "Who is taking her?"

His legs scrambled, trying to push off, and Thomas sent a kick to his right kneecap. The man wailed. He looked up at Callum. "Yer too late."

"What the hell are you talking about?" Callum growled.

"Yer too late. They probably already have her."

Rage surged through his veins and Callum released his grip on the man's jaw and punched him.

Hard.

Too hard and the man was out cold.

Callum's head fell back to the curved stone ceiling, his eyes closing.

"Well, fuck," Thomas said, his voice dry.

Callum dropped to his butt, sitting on the cold stone floor, resting his arms on his upturned knees as he looked at Thomas. "Get a cold bucket of water. Probably two or three."

Hours.

It took hours and they had nothing. No information on where Nemity could possibly be.

All damn night they kept having to throw cold water on the brute because the ass kept passing out on them.

And now it was morning, and Callum was desperate.

The man hadn't told them much of anything—not even who'd hired him. The bastard didn't even know. His cousin had pulled him into the job.

Leaning against the stone wall, Callum tried to still the shake in his arms as he watched Thomas creep into the cell with the fifth bucket of cold water and dump it on the man's face.

The brute sputtered, choking on the water in his throat, and turned to his side, coughing. The exact thing that would cause the most pain, for the number of ribs Callum had broken on him.

Enough of this weak, whiny muck.

Callum shoved himself off the wall and strolled over to the brute, pulling free the dagger he always carried in his boot.

He held the blade in front of the brute's nose so that the man couldn't avoid what he was looking at.

"We've broken what seems to be useful. Fingers. Toes. Ribs. Ankle. Leg. Arm. Nose. So now I start flaying the skin from your body as you watch. That's why I left your eyes as wide open as the day you were born. I want you to see what's happening to you. This is your last chance to tell me where they would have taken her." Brutal, and he used to have integrity in his interrogations. But in this instance, there was no line, no boundary he wouldn't cross for Nemity. That's how crystal clear everything in his life had just become during the last few hours.

She was the only thing that mattered.

Callum inclined his head toward the brute's one working arm and Thomas stepped on it, locking it into place.

The brute's broken feet started to scrape against the stone floor, trying to get away.

Pathetic, really. There was no escaping this.

"Wait. No. I told ye. I dinnae ken anything."

"You know something."

"Just what I told ye. We were—we were supposed to keep her alive—alive until..." The man clamped his mouth closed.

Callum set the tip of the knife under his chin. "Until what?"

"Until we were told to get rid of her. Something needed to be found first. She had to be alive in case it couldn't be found—I dinnae ken what it was. I just heard two of 'em jabberin' about it."

"Not enough information." Callum made sure to keep his words at a chilling, slow pace, a tortuous death vowed in the lining of his voice. He set the edge of the blade onto the man's upper chest, digging the length of it into his skin. "I may have to saw at it a bit to get it going. Try not to squirm."

He pressed hard, drawing a line of blood as the edge sank into skin.

"Stop. Stop. Please." Blood and snot splattered up from the man's mouth. "Cabin. Cabin. I—I dinnae ken where—it's abandoned—a gamekeeper cabin."

The detachment on his face stone cold, Callum glanced at the man's eyes. "Be more fucking specific." He pulled the knife, digging it in just under the skin.

The man wailed, the scream echoing off the stone around them. "I dinnae ken, I dinnae ken." More spittle and blood splattered out with each word. "There's a tree."

"A fucking tree?" Callum leaned over him, his top lip curling in a snarl. "That's what you're going to give me?"

"A tree—a tree—it's just beyond the lass's land."

"I know it," Thomas shouted.

Leaving his dagger lodged under the brute's skin, Callum looked up at Thomas.

Thomas nodded to him. "It's on the outer border of the Springfell lands. I ride the outside line of the estate every few months and I noticed last winter when there weren't leaves on the trees. There's an abandoned gamekeeper's cottage just beyond the border, and there is an odd ancient oak by it—it looked to be split by lightning long ago, three thick trees growing out of one enormous trunk. It has to be it."

Callum nodded, sliding his dagger out from under the man's skin, digging the blade downward as he did for maximum pain.

The man wailed, breaking into sobs, blubbering. "I told ye. I told ye. Let me go. Let me go. Let me go."

"Let you go?" With those words, something snapped in Thomas and he straddled the man, throwing his fists, punching him, again and again and again. Blood splattering everywhere. The brute's head lolling about, unconscious.

So vicious that it took Callum a moment to react, he was so shocked by the fury pouring out of Thomas. Usually it was him that had to be talked down from fury.

Callum swung an arm around Thomas's torso and yanked him off of the brute, throwing him into the wall. "We have to keep him alive—alive—in case he's lying."

Thomas ignored him and charged at the brute again.

Callum caught him and dragged him out into the hallway outside the cell. With the slope of the undercroft brushing against his head, he flung Thomas away from him.

Thomas rammed into a stone wall and spun, crumbling down against the stone, bent over with his hands on his knees, heaving breath after breath.

Callum stared at him for a long moment, waiting for Thomas to make a dive toward the door of the cell.

He didn't.

Because he was wrecked. Wrecked from head to toe.

Callum walked over to him, holding out his hand to Thomas. "Shit, man. What happened to you when you were gone all those years?"

His look not moving from the stone floor, Thomas shook his head, wiping the side of his face, his voice haunted.

"Hell."

A whisper, barely audible.

Callum nodded. It certainly did look like it.

Thomas took Callum's hand. He let Callum haul him upright, then set his hand in front of his eyes, pinching the bridge of his nose. "Hell is what happened to me."

Callum's look set hard on him. "We don't have time for hell. Not now. Now we need to ride."

Thomas's look snapped to Callum. He nodded.

CHAPTER 30

Callum had more steel strapped to his body than he usually did for something like this.

His brawn alone usually got him out of most situations.

But with Nemity on the line—his whole future on the line—he wasn't about to take any chances.

It had been hours since he and Thomas had finally broken that waste of a human that had helped kidnap Nemity. Far too long. It had taken two grueling hours in the cold dark with the wind whipping at them to get to the land adjacent to the Springfell estate, and then another hour in the early morning light for Thomas to remember exactly where he had seen the abandoned gamekeeper's cottage—now just a rotting set of boards with a half-deteriorated thatched roof.

They'd stopped a good distance away once they spotted it and Callum was able to finally let out the breath that had been strangled in his throat for the last several hours.

His biggest fear was that they'd killed her already—but three brutes were in front of the cottage, clearly guarding something inside.

The three men sat just outside the door of the cottage

around a small fire. Two of them on the length of a rotted log that had once served as a bench. One on the ground had his feet propped up on a stump as he leaned back against another rotted log.

They were close enough to guard the rough door that sat crooked in the doorframe, but not close enough that sparks from the fire would catch onto the old boards that served as walls. The thick and brawny man that sat on the log leaned forward, a blade in one hand flicking out shards of wood from a branch. Almost as if he was whittling, except the only thing he was creating was a mess of shavings piled onto his boots.

None of them spoke and the lot of them looked like they'd just woken up.

Which was good.

He liked slow moving men in the morning, one of his preferred times to attack.

Callum looked across the forest, searching amongst the trees.

That he had to search was a good sign. At least Thomas knew enough to be silent in his approach.

There he was. About the same distance away. Their approach in lockstep.

Callum slowly lifted his left hand high in the air and waited for Thomas to see him.

Thomas had stopped moving and he caught Callum's eye.

Callum pointed to the group around the fire.

Thomas held up two fingers, then pointed to himself.

Huh. Turned out Thomas had some steel ballocks on him.

Normally, Callum would be rankled by someone taking on more men than him, but if he only had to dispatch one man to get to Nemity, all the better. Let Thomas have the fun.

Callum nodded, and both of them started creeping closer

to the brutes, his stare locking onto the biggest one of the bunch. It was the least he could do, if Thomas was going to take on two of them.

A twig snapped across the way—Thomas.

Callum wasn't the only one that heard it, and all three men sprang onto their feet, pulling blades and searching around.

Time to attack. He didn't want any of the brutes getting any ideas about going into the cabin and hurting Nemity.

He charged out of the cover of the woods at the same time as Thomas did, who had drawn all their attention.

It wasn't until he was at the back of the biggest brute that the man realized another attacker was bearing down on him.

Across from Callum, Thomas kicked one man in the gut as he deflected the blade swinging at him from the other.

The tip of a dagger cut through the air, aimed at Callum's throat, and he caught the bastard's wrist just before the steel made contact. His grip tightened on the man's arm, twisting it, and the man yelped.

The blade fell out of his hand and the brute scrambled, his leg kicking up as he tried to pull another blade free from his boot.

Not happening.

Callum dropped the man's arm and clamped his hands onto the brute's head and twisted. Snapping his neck in one clean, quick move.

The brute dropped in front of him and Callum looked across the fire to Thomas. One of his opponents was in the dirt, face down, alive or dead it was hard to tell. Thomas parried daggers with the other one—a small, wily bastard that was going to be fast and hard to catch.

Thomas would deal with him.

For the amount of rage he'd seen in Thomas in the undercrofts at Ravenstone when he beat that man, Callum didn't think twice about who would be the victor.

Thomas held a rage in him that would decimate anyone in his path.

Callum turned to the cabin, running to the door, but then called over his shoulder. "We need one alive."

He wasn't sure if Thomas heard him or not, but he wasn't going to repeat it. It would be a hell of a lot easier to figure out who had sent these men if they had one to interrogate—because by the looks of them, they were hired steel, nothing more. But Thomas was going to do what he was going to do and Callum wasn't going to stop him.

These bastards took Nemity.

The quick death he'd already doled out was far too gracious a punishment.

He kicked in the door, his eyes taking a moment to adjust to the darkness inside.

There. On the barren dirt ground, a lump.

Nemity.

The rest of the breath he'd had stuck in his lungs seeped out in rage.

On her side, she lay with her knees curled up into her body, her ankles bound by a tight rope. Boots gone. Her arms were tied behind her back.

The whole of her body shook.

Even as she twisted her head to look toward the door and she saw him, screaming against the gag tied tight around her head, her body trembled.

Two lunging steps and he slid on his knees to her, his blade drawn and sawing at the rope cutting into her wrists.

The rope broke free and she didn't move her arms—couldn't move her arms except for the shake in them.

He moved down to her legs, the muscles in his arm straining as he ripped his steel through the thick ropes.

She still hadn't moved from the position on her side, her entire body convulsing.

Panic seized his chest and he rolled her onto her back, hovering over her as he slid the blade underneath the rag tied around her head that cut into her mouth, and yanked outward. He ripped the cloth away from her face, throwing it off to the side.

"Nemity, what in the hell?" He set his hand onto the side of her face, trying to stop the trembling, and then he realized why her body was shaking uncontrollably.

She was freezing. Her skin cold to the touch, her clothes wet. Her teeth chattering now that the cloth was out of her mouth.

He looked up. The roof of the cottage was nonexistent over the top of her. She must have been lying in the rain and cold all night.

But her eyes. For all that she convulsed, her eyes had found him, and were locked onto his face. Alert and terrified, yet full of relief.

"Those damn fucking bastards." He couldn't keep his growl from roaring out as he gathered her body in his arms and stood, wrapping her as tightly to his chest as he could.

She was even colder pressed against him.

He stepped out of the cabin.

Thomas stood by the fire, heaving, looking like he was waging a war on keeping his rage under control.

The smaller, wiry man he'd been clashing blades with was prone on the ground by his feet, blood pooling onto the dirt under his split neck.

Callum glanced to the other man on the ground. No gaping wound as far as he could see. "That one alive?"

Thomas didn't look at him, but nodded.

"Good. There's rope in the cabin. Tie him up, lug him to your horse, and tie him to the saddle. If he can walk, fine. If he can't, drag the fucking dung heap back to manor and then get the magistrate."

Thomas nodded, then heaved a seething breath and blinked hard. He forced his head to turn to Callum and finally looked at him.

His eyes ran over the parts of Nemity he could see, his words croaking out raw. "Is she injured?"

"I don't know yet. She's frozen—shaking so hard from it I couldn't check. I'm going to get her warm."

Thomas nodded, then turned, dazed, to get the rope from the cottage.

Locking Nemity tight in his grip, Callum took off running though the forest, aimed for his horse.

He needed to get her warm.

CHAPTER 31

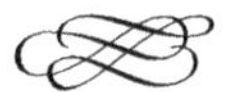

Cold.

So much cold, deep in her bones, it was the only thing in her mind, even though she knew, in a very distant way, that Callum had found her.

He was carrying her, clamped against his body.

Cold. Cold. Cold.

Freezing ice ravaging her muscles, tearing them apart from the inside out. Her teeth cracking against each other. Her stomach a hard rock of pain. Her eyes clamped tightly closed, her body shook so hard she felt like she was going to faint every time her eyes opened.

Cold.

Then suddenly, something enveloping her.

Soft, liquid.

Her muscles so tense, she couldn't feel what was really happening, and she still couldn't force her eyes to open.

Movement, a mass behind her.

Callum. Callum had her.

He was wrapped around her, and then he wasn't, but now his body wrapped around her again.

Then he was gone.

Hands moving around her body. Pulling. Tugging. Ripping.

Then suddenly, the warmth of the liquid around her flooding against her skin. Shocking it, almost like stinging embers from a fire.

"Wh—wh—wh—where?" It took monumental effort to get the air for the word out of her lungs, then formed on her spasming tongue and out past her clanking teeth.

"I brought you to the spring." Callum's lips moved against her ear and the heat of his breath singed her skin. "I couldn't think of anything else close. Even if I got you to the manor, water would have to be heated. This was quickest." His hands wrapped around her, spinning her, and he pulled her against the hard planes of him. "Just lean back on me."

She didn't consciously choose to do as instructed, because he just manipulated her body in place against the length of him. He sank her down into the water far enough at an angle so just her mouth and nose and the top of her head were in the air.

When she finally managed to open her eyes, the surface of the water around her rippled with her quaking.

His body propping her up from behind, Callum started rubbing his hands up and down her arms, pressing in on all the muscles, trying to force the heat of the water into her bones.

It took a long time.

What seemed like forever, but could have been fifteen minutes or fifteen hours. Yet his hands continued their pattern, up and down her arms, back and forth across her belly, down the outer muscles of her thighs and back up the top of her legs.

Until, finally, her fingers twitched instead of shook, and

she curled them into fists and unfurled them, loosening the muscles. Doing the same thing with her toes.

Stretching her legs out and her toes touched onto calves.

Naked calves.

She wiggled the length of her body.

No clothes between them.

None.

"Y—y—y—y—y—you're naked." As much as her body had started to feel normal again, the core of her still spewed up freezing air that stuttered her speech.

"I am that."

She twisted her body to the side so she could lift her head out of the water and look up at Callum.

He sighed at her accusing eyes. "I'm not trying to trap you in here naked for my own nefarious purposes. I knew I was going to need to tear your dress off so the water could get to your skin—it was soaked anyway. I took off my own clothes so they would stay dry. After you're warm, you'll need something to wear back to the house."

Her lips parted, but she couldn't even get a "fine" out—only a pathetic grumble.

His hand lifted from the water, his warm thumb brushing wet hair away from her forehead as his eyes searched her face. "Damn, your lips are still blue." He spun her body on top of him so their front sides tangled against each other, and he leaned forward, pressing his lips to hers, sucking her lower lip between his teeth as his tongue ran over it repeatedly.

She knew he was doing it, but could only feel it in a numb, far off way.

Satisfied with her lower lip, he moved onto her upper lip. Back and forth his tongue went.

By the time he was done, she could feel the swipes of his

tongue quite clearly and it was far more sensual than merely an effort to warm her lips.

At least to her. Maybe just a chore for him.

She tilted her head back, pulling her lips from his. "You're honestly not trying anything right now?"

He sighed like she had just stolen his favorite food from him, and his left hand under the water slid around her backside and squeezed. Another motion she felt perfectly clear.

"I don't think you're ready for me right now." He shook his head. "Hell, I'm not ready for you right now."

She studied his face. His jawline was taut—clearly had been for a long time for the strain of the muscles.

"What?" She lifted her hand out of the water, trailing the tips of her fingers along his jaw. "Wait. You are angry."

"I am bloody furious."

"Why?" Her brow furrowed, or at least she thought it furrowed. That part of her body was still slightly numb, even with the steam from the water bathing it in warm droplets.

His glare sliced into her. "I told you not to do a damn thing when I left."

"But I didn't do anything."

"You got yourself kidnapped, that's something." He closed his eyes, shaking his head, then adjusted his left thigh upward so she was sitting on it instead of slipping down his body.

His eyes opened, his stare eating into her as both of his hands came out of the water and his palms clasped onto the sides of her face. His voice hitched. "I know it wasn't your fault, but damn, you nearly shredded my heart into wisps of blood and ash when I learned you were taken."

Her breath caught in her throat. "I did?"

His fingers dug into the thick of her wet hair. "Hell, Nemity, of course you did."

"But—but I thought—"

His look ran across her face, then he sighed. "You thought I didn't want you? Why would you think that?"

Her fingers moved onto his bare chest. "In the stables, you said you were confused."

"Just because I was confused never meant—for one second—that I didn't want you. I always have." His thumbs came forward, running along the outer edges of her lips. "What wanting you would mean for the rest of my life was what I was confused about."

"But you left, you told me to stop, and you left me."

"Yes, I told you to stop because I didn't want you to ask me to marry you."

Her head tilted back, her eyes narrowing at him. "You don't know I was going to ask that."

His right eyebrow cocked. "Were you?"

Her mouth clamped closed.

"Exactly, and I didn't want that. My ego would never survive that and I needed to talk to Thomas first."

Her stomach flipped. "Why? About my money?"

"Yes."

She nodded, the pang that shot like a hot dagger through her chest making it hard to breathe. She knew how this part went and it cut her to the bone, even though she knew it was part of the deal. It always was.

Dignity.

She could at least attempt to keep her dignity about her. She tried to tilt her chin up, giving him a slight nod, which was hard to do with his hands still cupping her face. "Thomas showed you all the numbers?"

"Numbers?" His brow furrowed. "No. I didn't have him show me anything. I told him I was going to marry you."

"You didn't ask him?"

"Hell, no. I am marrying you no matter what that ass says. I told him I was going to marry you—if you'll have me, of course. And then I asked him to put your fortune in a trust that you can access anytime you want, that you can control. He'll still oversee it, unless you request for someone else to. A solicitor or someone of the like."

"What?" She grabbed his wrists and pulled his hold from her, pushing herself back from him, her stare frantic on his face for she was sure she hadn't heard him correctly. "You—you don't want access to my money? But I don't understand."

"I have my own fortune, Nemity. I told you about my grandfather."

"Yes, but…"

"I was his only heir and I have no other family." Even though she still had a grip on his wrists, his fingers wiggled down onto her thighs, digging into the muscles as he spoke. "My grandfather's money just sits around, making more money. I don't really keep track because I rarely have to use it."

Her jaw had dropped and she was having a hard time bringing it back up to its normal position. "Then what were you confused about?"

He shifted his right leg upward so both of his legs were supporting her underwater and he wrapped his hands under her butt, pulling her closer to him. The length of his hard cock nestled into the crux of her and she had to force herself to pay extra attention to what he was saying.

"I was confused because you were asking me to give up everything I know how to do, everything that I am good at, that I was put on this earth for—no, correction, you weren't asking that of me—I was asking that of myself. And it is a slippery bog to traverse when one's life purpose suddenly changes on him."

"It has?"

He nodded, his silver-grey eyes level with hers as his face moved closer. "I want you and Georgette and Jacob to be my purpose. I want to put babes in your womb and make them my purpose. I want the honor of making you laugh on the hour, every hour, merely because the sound of it soothes my rotten soul."

Her fingers unclenched from his wrists, sliding up his arms. "Your soul isn't rotten."

"It is what it is." He shrugged. "And this. When you aren't laughing, I want to be arguing with you about trivialities, because it entertains me like nothing else."

Her mind started fully working again at the worst possible moment, for her folds were already aching, desperate to draw him deep inside of her.

Chewing on her bottom lip, she had to force her body into submission before she started something that would take all rational thought out of her head.

Her right hand went onto his chest, her fingers tracing the dark ink that marked him, a reminder that life was never as easy as she wanted it to be. "But if I marry you, Charley said every door in society will be closed to us because everyone now knows about you being Vanessa's gardener. Georgette and Jacob's futures are at stake."

His head snapped back. "You talked to Charley?"

"Yes. Yesterday. He was in a mad dash to get to me before I accidentally married you. He said all of London knows you're a low-class fortune-hunting charlatan."

His lips drew to a hard line as his jaw ticked, shifting back and forth. She could see how hard he was trying to restrain himself from a string of blasphemies flying from his mouth.

He cleared his throat. "And what did you tell him?"

"I told him I didn't know what to do, because if I don't marry you, Lady Agnes will take away Georgette and Jacob. Then I went on a walk in the woods to clear my mind and that was when those brutes grabbed me."

His nostrils flared and he gave a hard nod. "And before you were taken, did you clear your mind?"

His whole body tensed under her.

She flattened her palm on his chest. It calmed him, but only slightly. "No. But the one thing I did realize as I was walking was that it wasn't just Georgette and Jacob I stood to lose. It was you. And that was the one thing that would destroy me above all others. But at that time, I didn't even know if you would ever be back for how you left me in the stables. I'd thought I'd already lost you and I was plotting how I could possibly go after you and convince you to marry me—dignity be damned."

His fingers tightened into the flesh of her butt, pressing her harder into him. "That is admirable."

She shook her head, having to expel a calming breath just to keep herself from lifting up and impaling herself onto his shaft. "But don't you see? Charley is right about all the doors that will be closed to Georgette and Jacob—and our own children. It is wrong—we'll be outcast from society. There is no good outcome here."

Water sloshed behind her as his right hand came up from her backside, and he sank his fingers into the back of her hair, cupping her head. "When does choosing love equate to wrong?"

Her breath hitched.

His voice dipped to a low rumble. "If doors close because of my past, do you care?"

"I don't care, but that's a choice for me—I cannot make that choice for others. Cannot ruin Georgette and Jacob's futures."

"When did living under society's rules ever give you peace? You are wild, my love, and you need to remain so. The future will be what it will be." He held her head in place, his stare swallowing her whole as his eyes, his voice, vibrated with intensity. "Georgette and Jacob will have both of us, and we can love them. Any children we have, we will love and cherish them just the same. Beyond that, beyond us, who cares? They will grow up happy and healthy and loved, and that is more than most sons and daughters of the *ton* get to experience. Plus, we don't have to stay in England, we can go anywhere."

The edges of her eyes crinkled, her breath rapid as she stared back at him, silent. Fighting internally, her head opposed to her heart.

His look bored into her, the intensity burning a hole straight to her soul. "If you want to battle this, Nemity, just know I am not going down on this one. I will fight you until I am bones in the ground to convince you of this. We have what we need right here. Right here between us, right now. There is no other option. Not for me." His fingers tightened in her hair. "So I ask you, when have you ever led with anything but your heart?"

And there it was.

Put so simple it was laughable that she'd ever even spent a moment's worth of confusion on the matter.

She always led with her heart. She didn't know another way.

She nodded. "You're right. You're right. I just—I was listening to Charley and I should have been listening to my heart, except I'd thought you'd already shattered my heart, so there was that."

His hand slipped down from the back of her head to slide in against her chest, his palm slick over her heart. "Is your heart back together now, secure and fortified and protected by the largest of all the guardians?"

She laughed. "It is."

He grinned. "Then we go boldly forth—together. But I will tell you, between my fortune and yours, I don't imagine anyone with a working brain would close any door to us. Titles may rule in theory, but the money always does in practicality. It's been that way for a long time and the only ones that don't realize it are in the era of Lady Agnes."

She leaned forward, her lips meeting his in a heated kiss. "Thank you for pointing out I was being ridiculous. Plus, I like that you were a gardener once. I think it is to be celebrated. You can work on the gardens here at Springfell."

He laughed. "Apparently, your friend Vanessa didn't notice that I was an awful gardener—I think I ruined that family's entire plum orchard during that mission."

Her eyes went wide. "You didn't."

"I did." He chuckled. "But I accomplished the task set out for me."

"Vanessa's uncle?"

He shook his head, setting his forefinger over her lips. "I don't talk about clients."

She laughed, nipping at the tip of his finger with her teeth. "You already did. You know your secrets won't always be safe from me."

"I am deathly afraid of that very thing." He kissed her on the nose. "Marry me, Nemity Wheldon, and all my secrets are yours."

With that, she finally allowed herself movement and lifted herself up, settling the tip of his shaft against her entrance. Her hand cupped his jawline as she looked down at him, their lips almost meeting. "I would love to do that very thing."

She sank down onto him.

His cock filling her, thick and pulsating with the blood pumping through him.

He'd been a master of restraint the entire time they were talking, and it showed, for he was voracious in attacking her body.

His lips, his tongue ravaging every spot on her he could reach. Neck. Breasts. Mouth. Chest.

She started slowly, lifting and descending methodically around his shaft, reveling in everything he was doing to her body.

Doing it slowly because the delayed gratification with him was so rewarding.

Doing it slowly because she could breathe real breaths again, the weight of everything that had been pounding down on her shoulders finally lifted.

His teeth captured her right nipple, sending a pang of wicked pleasure straight to her core. With a groan, she dropped on him, her thighs clenching his body as she gyrated her hips, making him hit the sensitive spot on her inner wall.

Bloody insanity.

He chuckled into her chest and she arched her back, giving him full access to anything he wanted to touch on her body.

Invitation taken, his hands ran all over, taking in every inch he could find. His left thumb slipped down between them, running circles around her nub as he rolled her left nipple between his teeth.

She sank into the thick cloud of pleasure filling her brain, sank into the rising tide in her muscles as he brought her closer and closer to release.

Then he shifted forward on the bench deep underwater and pulled her legs free from his sides, wrapping them behind him. Angling his body straighter, his shaft burrowed deeper into her body, to places he'd never reached before and she lost her mind.

Her hands locked onto his shoulders and she rode him, hard, water sloshing everywhere, screams coming from both of them with every breath. His cock consuming her from the inside out with every buck of his hips.

A growl started deep in his chest, and he shifted, going savage as he grabbed her hips to hold her steady against his raw thrusts.

Sending her over the precipice, a scream stuck in her throat for how intense her explosion was, ripping apart her body into thousands of floating pieces.

Her inner walls contracted around his shaft, and his growl pitched deep into a roar as he slammed up into her, his cock expanding with surges.

Her hips continued to circle him, squeezing every last drop of pleasure out of this for both of them.

Until she was spent, her muscles falling to exhaustion, and she collapsed forward on him.

A peace like she'd never felt warming her veins.

She loved this man.

And she knew, down to the darkest speck of her soul, he loved her.

That he lived to protect her. To make her laugh. To be reason when she needed it. To be wild when she needed it more.

She knew that he would never let her drift away from him because she was his soul, just the same as he was hers.

CHAPTER 32

Callum lifted her down from his horse, her bare legs sliding against the hard ridges of his stomach. With just his coat on, the front of his torso was bare, the cords of muscles tightening as her thighs brushed against his skin.

He'd graciously layered her under his lawn shirt, waistcoat and overcoat, as her dress was both sopping wet and ripped to shreds. He'd donned his coat alone, open at the front on the ride back, so her body was as close to his heat as possible. It had chased off the chill during the ride, but now that they were back at the manor, she realized how very naked the lower half of her was.

He set her onto her bare feet, keeping his hands circled around her waist. "You go on in." He motioned with his head to Springfell's west facing door next to them. "I need to stop by the stables first to see if Thomas made it back already with that miserable heap of dung that had you captive. I have some questions that need answers."

She nodded, looking over her shoulder down the hill to the stables. "How did you even manage to find me today?"

"My men from the Guardians had captured one of the

ruffians that had abducted you weeks ago. Thomas had him secured in the Ravenstone undercrofts, so after informing Thomas that I was marrying you, we went down to interrogate him together."

She couldn't stop a cringe from rolling across her face. As much as she loved Callum's gentle hands on her skin, she imagined those very same hands could do unspeakable damage to a body. "What did you find out?"

"We didn't get from him who'd hired him—the ass didn't even know. His cousin pulled him into the job. But he did know that his cousin and the other two men were about to take you again, and he knew where they were supposed to bring you. That's how we knew where to find you in that gamekeeper's cottage. Which was fortunate, but we still don't know who hired them. And this is not done until I find the bastard that hired them—find out why."

She nodded, her forehead dropping forward and landing on the slice of his bare chest showing between the lapels of his coat. Her lips pressed into his skin. "Thank you for finding me, for coming after me."

He kissed the top of her head. "To the ends of the earth, Nem."

She tilted her head back. "Do you want your shirt back? I can quickly peel it off."

"No. It would just get ruined with the blood I'm about to spill."

She shuddered, but nodded.

Callum was going to do what he was going to do and she wasn't about to ask him to be anything other than what he was. And that was her protector, through and through. "I'll sneak in and get up to my room, change, and then arrange for a bath for you to be readied."

He gave her a quick kiss and released her, then tugged on the reins of the horse, walking it down to the stables.

Nemity slipped into the house, closing the door quietly so none of the servants heard her. She paused with her hand on the door, listening. Echoes of Georgette and Jacob reached her—they were muffled and far away—probably in the library or study, if she had to guess. She darted toward the servants' staircase to get to her room and a change of clothes before any of the staff or the children saw her with her bare legs peeking out from under Callum's overcoat.

Moving quickly through the house in her bare feet as quietly as she could, she slid into her room, turning to close the door behind her.

Success.

The door had no sooner closed when a chill snaked down her spine.

Something wasn't right.

Slowly, her fingers wide at her sides, she spun around.

Her room was in shambles.

Drawers pulled out of the chest and overturned on the floor, her garments scattered about. Her bed ripped apart, stuffing loose and the mattress askew on the bed frame. Papers all across the floor from her secretary against the far wall, with part of the wood splintered on the center drawer.

Utter chaos.

She walked to the middle of the room, looking around, her mind whirling.

Rustling.

Rustling coming from her dressing room.

Just as she started to take a step back toward the door to escape, Charley walked past the doorway in her dressing room, moving from left to right. He didn't see her.

Her hand flat on her chest, she walked over to her dressing room. "Charley. You scared me half to my grave. What happened in here?"

He jumped, spinning half toward her. "How did you get out?"

Her brow furrowed. "Get out? Get out of what?"

He shook his head, scratching at the side of his face. "Nothing. It's of no bother."

"No bother? You must have seen my room—what happened in here? Have you been—"

She froze.

What was in Charley's hand?

Mostly hidden behind his leg. Just the corner peeked out, but she would recognize the tooled leather cover anywhere. The distinctive rounded edge of it. How the floral pattern in the leather had worn, turning the leather into soft fuzz in places.

Her gaze lifted to his face. "Wait. What do you have in your hand?"

"Nothing." He half smiled, surprise on his face as he angled his arm to fully hide his hand and the journal, and he walked toward her, his movements forcing her to back up into the main chamber. "What I want to know is why in the world you think traipsing about in a man's shirt and overcoat with your legs half bare is at all appropriate. You know that I usually look upon your exploits with good cheer, Nemity, but even this is beyond my forgiving sense of propriety."

She glanced down at her bare legs, then looked up at him, her eyes narrowing. "Charley, how do you know about my mother's journal?"

His eyebrows lifted in confusion, then he pulled his hand free and looked down at it. "Oh, you mean this thing? It was your mother's journal?"

"It is."

"I saw your room torn apart like this and I was looking around, making sure no one was still in here." His free hand swung around him. "I don't know how this happened—I never heard anything out of the ordinary last night. I stayed up until near dawn, as I was worried about you not returning—I even sent Mr. Youngstrom out looking for you —but then I fell asleep down in the study. I just woke, and came up here to see if you'd arrived home and retired without waking me."

"Well, I'm here now." She advanced on him, her arm stretching out to grab the journal from him. "Give me the journal, Charley."

He jerked a step away from her, holding the journal out of her reach.

"Charley." She lunged forward to grab it and he twisted it away from her.

Lifting it far beyond her reach, words hissed from him. "I need it."

Bloody hell.

It hit her, quite clearly, in that second. All of it in one blinding, horrifying flash of light.

She stumbled backward, sinking down onto the arm of the wingback chair by the fireplace, her stare on the papers strewn about Charley's dark boots.

"You." A strangled whisper from her throat. "It was you."

"What do you mean, Pip? Me what?"

Her dazed look lifted to him. "Put the journal down, Charley."

He stilled, staring down at her. "What?"

Her voice solidified into iron, her glare slicing through him. "I said, put the journal down."

"Whatever you are thinking, Nemity, you are thinking wrong." His head shook, his fingers still clutching the journal. "You know me, you—"

She heaved a breath, still not able to recognize what was in her head as the truth. This was Charley. *Charley.*

Still, she forced words out, her eyes going to pinpricks on him. "How long did your affair with my mother go on?"

At that, his head snapped back, his face blanching. "What?"

She'd never seen him look guiltier.

Anger coursing through her veins, she shoved herself up from the chair, advancing on him. "I said, how long did your affair with my mother go on?"

"Nemity—"

"She doesn't name you in there, of course, like she named so many others, if that is what you're worried about. But it makes sense, she would have wanted to protect you." Her arm flew up at her side. "You were the one at the end. The one that wanted to marry her."

"Nemity, I—I—"

"Don't lie to me now, Charley. Don't you dare." Her words hissed. "You owe me that. You owe me the truth."

His face fell, his shoulders drooping. His head dropped back, his eyes closing as his head shook. "You're right. It was me." His eyes opened and his look centered on her, pleading. "But you have to know, I loved her—I loved your mother desperately. I wanted to marry her. I asked a thousand times."

Nemity's stare went down to the journal he still clutched in his left hand, the leather binding bending, his knuckles white for how hard he clutched it. "She wouldn't have you. That is the crux of it, isn't it?"

"No. She wouldn't." He heaved a sigh. "Though she loved me as well, you should know that. She loved me enough to want me to marry someone young—to have children, have a family."

"But you wouldn't give her up."

Tears welled in his eyes as his top lip lifted in a twitch. "I couldn't."

"Did you kill her Charley?" Rage rolled and folded into a

hard, throbbing ball in her stomach. "That day she came back here before me? Did you kill her? You'd already left London before us and she was sad that day—sad and she wouldn't tell me why. She just wanted to be alone. It was why she travelled up here by herself. Oh, hell..." She choked out a garbled chuckle, her eyes closing as her hand lifted to rub across her brow. "Or did she come here by herself because she knew you were meeting her? You were here, weren't you?"

Silence.

She opened her eyes, staring at him.

Guilt seeped from his eyes as his head slowly shook. His body clearly wanting to deny what his mind knew was truth.

"Nemity, are you in—" Behind her, Callum had opened the door and stepped into the room, his words dropping off the moment he saw the room in shambles and her face. "What the hell?"

In a blinding blink, Charley dropped the journal, grabbed her arm, and twisted her hard into his body.

The cold steel of a dagger pressed long across her neck.

Where in the bloody hell had Charley gotten a dagger from? Why did he have one on his body when he never did? Charley didn't have a shred of violence in him.

Except...except...except...

Her mother.

The last desperate excuses rolling through her mind trying to protect Charley—to reason out what was happening right now—dissolved. Washed away with the fury flooding her.

Charley killed her mother. She knew it in her bones. Charley had killed her.

Callum threw his hands up, cautious, trying to calm Charley. "Charley, what are you doing? This isn't you. You have a fucking blade against Nemity's throat. Nemity—you adore Nemity. You don't want to hurt her."

"I'm leaving here, Cal. You can't stop me—you won't." He screamed the words.

Frozen still when Charley had grabbed her, panic now seared into all of Nemity's muscles, demanding she do something—anything—to get out of Charley's grip. Her body coiled, ready to slam an elbow into his face to break out of his grip. But then her eyes locked onto Callum's and he glanced at her.

Calm. Calm. Calm.

He didn't need to say it. She could read it in his eyes.

Charley's head dropped, his voice snarling in her ear. "Nemity, you don't want this blade to slip, do you?"

She couldn't answer, couldn't move.

"I assume your silence means agreement. We are bending, you and I, and you are going to pick up the journal."

His knees cut into the back of her legs, forcing her to bend, her torso remaining upright and tight against him. Unable to look down for the knife at her throat, her left fingers tapped along the floor, hitting clothing, paper, and there, the leather. The smoothness of the worn embossed leather familiar under her fingers. She picked it up.

"Good, now stand."

Her legs stiff, Charley more pulled her up than her standing on her own.

"Move out of the way, Cal." The blade pressed harder against her neck.

Callum's hands lifted high beside his head. "I'm moving. Moving. Don't hurt her." The debris of the room shifting about his feet, Callum shuffled off to the side, leaving a clear pathway to the door.

"Move, Nemity," Charley barked.

Her feet didn't pick up.

"I said, move," Charley shouted in her ear and he started to drag her toward the door.

He spun them as they passed Callum, moving sideways, then backward so he could watch Callum as he stepped out of her room and into the hallway.

Farther down the hall. Toward the center of the railing that was open down to the foyer between the two staircases.

His hands still up in the air on either side of his head, Callum crept along behind them, keeping a distance, his stare locked onto Charley.

Charley made sure to keep her in between them. Made sure that the blade on her neck didn't slip away from being able to deliver instant death.

"You aren't going to make it far, Charley. Just let Nemity go." For how calm Callum's voice was, she could hear the restrained growl vibrating in his words.

"No." Charley shifted, exasperated, behind her. "I am leaving here and you are letting me." More steps backward.

Callum shook his head. "There is nowhere to go, Charley."

"There are a thousand places to go."

Callum's lips pulled to a tight line. "No. Anywhere you go, I will hunt you down."

"You won't be able to find me," Charley roared, spit flying from his mouth and landing on her cheek.

Callum's look went impossibly hard, his voice granite. "Then you don't know me."

"Charley, please, please. Just let me go," Nemity pleaded, hoping her voice would calm him. "You can have the journal. It's yours. Please. I don't want you hurt."

"You don't want me hurt?" His caustic laugh rang eerie into the air. "You're the whole damn reason she hurt me."

"What?" The word whispered out of her mouth because the blade had pressed down hard against her windpipe and she couldn't afford real words.

His mouth went onto her ear, his words hot and furious. "She wouldn't marry me because of you, Nemity."

His hands still high in the air, Callum's fingers clenched. "Let Nemity go—she didn't do anything to you."

"She did everything to me." His feet stopped moving backward, his lips moving away from her ear as his voice got louder. "Nemity was the whole damn reason she wouldn't marry me. She said she couldn't afford the scandal, couldn't afford to ruin Nemity's future so she tossed me aside. Tossed me aside like I was used rubbish. Just like all the others in the journal. She used me and threw me away. I loved her and tried to make her see reason, tried to make her love me, but she refused me. I tried, but she…"

He cut himself off, the raw howl of a wounded animal erupting from his mouth.

Nemity's nostrils flared, her stare on Callum, but he wasn't looking at her. He refused to take his eyes off of Charley, ready to lunge at the first opportunity. But there were no opportunities.

Shit.

Callum wasn't going to make a move with the blade this precarious on her neck. She had to do something before Charley got her down to the stables and onto a horse.

"You're wrong, Charley, wrong," she whispered the words. "So wrong. She did love you. It was in the journal, how much she loved you."

"What?" His chin bumped into her head as he looked down at the journal in her hand.

All Callum needed.

He lunged forward, crashing into their bodies and knocking both her and Charley over the staircase railing.

She went flying as both of Charley's arms flung out, dropping away from her.

Weightless in the air.

Falling. Falling.

Then a sudden hand around her calf. Slipping against her skin. No grip.

Fingers clamped around her ankle and she jerked to a brutal stop, swinging hard in the air. Dangling, the full weight of her body crashed into the wall just below the railing.

Then the thud far below her.

Upside down. Hanging over the long drop.

Charley below her.

Callum above her.

She craned her neck, looking upward.

All of the muscles along his neck and in his face were strained. "I got you. Nem. I got you."

He started to pull her up, but all she could concentrate on were his silver eyes, reflecting the world around him, a burst of light at the top of his irises guiding her home.

CHAPTER 33

Callum yanked Nemity the rest of the way over the railing, his heart near to beating a hole clear through his chest.

He hadn't meant to send her flying with Charley.

His overconfidence in his own abilities sometimes surprised him—and not in a good way.

Yet letting Nemity fall to her death was never going to happen. He would have jumped after her, wrapping himself around her and cradling her fall if he'd needed to.

Her back slipping along the railing, her bare feet landed on the floor and her legs instantly crumpled.

A blessing, really, for it gave him the opportunity to clamp his arms fully around her, clutching her to his chest.

Something he needed for himself more than anything at the moment.

She huddled into him, hiding for a long minute, though it could have lasted hours and it still wouldn't have calmed his heart, calmed the manic energy in his body.

He'd almost lost her.

He never knew one second in time could crush his entire

being, but that moment when she was flying through the air, just out of his reach, had nearly sent him to his grave.

"Oh, no." Mr. Flourin, Nemity's butler, came running into the foyer.

Holding her away from the railing, Callum leaned over the edge, looking down at Mr. Flourin. "Flourin, make sure the children and Lady Agnes don't see this—then get a footman to help move him out of here. And tell Lord Hedstrom what has happened—he's in the stables."

Flustered, Mr. Flourin's hands shook at his sides. "Y-y-yes sir." He disappeared back from where he came, his fast footfalls echoing down the main corridor, presumably to wherever the children were with Mrs. Jorge.

Nemity pulled slightly out of his hold, and as much as it hurt deep in his gut to give her even a slice of space, he resisted clamping a hand to the back of her head to keep her captured against his chest.

He looked down at her. "Didn't get nicked, did you?" He lifted her chin and he angled his head down to the side to inspect her neck.

"No. Not that I can feel." Her hand came up, her fingers running along her neck. Her eyes met his. "I could have done without getting shoved over the railing, though."

"I was never going to let you fall, Nem."

She stared at him for a long moment, reading intention in his eyes. Her voice came in a rough whisper. "I know that. I trust that."

He exhaled a sigh. He'd never needed to hear those words more from her lips.

Not willing to let her body have any space from his, he wrapped his arms tight around her torso and picked her up, walking back to her room. He walked in and set her down on the wingback chair next to the fireplace.

He didn't really want to bring her in here with the mess

that Charley had obviously made, but she needed clothes and he wasn't about to leave her more than five feet from him.

"I'll go scrounge a dress up—which one?"

She looked around the room, dazed as her gaze shifted from one ripped apart spot to the next. Her numb stare lifted to him. "It doesn't matter. A day dress. Whichever one you come across first."

He nodded and disappeared into her adjoining dressing room.

Dresses were crumpled on the floor, stockings, shifts, stays, boots, all in disarray, every corner of the room overturned.

He bent over and picked up two dresses, shaking them out. One peach. One blue. Both looked like day dresses, but he'd never had an eye to tell a day dress from a walking dress from a carriage dress.

He stood for a long moment, staring at them. Taking far too much time deciding which one she would want more in this moment.

Blue. Blue would at least match her eyes.

He gently set the peach dress down and hung the blue dress over his arm, trying to straighten it and tug out the wrinkles that had creased into the fabric.

Stepping back into her bedroom, he stepped around the papers and overturned drawers and stuffing from the bed that scattered across the floor.

"Will this do?"

She looked up at him, her eyes still dazed, then looked at the dress he held out to her. "Yes." The word croaked out.

She suddenly shook her head and inhaled a deep breath that she held in her lungs for a long moment. "Yes. Thank you." Her voice came out stronger the second time she tried words.

He held his hand down to her, she grabbed it, and he

pulled her to her feet. Behind her, he set the dress on the chair and moved in front of her, his hands sliding in to slough off his overcoat from her frame.

Her eyes big, she looked up at him. "I—I didn't see. Charley is dead?"

"Yes."

Her eyes closed, a pained cringe creasing the edges of her eyes. "Oh, Charley, what in the hell were you thinking?"

Studying her face, he treaded carefully, for he wasn't certain how she was taking any of this. "I know you loved him, I know—"

Her eyes flew open, her voice cutting as she interrupted him. "All the love I had for Charley disintegrated the moment I realized he was the one that killed my mother."

Stunned, his hands on her arms stopped and his overcoat fell from her body. "Charley killed your mother? That was why he sent a blade to your neck? How do you know that?"

"He told me—well, he didn't really tell me—it was more that he didn't deny it when I blurted it out. He was holding my mother's journal—I had it hidden in my dressing room. I walked in and he had torn apart my room and he was holding the journal."

"That's what you were hiding from me that second day I was here—her journal?"

She nodded.

"What's in it?"

"The answers, apparently, I've been searching for since her death." Her hand lifted to her face, her fingers rubbing across her eyes like she wanted to make the last half hour just disappear. "The journal has details of every affair she had with a man after my father died. Many of them were with notable people, and she named them. She named all of them except for the last man she was having an affair with. That was the answer that I was always searching for."

"Who was it?"

"Charley."

"What? That wasn't just the rantings of a madman?" His eyes went huge, his breath catching in his throat. He'd been trying to piece together what Charley had been screaming about, but it hadn't made any obvious sense. His eyebrows lifted. "Charley? Your cousin, Charley? He had an affair with your mother? You are sure?"

Her shoulders lifted, and she looked so damn frail drowning in his lawn shirt. "He didn't deny that either. And he knew what was written in her journal, that was why he was after it. He knew the value it had—he would be able to blackmail some of the most powerful men in London with it."

His chest lifted in a heavy breath. "That's why you hid it from me."

Her look lifted to him. "I didn't know to trust you at the time."

"Why would she have something like that?"

Her head shook. "She kept everyone in there—everyone she was intimate with. I don't know why. As leverage, I imagine, in case she ever needed it. My mother was so canny, I can only think that was the reason."

"You've read it fully?"

"I have. So many times. Searching for clues as to who killed her. And there are so many secrets in it. So many that would destroy the lives of many of the men in the *ton*. I found it after she died, and I guess Charley knew about it. Knew what was in there. But that he would hurt me to get to it…that he would set a blade to my neck…I cannot believe…" A shudder ran through her body, sadness carving into her eyes.

He needed to tell her—after what had just happened, what she'd been through—she needed to know the truth. He had thought to keep what he'd learned to himself, for it would only hurt her, but she needed to know.

He set his hands on her shoulders. "Nem, this is exactly why Thomas sent me to protect you."

"What?" Her head jerked back, her eyes wide as she stared at him. "Thomas knows about the journal as well?"

"No." His lips pulled back as he sucked in a breath. "He suspected that Charley was after the money—your mother's money—your money."

Her brow furrowed. "What? No. Charley never..." Her look dropped away from him, her voice trailing off.

"Thomas knew it before anyone else. It's why he hired me—to find out what Charley was up to. There were the accidents that happened to Thomas, yes, but Thomas suspected something even deeper of his brother after you were abducted that first time. That was why he was trying to keep Charley away from you."

"He tried to keep Charley away from me?"

"Yes—keeping him away from you was a direct order. You didn't notice how quick Thomas was to demand Charley returned to Ravenstone with him after he brought me here?"

"No." Her head shook. "I thought that was Thomas being Thomas—being a tyrant just because he could."

"Think about it—it would have made complete sense to have Charley stay with you while I was here—for propriety's sake alone, it would have been advisable. Charley was right about that. But Thomas wasn't about to risk it. He had all these suspicions of his brother, but no way to prove them."

"Why didn't you tell me?" Her voice caught, her blue eyes wounded.

His hands slipped down onto her upper arms, rubbing. "You believed in Charley. You believed in him so damn much that I didn't want to ruin that belief you had in him—I didn't want to break your heart. There was the possibility I was wrong—that Thomas was wrong. You convinced me of that. You and your faith in him."

"But I was wrong." Her face crumpled. "How…how could I not have known? All these years. All these years he stood by my side, carried me through the horror of my mother's death, when he was the one that sank a blade into her. He—he was my best friend and all along…all along…" Her voice tapered off, a sob choking her.

He wrapped his arms around her. "There was no way you could have known. But if it was Charley's plan all along to get rid of you, it is diabolical how much sense it makes."

"How?" She murmured into his chest.

"If you died, where does your money go?"

"Thomas would get it."

"So your money goes to Thomas, and then Thomas is framed for killing you. Charley wasn't successful in killing his brother and raised too many suspicions in doing so. So what does he do next? In killing you and framing Thomas, who gets everything he's ever wanted in the end?"

Her head pulled back, her eyes wide as she looked up at him. "Charley."

His right cheek lifted as he nodded. "Charley."

Her eyes closed, her body swaying slightly in his arms. "He got everything but my mother."

"Everything but her."

It took her a long moment to open her eyes to him. "But I…I just cannot believe it of him."

"Then you need to sit down for this next bit I'm going to tell you."

"What?" She eyed him, heavy suspicion lining her blue eyes.

She looked like she was about to be sick, so he maneuvered her backward until she was sitting on the chair, and then he dropped to sit on his heels in front of her, his hands wrapping over her bare knees.

"When we were in London, do you remember those few times I left you at your townhouse with my four men outside guarding?"

"Yes?" Her brow wrinkled.

"I was investigating. I visited with both the men that you had been engaged to."

Her head angled to the side, her eyes searching his face. "Why would you do that?"

"Because of you. I couldn't quite stand the fact that you had been used by them and I was thinking to mete out a bit of justice to them."

"Cal—"

"I know." His hand flew up. "I know. But for how they treated you—they hurt you, Nem, so I thought it appropriate. Aside from the fact that I couldn't quite believe that you so egregiously misjudged not just one man, but two."

Her hand flickered upward. "Well, apparently, I am an awful judge of character."

"Except no, I don't think you are." His hand lifted and slid in along her neck. "I think you were just too close to a master manipulator. I think you grew up with that manipulator so you would never have suspected him of being so."

"Charley?" Her eyes went wide. "Why do you say that?"

"I talked to both of those men that you were engaged to. I visited them for some time and talked to their wives and their staff at their homes. They aren't who you thought they were."

"No?" Her jaw dropped.

"No." He shook his head. "They are actually nice men. Your instincts weren't wrong. Their families, their maids and cooks and footmen all attested to it."

Her brow impossibly wrinkled, her mouth opened and

closed again and again before words made it out. "What? But…but how?"

"The first one you overheard with the vicar before the wedding—he was repeating back what the vicar told him he would have to do in order to tame you—you only caught part of the conversation. The second man, he actually does enjoy women, and he has two children to show for it. Though you weren't wrong in what you walked in on with him—it is just that he also enjoys men, and he and his wife are in an arrangement of some sort with another man. A bond between the three of them."

Confusion clouded her eyes for a moment and then a spark lit up the blue in her irises. A smile curved onto her face. "Two men…"

His eyes narrowed at her. "Don't even think it."

She looked at him, laughing as she set her hand along his cheek. "You are easily two men put together so you are all that I can handle." Her look drifted off. "But another mouth…"

He dropped onto his knees, leaning forward and pulling her toward him until he could run his teeth up her neck, a growl in his throat. "Don't even think it—I am not a man who is going to share you."

Still laughing, she wrapped her hands around his neck, spreading her legs apart to let him pull her even closer to him. "Believe me, you are more than enough—too much sometimes."

He pulled back to look at her. "Don't forget it."

"I won't."

He stared into her eyes for a long moment, losing himself in the fortune of fate that had delivered him into her arms.

Her hand slid up along the side of his face. "I don't know if I should be happy or aghast that you visited them and poked into their lives."

"Be happy, for what I found out."

"But that means that I ruined my life again and again for no reason."

"Before you put that on yourself, tell me, how did you meet both of your fiancés?"

"I…" Her lips pursed for a long moment, her look going to the corner of the ceiling. "I guess I met them through Charley, if I remember correctly. He was always introducing me to people."

"And how was it that you happened to be outside that cubby at the church to hear your fiancé talking to the vicar?"

She looked up, thinking again. "Charley was with me, he walked me out to the gardens and back again, that was why we passed the cubby to begin with."

Callum nodded. "And the fiancé you walked into the intimate moment with?"

Her head nodded, the pieces falling into place. "I was at his house and Charley was leaving and told me he was in his study."

"And then he tried to convince you not to marry me."

She collapsed back against the chair, shock rolling across her face. "How…why would he do this to me—for years?"

"He never wanted you to get married."

"Because the fortune would go to my husband."

"And be out of his reach."

Her hands curled into a fist, her eyes sparking in fire. "That repulsive ass."

The door to her room flung open, Thomas bursting in. "Nemity, here you are."

Both Callum and Nemity turned to Thomas striding into the room.

Stopping in the middle of the mess of her room, he bent over, heaving breath after breath. He waved a hand in their general direction. "What the hell happened? Why are you only in a shirt? Are you injured?"

"No." Nemity shook her head. "No, I am fine."

"But what happened?" He pulled himself upright, his hand still flying about in the air. "A maid said someone died, then she scampered off. I've been running all over looking for you."

Callum stood up, moving in front of Thomas and grabbing his arms. "Did the maid tell you who?"

"No—if there was another one of those bastards in here after—"

"It was Charley, Thomas. Charley died."

Thomas froze, blinking, and then his stare centered on Callum. "Charley?"

Callum nodded, his look hard. His look alone telling Thomas all he needed to know. "You were right on all counts. He was behind it all. I will verify with that man you have secured in the stables. But it was Charley. And he killed Nemity's mother."

Thomas looked to Nemity over Callum's shoulder. "Your mother?"

Her lips pulling inward, she nodded.

"No...I...I...didn't want to believe..." He knocked Callum's hands off of him and staggered to the side, his shoulder crunching against the doorframe. He grabbed it to steady himself, then looked to Nemity, and his face crumbled. "Nemity, I am sorry, I am so sorry...I... He never told me where he was that night your mother died. I asked."

Nemity stood up from the chair. Not moving forward. Not moving backward.

His face twisted, tortured. "I asked and then I suspected, but I couldn't believe it...didn't want to believe it."

His head fell forward as his right arm wrapped around his middle. He dragged his gaze back up to her. "I'm so sorry.

But he's my brother, Nemity. My younger brother. I wanted to protect him. I didn't want to think that of him. He's my brother." His last words choked out and he turned, stumbling away from the room.

Callum stared at the empty doorway as he moved over to Nemity and slid an arm around her shoulders. He'd stay with her if she needed him, but she seemed much sturdier than she did when they'd first gotten in here. "I should go after him."

"No." Nemity drew in a deep breath and sighed it out. She looked up at him. "No, I think this one is for me to do."

He stared at her for a long moment. She was going to fight him on it. He nodded. "I'll go visit that bastard that had abducted you in the stables. I'll verify what I can."

She nodded, then pulled off his lawn shirt and picked up her dress. Foregoing any shift or stays, he quickly helped her into it.

"Thank you." She went to her toes to kiss him, then moved around him, hurrying out the door. "Thomas. Thomas. Thomas."

Her voice calling down the stairs echoed up to him.

Callum looked around Nemity's room. The mess, the destruction that Charley had caused spreading a wide path.

He bent over, picking up several crumpled pieces of paper to start cleaning, then he stilled, staring at the papers in his hand as he realized the futility of it. It would be days before her room could be righted from being torn apart.

He dropped the papers to the floor.

Better yet, it was time they moved into a room of their own. Together.

CHAPTER 34

"Thomas—Thomas—stop. Just stop. Stop. Ouch."

He kept charging forth in front of her, his long strides taking him across the wide lawn into the fog that had rolled in across the land.

She hopped on the ball of the foot that had just been poked with a stick, and then sped up, nearing him as he walked by the far end of the grand pond that abutted the lawn. She lunged forward to catch Thomas's arm.

He turned back to her, his top lip pulled tight in a snarl as he tried to shake her grip off his arm. "Leave me alone, Nemity. Just leave me alone."

"No." Her hand clamped tighter onto him and she jumped in front of him before he could escape her again. "No. You don't get to toss me aside again."

"Fuck." He turned away from her, running his hand through his hair. "I am a fucking ass, Nemity. Again."

Her head bobbed. "Yes. Yes, you are. But you are also the only family I have left, and I would rather not lose you over this. Over Charley. Over whatever in the hell has been happening to you since you returned to England."

"Nothing has been happening to me."

"No?"

"No."

"And you think me delusional?"

"Nemity—"

"Just stop and listen to me, for once." She stepped closer to him, her neck craning to look up at him. "I don't blame you. I don't blame you for what Charley did—has done to me. You didn't know. And you couldn't control him any more than you have been able to control me. This wasn't your fault."

His head tilted back, his hand slapping on his leg. "He was my brother, Nemity. My little brother." His face crumpled with the words.

"I know. I know. I loved him just the same. But I don't think we knew him. Not really."

His head swung back and forth and he seethed out a sigh. "If I ever did."

"No. We did." Her words slowed, her voice going soft. "In that time before you left, we did know him. All of us could laugh then. Play. Be careless. We knew him then."

"Then what happened?" He stumbled a few steps to the side and sank onto the stone edge of the pond, his hands landing on his thighs, his shoulders hanging.

She stared down at him for a long moment. No matter what his actions as of late, there it was. The boy that she'd once known—hell, he hadn't always been an old man to her. The boy that always took care of her and Charley—got them out of scrape after scrape. The wise one. The cautious one. The serious one. He'd always been all of those things, so she and Charley could be the fun, carefree ones.

But the boy was still in there, still wanting to take care of his younger brother, still wanting to take care of her.

"Life?" Her shoulders lifted. "Life happened? It happened

to all of us. Some of the rubbish is of our own making. Some of it is of others' making." Her heart heavy, she shuffled forward, sinking onto the pond's stone edge next to him. "But here we are now."

He leaned forward, burying his face in his hands for a long moment.

She sat in silence next to him. Waiting.

His hands dropped away from his face, but he didn't look at her. "So what do we do with being here now?"

Her fingers curled, undecided, and then she set her hand on his shoulder. "We keep on living."

Nodding to himself, he drew in a deep breath and glanced at her, his voice hoarse. "I am sorry I threw you out of the carriage." His head dipped downward, his eyes hidden, unable to look at her. "I...I don't really know what happened to me, all I knew in that moment was that I didn't want to hurt you—or the children—I didn't trust myself."

Her chest expanded with a sharp intake of breath. She'd never heard him apologize for anything in his life and he'd just said sorry twice in the last fifteen minutes.

She squeezed his shoulder. "I didn't understand why you did it. Not right away, but I figured it out—what happened in the carriage wasn't about me. It was about you."

He looked to her. "It was a little bit about you."

She laughed, her hand dropping onto her lap. "I'll give you that. Just a little bit, though. I blame you, but I don't blame you. And Callum found us, so all was well enough. You scared me, though."

"It's good to be scared once in a while."

She shook her head, chuckling as she leaned her shoulder into him. "Aaahh, no. I did not care for it at all."

He laughed, then nodded, running his hand through his hair. "You love Cal, don't you?"

"I do."

Thomas's head tipped down, his gaze going serious on her. "Do you know what he is?"

"A guardian?" Her eyebrows lifted. "Yes, he told me."

His mouth pulled to the side, annoyed. "He's not supposed to tell anyone, anything."

"Except some things override silly vows."

"This is one of them?"

She nodded. "It is."

He inclined his head to her, then leaned forward, his forearms resting on the top of his knees as his stare dropped to the ground. He scuffed at the grass with the toe of his boot. "He doesn't want your money, you know."

"I do."

He glanced back at her. "For that alone, I mark my name in support of you two marrying. Though the ass didn't even give me a chance to give my blessing."

"I heard." She grinned.

"No. He's a barbarian, that one." He scratched the back of his head. "Just came in and declared he was going to marry you, no matter what I said."

The image in her head of Callum going toe-to-toe with Thomas warmed her heart. "Then count me lucky that he feels that way."

His right eyebrow lifted. "He's tamed you, then?"

She shook her head, a smile on her lips. "No. It's more that I've turned him wild."

Thomas laughed. Real, soul-shaking laughter that made him tilt his head back, his laughter drifting into the thick fog.

"It's nice we have your approval." A smile beaming wide on her face, she flipped her hand over, holding it out to him. "Come back to the manor with me?"

He shook his head, looking into the haze of the fog. "I'd rather remove myself to Ravenstone."

"I know you would, but I would also like you to attend

our nuptials. Callum said the clergyman should be arriving in the next few hours, if the fog hasn't delayed him."

"That soon?"

She nodded. "That soon. Callum is my future, and I intend for my life to start anew today."

He glanced down at her hand, hesitated, and then took it.

Progress.

She'd take it.

CHAPTER 35

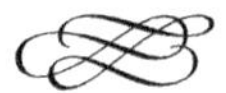

Stepping out of Georgette's room where she and Callum had just tucked Georgette and Jacob into bed together, she looked over her shoulder to Callum as he quietly closed the door.

He'd been telling them a tale of how he once had to swim out to a ship in the sea that had half sunk to rescue a friend of his that had been set upon by pirates.

Just enough imagination layered over what she presumed was a real story, that it made a fantastical tale. And long enough that both of the children had fallen asleep to the soothing cadence of his low voice.

She grinned at him, the happiness in her chest exploding so hard the grin didn't do it justice.

He caught her silly grin, smiled, and then lunged at her, swooping her up into his arms, her legs dangling over his forearm.

She laughed as he carried her down the hallway and stopped at the door to one of the many bedrooms in this wing of the house.

Dipping the top half of her body down, he flicked out his

right hand from her back and turned the doorknob, then stepped into the room.

Her eyes went big. "What is this?"

This bedroom, which she had never paid much attention to unless there were guests at Springfell, was filled with lit candles, a fire in the fireplace, and much of her belongings from her room. The large bed made perfectly with a dark blue silk coverlet and pillows. Everything in it fresh and clean.

Callum stepped farther into the room, still carrying her. "With your chambers in shambles, I asked Mrs. Jorge which room would be suitable to move into, then helped her and the maid and the footman bring all your clothing and items in while you were getting ready for our nuptials."

Her hand going to his chest, she looked up at him, tears welling in her eyes. "You did?"

"I did." He set her down, then pointed to the wide wall of windows with the drapes open. "Mrs. Jorge said this room has the best view of the gardens, and if it were up to her, this is where she would imagine you would want to awake every day. The best view of the gardens and the forest beyond."

Nemity moved over to the windows, nodding. It was dark out, but torches were lit all the way down to the grand pond, setting a warm glow across the estate. This was the perfect spot to wake up, and she'd never even thought about moving into here.

Callum wrapped his arms around her from behind, looking out along the land.

Her fingers wrapped around his arms holding her. "This is perfect. Perfect. Thank you."

"Good." His head dipped, kissing her brow.

She looked to the right at the door to the adjoining dressing room. "Did you bring your own clothes in here as well?"

"A few items." He shrugged as he pointed to the dressing room door. "That dressing room is expansive, but your wardrobe does take up most of the space, I'm afraid."

She chuckled. "I do own a lot of finery." She looked to the left, her lips pulling to the side as she surveyed that half of the room. She spun in his arms, looking up at him. "Well then, we will need to put in a new door into that side of the room to convert the next room over into your dressing and late-night drinking room."

He glanced to that wall, then looked down to her. "As long as you're in my bed, I'll never have need of late-night drinks."

His head dipped down to her, his kiss searing, but slow. Lazy. Like he had all the time in the world to imprint himself onto her. Not that he needed to.

She was his.

His fingers untied the knotted sash at the back of her dress, then slipped under the top edges of her sleeves, pushing them down from her shoulders.

A groan caught in her throat and she pulled away from the kiss. "We promised we would be back downstairs."

Callum didn't accept her pull away, and his lips dove down to her neck, teasing the delicate lines that sent shivers along her bare arms. "I think we'll be forgiven for disappearing for the night."

The groan made it up out of her throat. "Thomas is going to kill us."

"Probably." He tugged down her dress past her breasts and slid it down her body to pool on the floor. "I cannot believe you got Thomas to stay for the wedding."

She smiled, her fingers diving into his hair as his lips went lower. "I can be persuasive."

"You guilted him, didn't you?"

She laughed. "Maybe. And did you see his face when we left him in the drawing room to entertain Lady Agnes?"

"I did." Callum chuckled as he undid her stays. "I thought he was going to throw a knife at your back just so some blood would flow and he could get out of it."

His lips slid over her right nipple and her head fell back as pleasure shot down through her belly to the crux of her. "It's his punishment for what he did to us in the carriage."

"Did he apologize?" His words were muffled as he rolled her nipple between his teeth.

"He did." Her hands slipped down from his hair to untie his cravat. "But I stand by this being his punishment. He needs some uncomfortableness in his life. Besides, I think Lady Agnes always liked him when he was younger, so she was delighted to be sitting next to him at dinner."

Callum chuckled as her stays dropped to the floor and he switched to her left breast. "You can be cruel."

"Also a delight."

"My delight."

Her back arched, setting her breast fully into his mouth as she dropped his cravat to the floor. Her thoughts were starting to get muddled, but she wanted to get the business of Thomas out of their way before she fully captured her husband in bed. "I worry about him."

"It's not unwarranted." Callum slid her chemise off her shoulders and sent it to the floor. "Is he a danger to himself? Maybe. He's a danger to others? Maybe. Look at what he did to you, and you were the one—the only one—he cared enough about to protect."

Her fingers dove under the lapels of his coat and she tugged it off his frame. "Well, we need to help him."

He dropped to his knees, leaving a trail of kisses down her belly as he tugged off her slippers, then stripped off one of her stockings, followed by the other. He looked up at her, his chin dipping into her lower belly. "Except how do you help someone that doesn't want to be helped?"

Her eyebrows lifted at him, a smile playing on her lips as she sank her fingers into his hair. "Do you know the answer to that, or are you really asking the question? Because I can see where this is headed."

He shrugged, then got to his feet. "Well, it would be devious."

"Does it matter if it's devious if it helps him?" She unbuttoned his waistcoat, dragging it from his arms and then pulled free his lawn shirt.

His fingers brushed against the side of her face, then moved back, curling into her hair and loosening pins, sending them to drop onto the pile of clothes at her feet. His look met hers. "You already know my moral code on that one—I've lived a life of deviousness for a long time."

"You don't think he'll be suspicious of any new staff in his household? He obviously knows about you."

He pulled his lawn shirt off over his head. "Of course he would be suspicious. He's not an idiot and he knows all about the Guardians."

She nodded, her mouth watering at the sight of his bare chest. "So, we would have to insert someone into his life that he won't suspect?"

Callum stepped close to her, sliding his hands down her back and he picked her up, pressing his naked skin against hers. "We probably need to insert two. One that he does suspect and one that he doesn't."

"Diabolical." She laughed. "You have an idea of who?"

"I do." He walked across the room and set her long on the bed.

"Good." She nodded as he pulled off one of his boots, then the other.

"Especially good because you are naked in the bed and I am done talking about Thomas."

She laughed, reaching her hand out to him. "Come here, husband."

She didn't have to make the demand twice. His trousers dropped off his legs and he climbed onto the foot of the bed, kissing a pathway up her naked body. Calf, inner thigh, veering into her folds for a few glorious moments, and then moving onto her belly, both of her breasts, her neck and then her lips.

This night was going to be long. And arduous. And every second of it extraordinary.

She smiled, the happiness in her chest increasing tenfold.

Full of disbelief that this was where she landed, after all this time, after all the heartaches.

Here. A family. Callum.

Everything she always dreamed of, everything she always wanted, with this man in her bed, hovering over her. She'd had to wait for it, sometimes impatiently, but it was finally here. A life worth celebrating.

She wasn't wrong about luck being on her side.

EPILOGUE

"There." On his knees, Callum grunted as fabric ripped under the blade of his dagger. "I almost have it."

Nemity shrieked. "Cold—too cold."

Damn.

Callum slid his blade away from the skin of her belly. Deuced hard to get a blade between her dress and her skin these days.

He glanced up at her face. "Isn't the whole point of this to get this one spot cold?"

"Yes." She scrunched her nose. "But not that cold."

He heaved a sigh, setting the blade down on her outstretched legs as he flipped up the bottom flap of the round hole he'd just cut into the middle of her dress over her belly, then adjusted all the mounds of blankets on the sofa around her—across her chest and arms, and moving up to wrap around her head with just her face peeking out.

He tucked the flap of fabric from her dress he'd just cut free under the thick blanket across her ribcage, then set his hand on her bare belly. "Is that better?'

Both of her hands wiggled out from the depths of the blankets and rubbed across her bare belly, scratching at the skin. "Yes." Her eyes closed, drawing in a deep breath as a gust of cold air from the open window behind her swirled around them. "Yes. Better. Better."

His brow furrowed at her pale complexion. "You are certain there is nothing to be done?"

"There is nothing." Her eyes stayed closed as she spoke, scratching her belly. "It is something just to suffer through. That is what the midwife said. And she says the same thing every time you bring her here every other day. It is the same thing the other midwife you had brought all the way from Edinburgh said. The nausea will most likely last for a few months and then dissipate."

"Except it has already been a month and a half, and those women aren't watching you nibble away at the crusts of bread, then inevitably heaving it out not but an hour after you eat. You're wasting away."

Her eyes opened to him and she pointed at her belly bared to the air. "This. This is a help. Trust me, Cal. I trust them, so trust me. You forget that Mrs. Jorge said my mother was the same with me—she could only nibble at food for three months before she felt better."

A frown set hard on his face. "Then you need to nibble more."

"Maybe in a little bit. Let me just let this last wave settle down, and then I'll try again." She pointed to the *Times* that he'd shoved off to the side of the sofa when the last dry heaves hit her. "Take my mind off the dizziness and read me more of the paper. Please."

He swallowed down the argument on his tongue. She sounded so damn exhausted.

He wanted—needed—her eating. Something. Anything.

They'd tried every food available, and nothing was sticking in her belly.

He'd give her fifteen more minutes, then he would try again to shove something down her throat.

Still on his knees, he picked up his blade just as the Yellow drawing room door opened.

Thomas stepped into the room, saw Callum's dagger hovering above Nemity on the sofa, and he flew into instant action, barreling across the room, aiming to tackle Callum, a roar bellowing from him. "What the hell?"

Callum jumped to his feet, dodging out of Thomas's way and throwing a hand up to stop him. Glaring at Thomas, he sheathed his blade. "Don't you knock?"

Thomas angled himself between Callum and Nemity. Foolish ass. "Mr. Flourin sent me in here—and I see you holding a blade above Nemity and I— " Thomas's words paused as he glanced over his shoulder down at her. "What in the bloody world is going on here?"

Callum looked down at his wife, assessing her current state as an outsider would. She was splayed out on the long sofa, mounds of pillows behind her, blankets covering every inch of her except for the round hole he'd made in her dress where her bare belly was exposed to the air.

Peculiar, yes.

He had to give the bewildered look on Thomas's face its due.

Thomas looked back to Callum. "And why is it freezing in here?"

Nemity poked her thumb toward the open window behind her. "The window is open."

Thomas took a step back so he could look at both Callum and Nemity at the same time, his brow furrowed. "Do tell me why the window is open in the middle of winter, and then why your belly is wide open to the air?"

Nemity glanced at Callum and grinned. He was freezing as well, moving about here in just his lawn shirt and trousers with little heat from the tall flames in the fireplace. But he wasn't letting Nemity go through this alone. Not after what he did to her—setting his seed so deep in her womb she was carrying his babe within a month of their wedding. Probably before it, even.

He wasn't a good enough man not to be inordinately proud at that fact. So he would suffer the cold if that is what she needed.

"Wait." Thomas stilled, his stare centering on Nemity. "What is wrong with you? You look like you are at death's door."

"Strike those words from this room," Callum growled.

Thomas glanced at Callum, then looked back to Nemity. "Fine—strike that. You look like hell caught you between its teeth, gnawed on you for a while, then spit you out."

"Charming." She gave him a sardonic smile.

His look swept up and down the mound of her body covered with all the blankets. "Seriously, Nemity, what is wrong with you?" Actual concern haunted his eyes. He shifted his stare to Callum.

Callum avoided his eyes, looking to Nemity. They hadn't shared this news with anyone outside of Springfell, so this was her call to make with her cousin.

She exhaled a long breath. "I am with child, Thomas. And it has been making me vomit every other hour for weeks now."

His eyes widened. "A babe? But you've only been married for two months."

She nodded, a true smile catching on her lips.

"And you haven't eaten? You need to eat, Nemity."

Her eyes lifted to the ceiling. "Thank you for that brilliant observation." She looked to Thomas. "I am trying. Believe me, Callum is doing everything he can to get food down my throat."

His hand motioned to her body. "Why are you buried under all the blankets but your belly is bare?"

Her hands settled across her stomach. "Because my belly is raging hot and the rest of me is freezing because I need the fresh air to calm my flipping stomach. Callum was very helpfully cutting a hole in my dress so my belly could breathe when you came in."

Thomas stared at her for a long moment, and then the ass had the audacity to chuckle—though he attempted to stifle it as he ran his hand across his face. He looked to Callum for confirmation of everything she was saying.

Callum nodded.

Thomas chuckled again. "Well, this is…this is good news. But why aren't you in bed?"

"We're trying to make life as normal as possible for Georgette and Jacob," Callum said.

Nemity nodded, or at least the blankets wrapped around her head moved like she was nodding under them. "They watched their mother sick in bed for a year, and I'll not do that to them. When they come in, I find a way to sit upright and pretend all is well enough."

"Admirable." Thomas looked out the row of windows overlooking the gardens, now dormant with the season. "Where are they?"

"They're down at the stables with Mr. Youngstrom working on training the puppy you found on your land and tossed into their hands two weeks ago." Callum pointedly cleared his throat. "The one you didn't even bother to find us to tell us about."

Thomas had the good sense to look sheepish for one

short second. "I wasn't sure what to do with it when I found it. Giving it to the children seemed the most obvious choice."

"Aside from the fact that you sprung it on us—the children do love it. They named it Slider," Nemity said. "You could have told us, though. Come and said hello."

"I had to get back to Ravenstone."

"As you always do." Nemity pinned a stare on him. "So why did you make the journey here today?"

"Oh. That." His arms folded over his ribcage and he set his stare on Callum. "What have you done?"

"Done with what?"

Thomas's voice went hard. "You're meddling."

Callum shook his head. "Meddling in what, Thomas? You're making no sense."

"Meddling in my life."

"What could you possibly be even talking about right now?" Nemity asked as she drew her hands back under the cover of the heavy blankets.

Thomas looked to Nemity then back to Callum. "After my last driver quit, my solicitor replaced him with a new driver that seems to have an unusual interest in my life—in my whereabouts."

Callum's brows lifted. "Don't you usually have to tell your driver your whereabouts when you use him?"

"Yes, but this—this man is suspicious. Either that or I'm going mad. But he is suspicious."

"How so?"

"Stop with the innocent questions." Thomas sliced a glare at Callum. "Is he one of your guardians?"

"How in the world could that even be arranged?" Nemity asked, drawing Thomas's attention. "Can you blame your last driver for quitting on you—look at the position you put him in when you left me."

"Granted, that was unfortunate. I made mistakes." Thomas heaved a sigh. "But when he quit he was replaced with this odd new driver."

"So get a different new driver, Thomas." Callum's hand flipped into the air. "You think Nemity or I have had any time—while dealing with this—to meddle in your life?"

"But—"

"It really is a rather conceited level you've managed to reach, Cousin," Nemity chimed in.

Thomas's mouth clamped closed, his jaw twitching.

For a few long seconds, he looked ready to blow into a rage, but then he looked to Callum, then to Nemity and her bare belly, and he bowed his head.

"Forgive my intrusion." His words strained out through gritted teeth. "Be well, Nemity. Please do manage to eat something that will stay in your belly."

Without waiting for a reply, Thomas stalked out of the room, swearing under his breath as he closed the door behind him.

Callum stared at the closed door for several moments before shaking his head and moving to the side of the sofa that held Nemity's feet.

He slid his hand under her calves and the pile of blankets atop, then lifted her legs, moving to sit down. Settling her feet on his lap, he pulled out the newspaper that had crumpled against the side of the cushions and began smoothing it straight.

She nudged his thigh with her heel. "Tell me what you're really thinking. He's getting worse, isn't he?"

Callum set the paper onto the arm of the sofa and slipped his hands under the pile of blankets to find her bare feet and he started rubbing them.

He considered for a moment what to tell her, then sighed.

"I would rather have Thomas worrying about going mad, than having him hating himself as he was when he was sinking deep into darkness—like he was when we last found him at Ravenstone a month ago. I think this is progress. He came here on his own accord. To yell at us, yes, but he came. At least he's obsessing about something outside of himself for a change."

"He still has so much anger in him, but then he goes and finds a puppy and gives it to Georgette and Jacob." She shook her head. "It is like the good in him is scratching for the surface, looking for a shard of wood to keep him afloat in the sea of his anger. But then in the next moment, he is swearing under his breath and storming off."

He looked to her, squeezing her feet. "He'll get there."

"How do you know?"

"I don't." He shrugged. "But one can only be angry at the world for so long, right?"

Nemity laughed. "Have you met Lady Agnes?"

He chuckled. "True."

Her toes wiggled under his fingers. "If he thinks he is going mad now, wait until he sees what is in store for him next." Even through her haze of nausea, a mischievous glint sparked in her eyes.

She leaned fully back into her pile of pillows, her face finally relaxing for the first time in what seemed like forever. Seeing it, he took a real breath, deep into his lungs. A cold, but real breath.

All would be well, if only because his wife plotting out the saving of her cousin would keep her mind off of her rebellious stomach. If Thomas thought for one second that Nemity would leave him alone to live his life in the sorrowful state it was currently in, he had another thing coming.

His stare shifted to the tall flames of the fire in front of them, and he continued to rub her feet, happy to sit in the comfortable silence before Georgette and Jacob and Slider came bounding back into the room. That was the worst—when Nemity put on a strained smile for them and all he could do was worry about her.

"I think you've finally done it." She'd opened her eyes and was staring at him, for how long, he didn't know.

"Done what? Achieved the perfect temperature for all parts of your body and that babe in there?"

She shook her head. "Tamed the lioness."

He laughed, full and hearty.

He shouldn't take that much pleasure in one little moment, not now when his wife was so miserable, but he couldn't quite help it. "I don't think I tamed anything. There's no taming the wild in you. You've simmered, yes, but the second this constant nausea passes, I dread the day that I'll be trying to drag you in from the forest with the babe heavy in your belly."

She smiled, nuzzling her cheek into the side of the blankets wrapping her head, the blinks of her eyes starting to grow heavy. "That will be nice. Springtime. I can almost feel it."

"Just imagine you're there, sitting on the side of the grotto where the sunlight comes down, and you're swishing your toes in the water, the smell of budding trees filling your nose."

She nodded, her eyes closing. "I can almost taste it. That spark of spring on my tongue with the scent of the linden trees filling the air. Georgette and Jacob splashing in the pool. Laughter ringing the air. When everything feels alive again."

She drifted off.

He sat, still, holding onto her feet, watching the soft lines of her face. Contentment sinking deep into his chest, into his soul.

His entire world, wrapped up in this one wild little wood nymph.

Somehow, her luck had spread, turning into his very own luck to hold for all of his days.

WHAT'S NEXT?

More in the same world!
Read the full ***Guardians of the Bones*** series: *Discreet Destruction, Shadows of Scandal, A Savage Deception, Wicked Reckoning*. Thomas's story is next, *Twisted Treachery*, available in late 2024.

ABOUT THE AUTHOR

K.J. Jackson is the *USA Today* bestselling author of the *Hold Your Breath, Lords of Fate, Lords of Action, Revelry's Tempest, Valor of Vinehill, Box of Draupnir, Exile, Guardians of the Bones, Creatures of Sin & Savagery,* and *Creatures of Sin & Seduction* series.

She specializes in historical and fantasy paranormal romance, loves to travel (road trips are the best!), and is a sucker for a good story in any genre. She lives in Minnesota with her husband, two children, and a dog who has taken the sport of bed-hogging to new heights.

Visit her at www.kjjackson.com